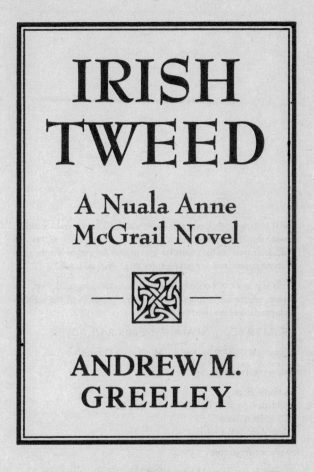

IRISH TWEED

A Nuala Anne McGrail Novel

ANDREW M. GREELEY

A TOM DOHERTY ASSOCIATES BOOK
NEW YORK

This is a work of fiction. All of the characters, organizations, and events portrayed in this novel are either products of the author's imagination or are used fictitiously.

IRISH TWEED: A NUALA ANNE MCGRAIL NOVEL

Copyright © 2009 by Andrew M. Greeley Enterprises, Ltd.

All rights reserved.

A Forge Book
Published by Tom Doherty Associates, LLC
175 Fifth Avenue
New York, NY 10010

www.tor-forge.com

Forge® is a registered trademark of Tom Doherty Associates, LLC.

ISBN 978-0-7653-6207-0

First Edition: February 2009
First Mass Market Edition: January 2010

Printed in the United States of America

0 9 8 7 6 5 4 3 2 1

Part of my story occurs in the era of the migration from Ireland that happened during the so-called little famine of the middle eighteen seventies when many men and women migrated from the West of Ireland to Chicago, which accounts for the preponderance of Mayo folks in our city. Among them were my two grandmothers, Annie Moran and Mary Laura Reynolds, good women who I, deprived of grandparents, had always wanted to meet. I dedicate this story to their honored memory and to the memory of all Irish immigrant women, whose sufferings we cannot even begin to imagine.

AG, June 1, 2008

— Note —

These stories are fiction. The events and people are all products of my imagination. The only person drawn from reality is Bishop Peter Muldoon, auxiliary of Chicago and then first Bishop of Rockford. He was pastor of St. Charles Borromeo Church in Chicago when my mother was growing up in that neighborhood. His kindness and goodness left an indelible image in her memory that I am happy to repeat. He was destined to be Archbishop of Chicago but was betrayed by his fellow priests—something that fellow priests often do. Rush Medical College and St. Joe's parish are real places, but their stories in this book are fictional. St. Joe's is a wonderful parish with a wonderful school; its only flaw is that my friends the Coynes have moved in across the street from them and hence the parish often appears in my stories—always, however, fictionalized.

There is verisimilitude, I believe, in my stories of late nineteenth-century medical education and practice in Chicago, but for history one could consult *Medicine in Chicago, 1850–1950*, by Thomas Neville Bonner. I have tried to give a hint of what the medical world was like when my parents were growing up—so very different from our own but, fortunately, very different from the previous quarter century. The inimitable Angela Agnes Tierney, MD, may not have been able to matriculate at Rush Medical College at the time I depict her entering the school, but a few years later she would have been able to do so. The struggle against plagues and disease in a large and very new city, I believe, was not unlike what I portray as the struggle between the followers of Pasteur and Lister, with their convictions about germs, and a slightly older generation who believed in miasmas and bloodletting. As for Irish women like Dr. Tierney, they are legion, then and now . . .

The battles at St. Joe's illustrate what can happen when errant clichés left over from Vatican Council II fall into the worldview of angry and unhappy humans, made bitter by the failure of the church leadership after the Council to implement the Council's vision.

There's never enough time, is there, Dermot Michael?
And when there is, isn't it too late?

Nuala Anne McGrail

IRISH
TWEED

— The First Battle —

 THE WOLFHOUNDS were howling. That wasn't right. When they were angry, normally they barked. Why were they making a fuss on this early September afternoon, dense with humidity? When they howled they were furious, ready to fight at the slightest notice. Where were they? I rolled over in my bed, trying to straighten out this puzzle. Normally the gentlest of God's creatures, hounds are big, terrifying monsters when they are offended. In the school yard, they adored and were adored by the kids. What would make them angry . . . Why would they howl? Only if someone for whom they were responsible was under attack? Who could that be?

Nuala Anne! My wife!

I jumped out of my bed, ignoring my pained muscles (thirty-six holes at Lost Dunes) and rushed to the window. Across the street the school yard was in chaos. Kids were swirling around in battle with one another. Nuala was in the middle of the fight. The hounds were trying to drag her across the yard so they could make short work of the bad guys. My four children were fully engaged—Mary Anne, just turned thirteen, helped her mother to restrain the hounds, eleven-year-old Micheal (Me-Hall, AKA the Mick) had pinned a big kid on the ground, nine-year-old Socra Marie and seven-year-old Patjo were pounding on the Mick's foe, and the new principal, her ascetic face twisted in rage, was screaming at my wife. Various other parents were engaged in battle to protect their own children from the Ostrogoths who were trying to beat them up.

Pulling on my jeans and Marquette sweatshirt, I charged down the outdoor stairs of our pre–Civil War three storey, wondering what the hell I was supposed to do. On the way down I noted that a woman, shaped rather like a bowling ball, rolled across the yard and knocked my three youngest to the ground. Frank Sauer, the parish priest and a classmate of my brother George, was nowhere to be seen. The unengaged children were chanting "Fight! Fight! Fight!"

Dr. Lorraine Fletcher, the principal, slapped Nuala Anne's face. The doggies went ballistic, Mary Anne grabbed their leashes so that her mother, a newly minted black belt, could kick Dr. Fletcher in the stomach and send her reeling into the mud of the yard . . .

"No! Doggies!" I shouted.

"Stop!" My valiant daughter shouted.

"Sit!" Her mother added the decisive word.

They did, of course.

Julie, our golden-haired nanny, pulled the human bowling ball off the Mick, who promptly slugged his assailant (as I presumed the lout on the ground must be), gathered his younger siblings, and redeployed to where his mother and father stood. I whistled a signal to my troops that we were to engage on a strategic retreat.

"I'm a-callin' the po-lice, over to the sixth precinct, and a-tellin' them that the polecats have taken over at

St. Joe's. I saw Nuala kick that polecat bitch after she done slapped her. I'll testify in court."

It was Cindasue Lou McCloud Murphy, Commander in the Yewnited States Coast Guard and some kind of gumshoe for the Secret Service. She had an arm around her son Peteyjack and the other arm around her daughter Katiesue.

"I wanna kick that phony bitch just once more," my wife, teeth clenched in determination, begged.

"Maire Phinoula Ain," I insisted, "You do not! . . . Julie, you and Mary Anne, get her mother back in the house before the cops come."

Somehow I now had responsibility for Maeve and Fiona. They had begun to howl again.

"Shut up!" I shouted at them.

Surprised, the two mutts fell into line with our retreating militia. I did not ordinarily presume to give them instructions. It may have been that my wife, who maintained some kind of creepy extrasensory communication links with them, had ordered them to chill out.

Inside our castle, everyone wanted to talk at the same time.

"Julie," I said, "I think we all need a hot chocolate with whipped cream . . . Sorcie, will you help her, please?"

Delighted to be given adult responsibility, our onetime-tiny neonate followed Julie to the kitchen.

I sat down on our antique couch next to me wife, who was quivering with many different explosive emotions. Mary Anne was on the other side, both of us helping Nuala to chill out.

The dogs arranged themselves at her feet, ready to resume the fight should the enemy return.

"I'm a-goin' out to talk to them thar cops, a-tellin' them that the little kids are rebellin' 'gainst the junior high school polecats who are a-takin' their money."

"Bobby Finnerty, if you need a name, ma'am."

Mary Anne kissed her mother's cheek.

"Ma, you were wonderful. The Revered teacher will be proud of you."

Later on, as supper time approached, the tangled lines of the story began to emerge. There had been a parents' meeting at the school. Father Sauer had introduced the new principal, a lean and hungry polecat, according to Cindasue, to whom everyone took an immediate dislike. She announced that henceforth St. Joe's would be a *Catholic* school because it would exercise the "fundamental option for the poor," which meant that no special favors would be granted to the children of the affluent or of celebrities or to children who were good athletes. Everyone would be equal and the only discrimination would be in favor of the poor. When asked about the bullying of little ones by "big kids" who were taking their money from them, she had replied that sometimes the poor may take revolutionary action to reestablish equality.

"That polecat just plain crazy."

"It means she selects the basketball team," Mary Anne explained, "not coach. And no seventh graders can play on the eighth-grade team."

"Guess who that means!" the Mick, still angry, shouted. "So this morning the bullies started pushing around the little kids like Sorci and Patjo."

"I pushed back," Patjo said.

"And so we organized our own revolution!" the Mick continued.

"Who is this 'we'?" I asked.

"Me and Liz Boyle."

Ms. Boyle was the local hellion, a sweet little blond with an enchanting smile.

"Good ally," I conceded.

"What kind of a Catholic place is this," my wife protested, "that has revolutions and counterrevolutions . . . I'm so ashamed of myself!"

"I'm not ashamed of you, Ma," Mary Anne said. "She had it coming!"

"Dermot Michael Coyne, you've raised a brood of bloody radicals!"

"Apples don't fall that far from their trees," I replied.

Fortunately the melee did not make the evening news.

"Nuala Anne in mob fight with kids!" she said. "Wouldn't that have been a great lead."

Wouldn't it now?

"I lost it altogether, Dermot Michael," my good wife said. "I should never have kicked that bitch in the stomach."

"You were just defending your kids, Ma." The Mick inched his way onto the now-crowded couch.

The whole lot of them, I told myself, were wild uhns from the West of Ireland. In times of trouble when the wolves were howling, my genes became recessive.

— 1 —

MY BEAUTIFUL wife, Nuala Anne, is
doing martial arts these days. Like everything she does, she's an enthusiast about
her program of "Self-Defense for Women."
One night every week, she dons her floppy white
clothes, tightens her black belt, and goes over to the
storefront on Clark Street to learn from "the Revered
Teacher" how to fend off and incapacitate would-be
assailants. Sometimes she brings along one of our snow-
white wolfhounds, which, she insists, are very popular with the group.

"'Tis not that I'm afraid of you, Dermot love," she
says anxiously as we wait in the parlor of our home on
Southport Avenue for the advent of Julie's date. "It's not
that kind of attack that I want to resist."

"We'll see," I say, not wanting to give up a talking
point in our culture of banter.

In some of our recent adventures me wife has battered, routed, and incapacitated troublesome males
with considerable éclat. The only resistance I encounter is symbolic, part of the games we play in bed—or
anywhere else when there is opportunity. However, I
rarely challenge her when she has a new idea. My chal-

lenge would make her feel guilty, but it wouldn't stop her. If me wife says she feels the need to learn taekwondo, I go along. Her instincts, I have learned in thirteen years of marriage, are usually dead on.

Fiona, our senior wolfhound, ambled in the room and sat at me wife's feet.

"Doesn't this one want to get a look at Julie's date," she said as she patted the compliant canine's massive head. "Just like that one that just went upstairs." "That one," was our Mary Anne (in the past also known as Nellie or Nelliecoyne), an auburn-haired beauty on the cusp of adulthood. Nuala Anne's conceit was that she had no control whatever over our eldest, and she was now my responsibility. This was pure fiction. The two of them had bonded long ago and, both being part witch, they communicated silently with one another. Against me, as I claimed. Nuala bonded with every woman that came into our sprawling antebellum house. That was the only way she could properly take care of them. Julie alone of our nannies resisted the link— mostly out of shyness, I thought. Instead she bonded with Mary Anne, which perhaps gave my wife an indirect link, not one which assuaged her Connemara sense of maternal responsibility.

"I'm sure her ma expects me to take care of her and herself all them thousands of miles away from Dublin at Loyola University, the poor little thing."

You must understand that the key words which began with *th-* emerged sounding like "dem," "dousands," and "ding"—the Irish language lacks a sound to correspond with our *th*. I had long since given up my battle to transform her dialect from Galwegan to Mercan. Yet when our oldest began to speak "the way they do back home," me wife would comment, "Won't dem kids at St. Ignatius College Prep laugh at you for being uncivilized."

"The ones from da Soudside won't even notice."

"Dermot Michael Coyne! You must do something about your daughter."

"Isn't it too late now, and yourself having spoiled her rotten?"

Thus we bantered with one another—outside our bedroom anyway.

Me wife is a beautiful woman, as I have said. In fact, she is many beautiful women, and an actress at that she was at TCD (Trinity College Dublin), as well as a singer. She slips from one persona into another with practiced ease—the shy and charming young singer from Carraoe in Connemara, the disciplined athlete who ran the marathon and played hoops with her daughter over in the school yard of St. Joe's, the stiff, shrewd investment broker at Arthur Andersen (who got out long before the bailiff arrived), the grand duchess sashaying down Michigan Avenue in the Easter Parade, oblivious to the hungry stares of men and the resentful expressions of women, the modest virgin who might have become a nun and who could outpray most of the women in the world (especially when our tiny neonate was dying), the ingenious slut with whom I slept.

I loved them all.

She was five feet nine inches tall, and had pale blue eyes which suggested a rare sunny day on Galway Bay, long thick black hair, and buttermilk-smooth skin. Her voice evoked, for me anyway, the sound of church bells heard from a distance over the bogs. I fell in love with her the first night I encountered her with a world economics textbook in O'Neil's Pub on the College Green (which hasn't been green for centuries) and she repudiated my efforts to "chat her up" with a dismissive, "Focking rich Yank." According to her, she knew then and there, as I gawked at her breasts while she was singing about Molly Malone—and weeping at poor Molly's fate—that she would have to sleep with me sometime.

She'd had a hard time at first in Yank Land—homesick, afraid of me and my family (all of whom adored her), hunted down by the feds as an illegal (which she wasn't), terrified at the prospect of becoming a concert singer. Marriage did not make life any easier—four pregnancies, one of them causing a sustained trauma of postpartum depression and another a premature little girl child, Socra Marie, who was now our tiny terrorist. And she had to live in the same house with me, the four kids, the cook, the nannies, and the hounds. I was the most difficult of them all.

"Me poor Dermot Michael, he doesn't do much of anything useful. He started his life as a gambler (read 'commodity trader'), then he retired and lived off his winnings and he just sits around daydreaming and writing poetry and stories."

"And I didn't say that you devour me with your hungry eyes all day long, did I?"

"You're the one who is a poet, woman of the house. And you didn't say either that I'm your spear-carrier, your Doctor Watson, your Captain Hastings, your Monsieur Flambeau."

"Actually you're my Baker Street Irregular."

You see, my Nuala Anne solves puzzles. According to Commander Culhane of the Sixth Precinct Detectives and Superintendent Michael Casey of Reliable Security, she is the best "natural" detective they have ever met, save perhaps for her good friend Blackie Ryan, sometime Rector of the Cathedral and now, "by the inattention of the Holy Spirit and ineptitude of the Holy See, Cardinal Archbishop of Chicago."

The doorbell rang.

"'Tis himself," my wife said.

That could have been a guess, a statement of probability, or a certainty. You see, my wife is fey. She even sees halos around people's heads (mine is silver and blue, if you're interested), a trait she shares with the good Mary Anne.

"Answer the door, Dermot Michael, and remember his name is not Finnbar Michael but Finnbar Me-*hall*, just like yours is Dir-*mud*."

"With the emphasis on mud."

I struggled to my feet and glanced at her quickly. Her body was turned at such an angle that her torso outlined itself against the floppy gown. My thoughts of lust or love, hard to say which or what combination of both was at work, that had teased my imagination all day, took over. Ah, it would be a fun night.

She knew of course about my fantasies almost before I did—and sometimes, maybe always, stirred them up. I learned how to read the glint in her eyes which was a signal that she wouldn't half mind. There was, I told myself, the required glint. It didn't follow that there would not be a show of resistance, hesitation, insistence that we both had a hard day tomorrow and should have a good night's sleep. This was all, I had come to realize, nothing more than symbolic behavior which meant, "yes, why not?" She would beg off on occasion, with a signal in her eyes.

One night after a particularly delightful romp, she said, "Isn't it a good thing now, Dermot Michael, that we enjoy this so much. Otherwise it would be difficult to live together, and meself an accountant and yourself a poet."

" 'Tis true," I said with the required sigh.

"And yourself telling me all along that I'm a beautiful woman and meself not believing it at all, at all."

"That's why God created us humans to be lovers."

" 'Tis true," she said.

So, of course, when I had looked out the window there was a small decrepit Asian-looking car, probably "previously owned" and maybe "previously owned" twice. A young man emerged, barely of medium height, six inches shorter than me and an inch or two shorter than Nuala. More than big enough for the diminutive Julie. He glanced up at the house, noted the stairway to the second floor, shrugged his shoulders and began, somewhat gingerly like all first-time guests, to ascend the stairs. He was wearing a dark suit (vaguely navy blue, perhaps) purchased off a rack somewhere. He was also wearing an Irish tweed hat, which he removed and stuffed into his jacket pocket halfway up the stairs. His hair was blond with bushy curls and his face was already tainted red—and not from climbing the stairs. Not handsome, not a man of power, but surely cute and perhaps even adorable.

He knocked on the door. I opened it promptly.

His smile was easy and charming.

"Good evening Mr. McGrail, Finnbar Burke. With your permission I'd like to take Julie Crean to the motion pictures tonight."

Very formal but still with a grin that forced me to grin.

I shook hands with him.

"I'm Dermot, Finnbar. Mr. McGrail is my father-in-law over across in Connemara. The woman of the house is the gorgeous woman behind me, my wife Nuala Anne McGrail."

"Dressed for combat, I see."

He was inundated by a stream of Irish, Galway dialect I expected.

He responded with his own stream.

Both of them showing off.

"Like all good Cork men," Nuala Anne observed, "you still have that patada in your mouth."

"And like all Connemara mystics you talk in plainchant."

More laughter. The young man was not devoid of wit.

"And here's your lovely date . . . Trailing after her are three witches who ought not to be here—Fiona, who is Julie's canine guardian, and two of my children, Mary Anne and Socra Marie. Shake hands with Mr. Burke, girls."

"Mary Anne" was pronounced "MA-ree-ahn."

The white hound claimed precedence and offered her paw respectfully. Finnbar Burke bent down, took the paw, and said some words in Irish. The huge dog stood up on her hind legs and kissed him. He hugged her and continued praising her in Irish.

"Fiona," Julie said, blushing furiously, "you'll be the ruination of us all!"

"And my daughters, Mary Anne and Socra Marie, who are now going to shake hands with you and return to their rooms to finish their homework."

They both shook hands with Julie's date and greeted him in Irish. Mary Anne wore her martial arts garments.

"Och, isn't it two fearsome women altogether? And a gorgeous wolfhound? Sure, Mr. Coyne, wouldn't you be havin' no security problems at all, at all?"

"Dermot! Isn't Mr. Coyne my uncle, the lawyer?"

"Galway lasses, I note," he said. "Good night, girls, study hard."

"Yes, Mr. Burke."

Julie, dressed at last in something more than jeans and sweatshirt, was gorgeous in a knit beige dress which clung nicely to her delightful body. She radiated joy, confidence, pleasure. She had a fella, and a nice fella, with a great smile and a quick wit. His admiration enveloped her. She lowered her eyes, embarrassed but pleased. It was perhaps the first time in her life that she had experienced male desire, respectful desire indeed, but still desire.

"We'll just go over to the Century to see the filum there about Cork during the Troubles and then stop for a pint at the Irish pub down the street."

The Wind in the Barley Fields was not, I thought, the ideal "filum" for a first date.

"We won't stay out too late," Julie assured us.

"Don't come home too early either," Nuala added.

She pecked at my cheek and then Nuala's, the first for both of us. Finnbar Burke took her hand and led her down the steps. He watched her on every step, his eyes drinking her in, like a man perishing with the thirst.

When I closed the door, Fiona curled up in front of it. She would stand guard till her charge returned.

"Upstairs, girls," the woman of the house repeated her orders . . . "No, not you, Fiona. You can wait till she comes home."

The hound raised her huge head as if to protest and then curled up in a complacent knot and promptly went to sleep.

"I think he's adorable," Mary Anne observed as she obeyed with no undue haste.

On the couch next to me, an antique from the Civil War subbasement and appropriately rehabbed, me spouse was weeping softly. I put my arm around her.

"They're both so young." She sighed her loudest West of Ireland sigh, which her friend Cardinal Blackie described as sounding like the beginning of a heavy asthma attack.

"Reminds you of O'Neil's Pub a long time ago, does it now?"

"'Tis true."

"In fact, she is three years older than you were that evening, and he's probably about the same age as I was."

"And he looks at her with the same glow in his eyes that you looked at me."

"And she blushes in response even as you did."

We both sighed again.

"We didn't know what we were doing, did we, Dermot Michael?"

"Woman, we did not!"

"Won't you have to take him out to Butterfield and see how good he is?"

"He plays golf?"

"Isn't that tweed cap he shoved in his pocket the symbol of the Old Head Links in Kinsale? Don't they say the wind there comes either from the North Pole or from Hell?"

"You'll have to come along and play with us."

"Only when you report how good he is."

Me spouse is a grand golfer altogether. Won the women's tournament at Portumna when she was seventeen. She claims she's too busy to play anymore, but in truth she's afraid that I'll beat her, which I do on very rare occasions. She hits her drives as long as I hit mine, which is not appropriate behavior for a wife, is it now?

"Well," she sighed again. "Don't we have one more responsibility and ourselves not having enough responsibilities as it is."

"What responsibility?"

"We have to take care of Julie and her fella. They don't have anyone else to take care of them."

"Two more children in our family?"

"If God didn't want us to take care of them, why would he have sent them here?"

"Give over, Nuala Anne. No one took care of us."

"Except our parents who taught us marital love by example and your family which took care of me as soon as I showed up. And themselves wondering if I wouldn't make something out of you."

"Which you didn't like at all, at all, if I remember right."

"They wanted me to remake you and meself liking you the way you were. And now they think I did remake you and themselves being wrong altogether. But they were there to help and still are. Your pa and ma take care of the kids, and His Riverance digs up all those manuscripts, and Cyndi keeps the feds off our backs."

My brother the priest is always accorded such respect. The Cardinal, one would expect, would deserve much more. However, he was simply Blackie.

"'Tis true," I admitted. "Don't Julie and Finnbar have families of their own?"

"Dermot they do not, and yourself knowing that. They came here to escape their families. God wants us to be their families while they're keeping company and courting."

I never quite understood the distinction.

"Orphans of the storm who rolled up on our beach?"

"You have the right of it now. God wants us to help them."

Well, that settled that.

"You have the right of it, woman of the house."

She sniffed as though that were self-evident.

"What do we know about them?"

"She doesn't confide in me, but your daughter keeps me informed."

"That one?"

"She tells me that she went to CUD, City University of Dublin, and himself to CUC, City University Cork—the bottom of the ladder, so to speak—and themselves both very clever, herself in a doctoral program at DePaul and her man down at your business school below on Illinois Street and doing very well indeed, if you please."

It wasn't my business school. It belonged to the University of Chicago. Or simply *The* University.

My wife was proud of her knowledge of the street maps of Chicago. If Finnbar Burke was doing well there, he was also a bright young man and probably a dangerous golfer.

My tranquility disappeared before my very eyes.

"And where does he work?"

"On Washington Street down below and isn't it for some Irish company that's buying a lot of American property and that cheap these days."

"Sounds un-American to me."

"We bought property in Ireland when it was cheap, why shouldn't they buy it in America when it's cheap?"

We both sighed again. This time I was faking it.

"Well," she said, "since you intend to have your way with me once again tonight, we'd better go upstairs and put the small ones to bed."

She spoke as one resigned to one more male assault, but her glowing eyes suggested that she could hardly wait. It ought not be that easy for a man to seduce his wife. But it is what it is.

I loosened the black belt and probed her sports bra. She sighed again and leaned on my shoulder.

"There's never enough time, is there, Dermot Michael? And when there is, isn't it too late?"

I think that was Irish bull.

"How is that one doing in her taekwondo?"

"Och, isn't the little witch catching up with me? She's not as strong yet, but isn't she pure grace? Lightning feet?"

"She'd never permit herself to beat you."

"She'd better not . . . Give over, Dermot Michael Coyne. We're not up in the bedroom yet."

I paused in my explorations.

Now don't youse be thinking I'm gonna tell you what me spouse looks like with her clothes off. Or what she's like when she is gasping for orgasm, fuhgeddaboudit. That's none of your business, is it?

"Did you go over to the parish while I was up above perfecting the womanly art?"

"Woman, I did."

"And?"

"The principal—Dr. Fletcher—didn't have time to talk with me. So I asked her when I could have an appointment, and didn't she say, she never had time to talk to the children of the rich and famous. 'The school,' she informed me, 'is exercising the fundamental option for the poor.'"

"Bitch! . . . What did that eejit priest have to say?"

She had leapt off the couch and the *gi* of her martial arts garb fell open. I gulped at the sight of her wondrous breasts behind the discipline of the bra. My fingers twitched a little.

"Sit down, what would the kids think!"

That was her favorite line about our occasional affection when they might see us.

She drew the *gi* together and sat on the couch next to me, her body tense with fury.

Dr. Lorraine Fletcher was a thin, not to say skinny, former nun with a Ph.D. in education from Chicago Circle and Technicolor hair which changed its hue frequently. She was an intense feminist who did not suffer fools lightly. By definition all men were fools. I wondered why, with a Ph.D., she was a principal in a Catholic grammar school.

"The priest said that he supported any decisions that the principal made and would not discuss them with me. He supported lay authority in the schools."

" 'But,' I says to him, 'aren't the parents laity too?' "

"And he says?"

"He says that he's not afraid of the Cardinal or my brother or the school office or anyone else because the laity supports him completely. He added that it is natural and healthy that the ordinary kids resent those who get good marks or are good athletes. A little bit of bully action is good for everyone."

Our priest supported the principal's theory that some of those who are not good athletes should be on the varsity teams even if that meant the stars should have to sit on the bench. There was open warfare between the coach and the principal, with the laity of course supporting the coach, save for the parents of those who weren't good athletes. The school was, as Mr. Dooley would have said, in a state of chaos.

"So you said?" Me wife was growing angry at me for not "putting that friggin' amadon in his place."

"I said that if the bullies continued to mistreat my children, we would withdraw from the school and I would ask my sister to seek an injunction against the school."

"And that scared him?"

"He said he was not afraid of Cyndi Hurley either."

"Then he's a real eejit altogether!"

"'Tis true."

My sister lives in the Joliet diocese west of Chicago and had scared the living daylights out of their Chancery on the subject of bullying. She had forced them to hire security guards to end violence in the yard of one of their schools.

Julie and Fiona would take the four kids to school every morning and bring them home at noon and in the evening. Maeve had joined them recently. The kids ordered their ma to stay out of the fight. The tense days were Julie's days off, when Nuala or I would escort the entourage. Wolfhounds love kids and like to play with them. They also can sniff hostility a mile away. So they would snarl when someone hassled one of our kids. The principal ordered us to keep the wolfhounds out of the yard. We responded by keeping them on the sidewalk. We also hired Reliable Security to keep an eye on the school. Mike Casey, former superintendent of police, managed to have someone around every day, someone so discreet that no one would suspect that he or she was an off-duty cop. I would sit at the top of the stairs in front of our house—a sky-high stoop I called it—with a powerful TV camera monitoring the school yard during recess time, the dangerous hour of the day for our ring of bullies.

Me wife would instantly recognize the cop, of course. Fights in the school yard and nastiness to the talented committed by bullies were part of growing up. We had them in the school yard at River Forest in my day. They left me alone, because even then I was kind of big. Clumsy, but massive. I was the one to go into fights and break them up because even then I was a romantic. I also shut bullies up, unless they were girls. I refused to admit that girls could be bullies.

In the school across the street from us, however, the bullies and begrudgers had set the tone. Some parents, especially mothers, were urging their children to stand up for their rights. That meant they should fight the favoritism teachers displayed to smart kids, "good" kids, and athletes. Ms. O'Haloran made this "resistance" a cause of social justice. Our four were smart, good, and athletes. Worse still, their parents were celebrities, and were probably rich too. They also fought back, since each of them had quick tongues and could match insult for insult. Micheal Dermot, our older son, had a reputation for being tough, so he was generally left alone. Patjo, our youngest child, was big for first grade and could (and did) take on all comers.

"Only when they try to beat up on him," Socra Marie, his next oldest sibling, rushed to his defense. "Don't believe that Dr. Fletcher . . . She's a friggin' bitch."

"Socra Marie, you should never talk that way!"

"It's true, Ma." Her big sister intruded in the conversation. "She makes fun of Sorcie because she says it's a pagan name."

"And what do you say, Socra Marie?"

"I say that it's an Irish name and it can't be pagan."

Well, that settled that.

"There's a rumor among the kids that the grades in our next report cards will be distributed randomly . . . What does that mean, Da?"

"It means that grades will not be related to performance in school."

"Dumb kids get As and smart kids flunk?" the Mick protested. "That's not fair is it, Da?"

"It's as fair as replacing the good players on the teams with those who aren't so good."

"Friggin' bitch," Patjo said with a happy smile. If his sister said it, he could say it too.

"Hush, dear," his mother said. "Nice boys and girls don't use words like that."

"I'm not a nice boy, Ma. Dr. Fletcher said nice boys don't fight back."

"There's going to be a lot of trouble at the next parents' conferences," Nuala Anne said thoughtfully. "Grades are precious stones to parents. They'll be furious."

"It will end up on the Cardinal's desk," I predicted. "It will be interesting to see how he handles it."

"Stay out of it, Ma," Mary Anne urged. "We can take care of ourselves. Ms. Murphy says that most parents are already angry at them two polecats."

Ms. Murphy was Cindasue Lou McCloud Murphy from Stinkin' Crik, West Virginia, a commander in the Yewnited States Coast Guard who lived down the street from us. She was related to Cardinal Blackie by marriage and claimed that she was a "Hard-shell Baptist Catholic." She was some kind of spook for the Yewnited States Secret Service. Her two kids, Katiesue and Peteyjack were the ages of our two youngest, and the four were inseparable friends.

So, as we cuddled on the antique couch in the parlor, I felt that everything was under control, and I said so as I embraced my wife with some determination. She was quite content with this affection. Indeed, she was fading into one of her moods where the whole world was running out of control and poor Nuala Anne had to reorient it.

"Cindasue is on the case," I said tentatively.

"It's bad, Dermot Michael," she replied. "Really bad. There's evil over across in the school. Deep, mean twisted evil. Naturally, we'll have to fight it."

This was hardly the time or the place to argue with her. Just because there was evil around didn't mean it was any of our business. Except that it was not an argument which had ever worked with her before.

"Well," she said with the loudest sigh of the evening, "since you're determined to have your way with me tonight, we'd better tuck the kids into bed now or they'll know what we're doing." I held her closely as we climbed the stairs. She surrendered herself into my embrace. It would be one of our solemn high lovemaking nights.

At the head of the stairs we encountered Maeve who was patrolling the corridor to protect the small ones, an obligation that the two white giants had assumed for themselves on arrival. The hound would push her way into any room whose door was not closed. She led us first to the girls' room. Both daughters were sleeping peacefully.

We kissed them good night. They stirred slightly and went back to sleep. If we didn't pay our routine visit, we would hear about it from all four in the morning.

"Aren't they sweet little ones, Dermot Michael? Innocents!"

"Who can take care of themselves, thank you very much."

Then we turned to the boys' room where both our sons were also sound asleep, Patjo with his baseball glove on the pillow next to him—just in case there was a pop fly he had to chase.

Then we petted the "doggie," who had sniffed each of the children and licked both of our faces and returned to the girls' room. We went to our own.

"Close the door, Dermot."

With great ceremony I removed her clothes.

"I should take a shower," she argued with little conviction. "I smell of sweat."

"I've told you that it's an aphrodisiac."

"Och, Dermot, you're a desperate man altogether and yourself setting me on fire."

Despite fourteen years of marriage and four pregnancies and concerts every year and mysteries resolved, me wife was more sexually attractive than when we married. She was filled with what she called a holy determination to preserve her figure. I thought at first that it was for my benefit, then I decided it was for her own self-respect, then I knew it was a combination of both in an intricate pattern, and that I would never figure out and indeed shouldn't bother. She had also become more confident of her sexual attractiveness and of her lovemaking skills. She could drive me out of my mind just as she claimed I did her. As she removed my clothes and my temples pounded, I realized again that this she-demon from the bogs and the fog and the howling winds and the pounding sea of Connemara was quite beyond my analytic powers.

Lovemaking with Nuala Anne was always a joy, sometimes just a simple, satisfying joy, but on other occasions an explosive burst into another world where we floated together on the sea of eternity. A wild, fantastical spirit, she would sometimes even drag me along on our trip, even if it seemed, faint heart that I was, hesitant. We were dancing in the courtyard of God.

Then we would float back to earth again, more confident of ourselves and our family and our life. Joy superabundant.

"That was nice, Dermot love," she said, patting my chest. "You're improving."

— 2 —

A WOMAN shouldn't do those kinds of things, especially with her husband. As some women say to me, after five or six years, it's time to curtail sex. They want it all the time, of course. But you have to make them earn it. I pay no attention to that advice. Nor do I join in conversations about how difficult my man is, because I think that's dirty. Me Dermot is not a difficult man at all, at all. Doesn't he have the patience of a saint and meself sometimes a frigging witch altogether. He is a distraction, ogling me all the time and embarrassing me. How can a woman keep a proper house with four kids, two dogs, two nannies usually, a cook, and her man devouring her with his eyes all the time. And meself having to exercise, and go downtown for my voice lessons with Madam, and now attend sessions with the Revered Teacher. 'Tis not fitting to be gobbled up like he gobbles me. I have work to do, you ravening creature, give over.

I never say it, of course. It would break his heart, poor dear man. Besides, if he didn't look at me that way, wouldn't I be afraid that he had found someone else to devour with his soft blue eyes? And doesn't it feel good when someone who by now should be bored with you still wants you, even if it's all the time. What would have happened to me if he hadn't tried to chat me up in O'Neil's that cold autumn night? I'd be a lonely, frustrated, nasty woman—which I might be anyway, but at least one who is loved and knows how to love in return—just as the Holy Father, poor dear man, said in that letter of his. That's where God is.

Speaking of Yourself, thank You for me Dermot and me kids and me friends, and protect us from the evil that lurks all around, especially over across the street.

— 3 —

 AFTER THE choir Mass at Old St. Patrick's at which Nuala sings, we drove out *en famille* to River Forest to have dinner with my parents. They were careful to see that all the children and grandchildren in the clan were given equal opportunity to return to the castle, but they were especially eager to see us, in part because, as they insisted, ours were the best-behaved kids. In truth they also especially delighted them, because she talked so much like "Ma"—the original Mary Anne (and Nellie). Needless to say, me wife perceived that she had an audience and performed up to her highest standards of the beautiful but mildly crazy Irish immigrant woman.

My brother George the Priest was there, happy because he could see his favorite nieces and nephews. George was the Pastor of the Cathedral and was considered by his fellow priests to be Blackie's Blackie, a difficult act to follow.

"How's the situation at the parish?" he asked innocently.

George shares the family conventional wisdom that I am practically useless and managed to remember to pay my income tax only because my wife reminds me (in fact, she does all our taxes). They agree that whatever diminution of my uselessness might be, it all results from me wife's benign influence on me.

" 'Tis bull shite, Dermot Michael," she explodes.

" 'Tis true," I said, "but we all need our simple explanations."

George, however, has decided that I am a credible observer of the follies of the human condition.

"You been hearing complaints?" I said, following my wife's custom of answering a question with another question.

"Some."

"Well, Blackie will have to do something about it soon. It's a viper's tangle."

"So I gathered, though your literary allusion is the first I've heard."

"The place is worse than anything you might have heard. It could explode any time. Your very favorite niece is taking taekwondo lessons along with her mother, so she can fight off bullies in the school yard."

"Why do they go after her?" he asked, his face tightening.

"Because she is the best basketball player in the school and that's a form of repression that is not Christian."

"I can tell the boss this?"

"Be my guest."

"You can tell me more that I can tell him."

So I rehearsed the whole story.

"Is Frank sleeping with Dr. Fletcher?"

"Our friend Cindasue, who lives down the street, says in her own colorful lingo that you get two polecats together in the same holler, they go a-ruttin'. However, I don't think so. Not yet anyway."

"He wasn't a half bad pastor before this?"

"Old-fashioned but harmless. Midlife crisis maybe."

"You'll keep us posted?"

"Our kids say they can take care of themselves, but sure, so long as I am an anonymous source."

"You have Mike Casey keeping an eye on it?"

"Sure I do. But that's the deepest of deep background."

"Good idea . . . It's all the Vatican Council, Bro. All the old structures fell apart. That means more craziness, some left-wing, some right-wing, and some Katie-Bar-The-Door-Wing. There's no one around to say to people, 'That's the worst crock of bullshit I've ever heard.'"

He then went off to collect his favorite niece for a game of twenty-one on the old basketball court in the driveway.

"We call it twenty-four now, Uncle George. If you make the free throw and the layup, you get a shot from downtown."

"Sounds like fun."

Beware brother, you're in trouble.

My wife and my parents came out to watch.

Nuala clung to my arm to protect herself from the October chill.

"She won't beat him, will she?"

"Is the Pope still Catholic?"

George had some skills at the hoops in his days at Fenwick, and, while no Barack Obama, he had a pretty good eye.

Me child skunked him.

While the annihilation was transpiring, I whispered to me wife the gist of my conversation with George.

"Then everything will be all right," she said with a sigh of relief. "He knows about it, doesn't he?"

"Blackie? Sure he does. George wasn't surprised. He was very angry when I told him who was the prime target."

"Blackie will work it all out," she said confidently.

I wasn't so certain. Blackie was *the* cardinal, but his powers were limited. He couldn't close down the school and surround it with police, could he?

The Hurleys joined us for dessert after dinner. Their oldest, Josephina, or Josie, would attend St. Ignatius College Prep next year. She and Nellie—oops—Mary Anne had been friendly rivals for a long time. Against a new and scary high school, however, they would surely make common cause. They'd have a lock on it before their first week was over.

Dad cornered me as we were leaving and handed me a thick manila folder.

"You still interested in old manuscripts, Derm?"

I had presided over the publication of several old memoirs that my wife and I had rescued during the course of our problem solving. So my dad finally realized that I was not a complete waste—but it was still all because of Nuala's influence.

Give over! It's time you stop feeling sorry for yourself. Doesn't the whole family give you credit for bringing home such a wonderful bride.

My adversary had returned to torment me with his truisms.

"We found this in the old archives we brought out to the new campus from the old place down on Harrison Street. Someone decided that it was time to clean the place up. This looks like a pretty interesting story. Remarkable woman. One of the first women doctors we had in this town. Still something of a legend. She seems to have been a little fey, just like your Nuala."

I winced but to myself. Two fey women would not find a century of time any barrier to communication, not at all, at all.

"They're not a great deal of trouble," I said with phony confidence. "Not when you get to understand them."

I noted that the folder had somehow morphed into my hand.

"The Old Fella gave you a memoir, did he now?" Nuala said suspiciously. "I suppose it will be another dull story. Besides, Dermot love, we have more than enough on our platter, don't we now?"

"'Tis true," I said. "I won't pass it on unless I think it's something which you would want to read."

"Give me every single page! We owe a lot to the Old Fella and himself so nice to our kids."

My parents insisted that when we were going away somewhere, we were to leave our kids at their house. They would spoil the brats rotten, of course. But it was, as me wife proclaimed, good craic for both sides. Now that they were growing up and Mary Anne was the special agent in charge of the group as well as the acting precinct captain, the kids were generally well behaved. Nuala figured we owed my parents for their babysitting. I figured that they reveled in spoiling the kids

She has the right of it, like always.

Be quiet!

"What's her name?"

"Who?

"The woman who wrote the memoir?"

I opened the manuscript.

Nuala drives the car in our family when we have the whole clan. She insists that she is the better driver, "and yourself teaching me how to drive."

Moreover she argues that our fire-engine-red Lincoln Navigator is her car.

"Angela Tierney."

"Who was she?"

"Someone famous, though I've never heard of her."

"All the same," Nuala said, "she's someone we know very well. Isn't she from Carraoe?"

I shivered. We'd have this dead woman walking around our house for weeks.

We arrived at our house on Southport Street to find the night lights on—my wife had them in almost every room in the house—and the puppies sound asleep and upset when we had disturbed them. A note from Julie was pinned on the bulletin board.

"Nuala, would you ever let me Finnbar buy you a pint down below in the pub?"

"She's getting familiar with you, isn't she?"

"Haven't we had some talks about herself and her fella? Didn't she ask me about men?"

"A subject on which you are an expert?"

"Didn't I tell her that the secret was that we have to teach them, poor, clumsy, testosterone-driven boy children that they are, how to love us, and then they have to teach us how to love them . . . Isn't it all as simple as that?"

"No, it is not!"

Our elder daughter appeared with a note from Julie, asking her to take over for a half hour.

"Pa, I think you ought to go down to the pub and have a pint with them . . . I'll get all the kids in bed on time, well, not the Mick because he doesn't take orders from me anymore, and he shouldn't really. I'll ask him to. You call me on the cell phone every fifteen minutes, and I'll report."

Mary Anne knew which parent to address questions to in the circumstances. So we put on our dark leather jackets and, harp in my hand, we walked down to the corner pub. Flannery's by name, but with a Polish owner.

"Go on, say it, Dermot Michael Coyne."

"That the poor child is her mother's daughter and herself taking responsibility for the whole world? Why would I be surprised?"

She sighed loudly.

"So long as she doesn't take responsibility for the wrong people?"

"I only did it once," she said, squeezing my arm.

Everyone was happy to see us, especially the Yuppies, who were taking over West Lincoln Park. Me wife, to tell the truth and despite her national reputation as a concert singer, was in fact at her best when she was singing in a pub. She became the ur-Nuala, a peasant matron from the bogs of Connemara. Mary Anne was faithful to her promise.

"Mick is doing his arithmetic and the little kids are in bed and I'm reading a book by Graham Greene. He's a strange man, isn't he, Pa?"

Haunted by God, I think.

"Yeah . . ."

I had time to talk with Finnbar Burke, who was wearing his tattered "Old Head" cap, jeans and a tattered windbreaker over a T-shirt which proclaimed CORK CITY.

"You play much golf here?" I asked.

"Busy with work and school, but I wouldn't mind having a go at it."

"What's your handicap at Old Head?"

"Three on a day when I'm feeling good."

"That's impressive."

"It would be lower if I was better with a driver . . . Where do you play, Dermot, if it's not improper to ask?"

"I try to stay a moving target. When we're over across in the summer, it's Polerama, where they give me four and herself a three. She won the women's championship there when she was seventeen."

"She never did!" This was a cry of wonder, not disbelief.

"I don't play against her when we're home, as she calls it. She out-drives most of the men in the club."

"A wife who is wicked with the driver."

He had the strange Irish habit of echoing your last comment, though in different words. Me wife rarely did that, because it takes too much time.

"In the summer we play at a place near our home on the other side of the lake called Lost Dunes, where they give me a three because they like her."

"They have the sense to like a beautiful woman who hits a wicked driver . . . But I'm not sure I can afford to lose the golf balls that they tell me the place eats up."

"My home course is Ridgemoor out in my old neighborhood . . . Would you ever be able to shoot a round with me? I'll give you a five handicap, seeing that it's a new course for you."

"I'd rather play you even," he said firmly.

"It's a deal . . . When can you be free?"

"It's an Irish firm I work for, so we're relaxed about days off. My boss thinks I work too hard and meself going to school every night. How about Wednesday?"

"Wonderful! I'll pick you up . . . Where do you live?"

"You know the Adlon Hotel?"

"On Huron street?"

"It's one of our properties, and I have a small room down there. An easy walk from school . . . which is really hard, Dermot. They expect you to think. The golf game might clear me addled brain a bit."

"I am fairly warned."

We both laughed uneasily.

This cherubic little guy could prove dangerous.

The songfest ended with Nuala Anne singing the sad tale of Molly Malone.

As always, there were tears in everyone's eyes. Poor little Julie sobbed.

"Gotta get home to the brats!" Nuala exclaimed.

"Come back more often!" Flannery (née Osmanski) begged.

"We will, Seano!"

A local Yuppie, named Reilly I think, took me aside as we were going through the rituals of saying good-bye (which in Nuala's case dragged on like an old-style Solemn High Mass).

"What's going on across the street at the school? It sounds to me like they're deliberately trying to ruin it. The monkeys are running the zoo? Does Ryan know about it?"

"I don't see how he couldn't know about it. I'm sure he's being deluged with complaints."

"Do they pick on your kids?"

"Yeah, but mine want us to stay out of it . . . Why don't you write to the Cardinal yourself?"

"He won't hold it against us. Some of those guys do, you know."

"My brother's a priest, and he says that one should never, *never* mess with Blackie Ryan."

"Sounds good . . . He looks like such a diffident little guy."

"That's what makes him so dangerous."

Back at our house, Mary Anne and the dogs, all three of them yawning, went quietly to bed. Me wife departed to her exercise room and I went to the office to begin the story of Angela Tierney.

— 4 —

 THERE WERE three aged sheets of paper on top of the manuscript. One was a letter from Galway dated in 1875 to Mrs. Patrick Gaughan at a Union Park address in Chicago.

Dearest Mae,

It's been a long time since I've written you. There are hard times again here in the West of Ireland, the most god-forsaken part of the world, thanks to the English tyranny. We've been suffering from another famine, not like the big one back in '45, but bad enough, and the winter has been terrible cold all together. There's sickness too, some kind of affliction which wipes out whole families, even ones which seemed healthy are all dead in twenty-four hours, Lord have mercy on them. Then the weather has been terrible, bitter cold and piles of snow which melts and then turns to ice so that neither man nor beast can walk down the roads.

I am writing to you about a fourteen-year-old who is the only survivor of a family of six, two parents and four children. David kept her in quaran-

tine after the parish priest brought her to us. She did not, by the grace of God, succumb to the fever that killed the others in her family. David says she has a strong constitution which resists the miasma that spreads the fever. We kept her in quarantine even on the day her family was buried, the priest insisted. Neither David nor the priest nor the grave diggers have picked up the infection, thanks be to God, but the town lives in mortal terror of her. She is a pretty little thing with bright blue eyes and pale blond hair, like a Viking, very intelligent, plays the piano and picked up a little bit of French in our school—she works very hard. Our children love her but are afraid. There is, to tell the truth, no room for another child in our house though, poor weak little thing that she is, she does most of the housework.

We think of sending her to the orphanage down in Galway Town, but the nuns there are very rigid and will crush out of her what little spirit the poor child still has. We wonder if you would ever think of hiring her as a servant girl. She works very hard and never complains and her fare from Kinsale to New York would cost you only ten dollars and you could take it out of her pay until she has earned it. If you would be willing to hire her, send a draft to our bank in Galway and we will arrange for her transfer to Kinsale. David says I shouldn't ask this of you, but I say that you and Paddy have always been very generous and that this is a request that might save a great spirit. I ask God in advance to bless your generosity to poor little Angela Tierney.

Pray for all of us here. Ireland must have committed terrible sins to have earned so much of God's Holy Wrath.

Your Loving Cousin,
Agatha

The other slip of paper was a trans-Atlantic cable.

FIFTY DOLLARS FORWARDED YOUR ACCOUNT GALWAY
BANK. STOP. OBTAIN NON STEERAGE TICKET. STOP.
NEW YORK CENTRAL TICKET CHICAGO. STOP. BUY
CHILD PROPER CLOTHING. STOP. THANK YOU. STOP.

PGAUGHAN MD.

Then another letter.

Dearest Mae,

*David and I are grateful that you sent the money
for Angela's journey to America. She sailed from
Kinsale on the Duke of Kent yesterday. The ship
should arrive on December fifth. I hope you can
arrange to have someone meet her and put her on
the train to Chicago. It was a cold gray day, and the
poor child was silent as she left us to go on the
boat. I believe she wants to start her life over again
in America.*

Angela's baby brother, a cute, mischievous little tyke,
was the last to die. She laid him on the floor next to his
mother and covered him with the last sheet in the
house. When the police came to bury the family, they
would discover that the Tierneys kept a neat house to
the bitter end.

Angela herself rested on the floor among the bodies, rosary in her hand. There would be no one to
cover her. That did not matter—her soul would join
the rest of the family in heaven before morning. Jesus
and Mary would take her home. The smell of dead
bodies was terrible. Dust to dust, ashes to ashes. A terrible waste of ashes. Not my will, but thy will be done.
By morning her body would smell too. What would
her life have been like . . . foolish question. We will
all live again.

The sun woke her up in the morning. She was still alive. Why would God not take her as he had taken all the others? She heard snow sliding off their brand-new thatch roof. Water began to fall on the floor. The thaw for which they had hoped and prayed had finally come. Too late.

She still clutched her rosary. Eternal Rest grant unto them, O Lord, and may perpetual light shine upon them. May their souls and all the souls . . .

She should walk down to the parish house and tell the priest . . . wrap herself in Ma's Irish tweed blanket.

She wanted only to stay where she was and die. Maybe God didn't want her to die.

She struggled to her feet, went into the children's sleeping room, "borrowed" her sister's walking shoes and her brother's jacket, and her mother's blanket, walked around the bodies and paused at the door.

"Good-bye. I'll be with you soon. I've gone to get the priest."

Her mother favored her sister and brother. She felt guilty because she had taken their things. In heaven, she hoped, they would forgive her. Outside it was warm for the first time in weeks. The snow on the road was melting, she plunged into it, fell on her face, pushed herself up, and struggled down the road towards the parish house.

If the weather had changed yesterday morning, perhaps the doctor could have come and saved at least her mother and the baby. Or at least the priest might have anointed them. None of them wanted to die. Their pain was unbearable. They cursed one another and they cursed God.

"They didn't mean it, Lord, you know that."

Her ma had died while Angela held her hand.

"Why didn't you get the priest?" Ma had demanded.

"You told me not to leave the house."

"God damn your selfish little soul to hell for all eternity. Always thinking of yourself."

Those were the last words Ma had said.

"She didn't mean it, Lord, she was in terrible pain. Please forgive her."

Ma had loved her and she had loved Ma back. But they had fought all the time. Ma told her often that she was too smart for her own good.

Then she began to cry, for the first time since the family began to die.

I'm not going to die, she told herself. For some reason *you* decided I should live. I suppose I should say thank you.

Then, shivering and exhausted, she was at the parish house.

She knocked on the door. No answer.

She pounded harder and then shouted.

"Everyone is dead," she howled, gasping for breath.

His wolfhound howled in protest. Too early in the morning to wake the priest. The housekeeper wouldn't answer. Soaked to the skin from melting snow, she was trembling now. Maybe she would die after all.

Then the canon, in his long crimson robe, answered the door.

"Who are you child? Why do you dare to awaken me at this hour?"

"Angela Tierney, your reverence. My family is dead, all except me. They died yesterday, first my father and then everyone else, down to the poor little baby."

The canon shook his head as if to clear it from sleep.

The dog, MacCool, pushed his way out of the house and embraced her. For some reason she was one of his favorites.

"To ask you pray over them and to say the Mass for them."

He shook his head again. This was not a dream.

He took her little hand in his huge paw.

"I should have recognized you, Angela, and yourself with the Viking hair . . . I'll get dressed and we'll find the doctor."

He didn't ask her inside the house.

She waited outside, cold and now very hungry. Yes, she was going to live. Why, O Lord, why? Why didn't you take me home with the others?

More tears. Ma didn't approve of my weeping so much. She thought it was a sign of weakness.

The canon emerged, wearing the thick cloak he had brought home from his years in Rome. He handed Angela two big slices of soda bread slathered in butter.

"Eat it slowly, little one, your stomach is still unstable."

"Everyone in my family vomited as they were dying."

"Don't worry," he said gruffly. "God still loves you and so does this poor little town."

Angela wasn't sure that either still loved her. She wasn't sure about anything anymore. They came to the doctor's house. His trap and pony were waiting outside.

"Good morning, David," the canon said. "Miss Tierney here tells me that her whole family died yesterday."

"Dear God, no! Angie, how terrible."

"Everyone!"

"My parents and all the children. Their bodies are out there in the house."

"You feel all right?"

"I'm tired and terribly sad. I'm not sick. I vomited once in the house when my little Kevin died. I thought my turn would come during the night, but then the sun came out. I knew God wanted me to tell you and the canon. We must bury them properly."

He put his hand on her forehead, looked into her eyes, took her pulse.

"Was there something your family ate recently that you did not eat?"

Angela hesitated.

"Pa found our last lamb dead in the field. Ma insisted that we eat it for supper. I didn't want to because I loved the little thing."

"The baby ate some of it?"

"He's been terribly hungry."

The doctor looked at the priest.

"Poisoned," he said curtly. "Rotting meat."

"You're not going to die, Angela," the canon said softly. "Thanks be to God."

"We're going to have to put you in quarantine for a few days, Angela, so the people will know that you were not affected by the poison. Do you mind?"

"What's quarantine?"

"We'll put you in a small room in my surgery and isolate you from others. Just for a few days. There's lots of books in there. As I remember, you were quite a reader."

"Can't I go to the burial?"

"I'm afraid not. It's for your own good."

"I'll say a requiem Mass for them later," the canon said. "Just for you."

In Ireland in those days of famine burials were quick and requiem Masses were infrequent. Doctors disagreed about whether diseases were contagious and might be spread from one person to another. Later Angela would argue for contagion against miasmas. She never forgot the horror of a week in quarantine, cut off from everyone in the village as her family was buried in the old cemetery behind the church. Nor would she forget that her family had died from eating rotting meat. The quarantine was unnecessary but the doctor had to impose it so that the town would not be afraid that she still had the disease.

The small room had been a closet in the corner of

the doctor's surgery. There was a cot and a hard chair and a tiny window.

Poor Ma killed everyone but me—the thought haunted her through the days when food was brought to the door of her tiny prison and a knock would signal that she should open the door. She waited till she heard her good friend Eileen run away, and then opened the door. The Gaughans fed her well during those days, even though hard times affected the doctor too. She was taking the food out of the mouths of Eileen and her brothers and sisters. Some of her strength came back, and she still clung to her rosary. Yet she realized that she had no future. She had no family. In the West of Ireland, a time of famine meant you had to take care of yourself.

She would have to become a beggar, walking the muddy roads, seeking alms from people who had no alms to give.

She spent most of the time in the little room sleeping. She dreamed often that ma and pa and the childer were still alive.

The doctor came to see her the day of the funeral.

"It was a grand turnout, Angela. Grand altogether. The whole townland. They were greatly concerned about you. The canon explained what happened. People are dying of corrupted meat all over the West of Ireland . . . I don't think they'll be afraid of you . . . we'll see what they're saying in a day or two . . . Have you thought about what you want to do?"

She had not.

"I suppose I could become a beggar. I'm no use to anybody."

"There are much better alternatives. I'm not without influence in the orphanage down in Galway Town. They would teach you some skills. They are too rigid altogether. The life of orphans is not easy, but there will be food and a roof over your head."

"That would be better than walking the roads like the Travelers do."

"Agatha had another idea. She has a cousin who lives in Chicago, married to a doctor, who is a cousin of mine." He laughed uneasily. "Quite generous people. Wasn't she thinking of writing to her to ask if they could find use for an intelligent and hardworking young woman? She could send a letter."

"I can't remain here in the village," Angela said. "I don't want to add to the burdens of any other family."

America was both intriguing and terrifying. She squeezed her rosary and made a decision that would shape the rest of her life. The words were out of her mouth before she had a chance to consider them.

"If they would have me, I'd love to go to America."

Dr. David seemed surprised by her enthusiasm.

"It's a difficult trip, not as bad as back in '45 with the coffin ships. Most people survive them now, especially if they're young and in good health like you are. But I don't want to deceive you about the risks."

"Life is a risk, Dr. Dave," she said, the words again leaping out of her mouth.

"Well, I'll ask Agatha to write a letter, and we'll see what happens."

Angela was released from quarantine just before the canon said the requiem Mass for her family. All the young people her age in the townland came to the Mass. The canon preached powerfully. Angela did not understand anything he said, but she realized that the sermon and the ceremony did console her and most of the others in the church. Was that the way it was with Catholicism? Sometimes the sounds were enough. In his final words, the canon seemed to be saying that she was a child chosen by God for special deeds, and that everyone should pray that she rise to the challenges.

What if he were right?

Angela had never realized that she had so many friends. Maybe there was much she had not realized.

"Are you frightened, Angela?" Eileen asked as they walked back to the doctor's house.

"I suppose I should be. Now I don't think . . . well, the worst has already happened, hasn't it?"

"I don't want to lose you, Angela."

"We'll never lose one another, Eileen."

Though no one had asked her to help, Angela took over the responsibilities of keeping the doctor's surgery neat and clean—cleaner, Mrs. Gaughan said, than she had ever seen it.

"Child, you don't have to work," she said kindly.

"Och, Missus, I've been working all my life. Me ma, poor dear woman, used to say that cleanliness is next to godliness."

"Sure, that's a Protestant saying, isn't it? But sometimes, maybe, they're right."

Later in life, Angela would realize how important it was to maintain clean premises. "You should be able to eat off the floor," the Polish nun had said to her.

She had even started back to school and had rapidly kept up with the studies she had missed. She had become part of the doctor's family, a much more peaceful and pleasant family than the one she had lost. She loved her ma and pa and her brothers and sisters, but they were often very difficult to live with, no matter how hard Angela had struggled to keep them happy.

There was room for her in the doctor's house. "Sure, you don't eat more than a few bites," Eileen had said.

Then, one day, a post office man had come up from Galway with a cable from Chicago.

"They've sent money for your trip to America," Agatha said. "Sure, Angela, you don't have to go. Why don't you stay here with us?"

"Won't we be missing you something terrible?" Eileen groaned.

"It's up to you child. I could go into Galway tomorrow and buy the tickets or send a cable back, saying that you'd rather stay with us . . ."

I've lost one family this year and now I'm about to lose another.

"Hadn't I better go and them Yanks expecting me?" she said, the words again jumping out of her mouth.

It all happened quickly. She had a ticket for the *Duke of Kent*, a steam liner that everyone said was clean, safe, and fast, a note to someone who would meet her at Ellis Island and take her to Grand Central Station, and a ticket to Chicago . . . What a strange name for a city. But the Yanks were said to be strange people.

"They say the steerage," Uncle Dave insisted as they waited in the railroad station in Galway Town, "is better than first class was even twenty years ago. And you'll be there in no time."

"They're terrible nice people, aren't they now? They'll give you a wonderful start in America," Aunt Agatha said.

"I'll never see you again!" Eileen sobbed.

Angela hugged her friend.

"We will see each other again, Eiley. We surely will."

"I know . . . In heaven."

"In this world."

There had been no American wake before she left. Those who left for America were thought to be as good as dead. If they survived the trip, they might well die in the American slums. Very few would return to Ireland. But the American wakes, like the real wakes, were often orgies of drinking or lovemaking in the fields. It would be a waste of good money. She had lived off the doctor's family long enough. They should not have to spend more money to get rid of her. She should learn not to feel sorry for herself. Her friends from school had come over to the doctor's house to say good-bye as they put the tweed blanket, which held all her possessions, into the pony trap. Many tears were shed, but none of them were Angela's. She was leaving on a great adventure.

She had terrible dreams. Her mother came out of the grave, an angry, half-dead skeleton, and accused her of deserting the family, "and our bodies not cold in the ground. Isn't it the way you were when we were all alive. You thought only about yourself and your future. I hope the boat sinks."

"Ma, I'm going because God wants me to!"

"God will damn you to hell for all eternity because you killed us."

"Ma, I didn't! I didn't! The meat was poisoned."

"You were always a great one for thinking up excuses . . . Why don't you kill yourself and come to hell where we are . . . You belong here!"

She would wake up shivering and hot at the same time.

The dream was not true. It could not have been. She loved her mother and so did God. They were all in heaven. She prayed for them many times every day. They would watch over her and keep her safe on the journey to Chicago.

She had never been on a train before. The trip to Cork was miserable. The rain beat against the dirty windows but did not clean them off. The car was cold. Other travelers complained to the conductor, who told them that if they didn't like the train they could get off and walk.

The train was also late at the station in Cork City. She had to transfer to another train to get to Kinsale. No one in the train station could tell her where the train to Kinsale was.

"I need to get to the *Duke of Kent*," she told one uniformed train man.

"Shite, isn't that focker at Buckingham Palace?"

"Gypsies like you should be arrested."

"Go away or we will call the police."

Angela was swept away by a wave of despair, the same feeling she had experienced at the cottage when the baby died. She had failed to save his precious little life. There was no escape from her fate. America was a foolish dream. She'd die soon, sitting on the steps of the Cork Railway Station.

She dragged her rosary out of its honored pocket in her dress, not to toll her beads but to cling to her God, who was suddenly distant. She wept for the first time since she had fled the cottage.

"Now why would such a pretty little woman be weeping in such an unpretty place?"

She looked up at a sturdy country woman, from Clare by her accent and herself with two small ones in her arms with a third child clinging to the hand of his da, a cheerful-looking fella if there ever was one such.

"Don't I have a booking on the *Duke of Kent* and meself lost in this terrible city?"

"Are you the only childer in your family and going to Amerikay all by herself?"

"Aren't me brothers and sisters and me ma and pa all dead and buried and our house burned to the ground up above in Connemara?"

Annie Scanlan, for that was her name, folded Angela in her arms.

"Well now, don't you have a family to go over across with you to Amerikay?"

She slipped her rosary back into its proper place, told God she was sorry, and took the nervous second child out of its mother's crowded arms, and didn't the child sleep there all the way to Kinsale and the *Duke of Kent*?

—— 5 ——

WHILE THERE had been no American wake to send Angela off to America, the tradition was maintained by the steerage passengers of watching the steeples of the church disappear over the horizon the next morning. "The last time any of us will see poor Ole Ireland," Pete Scanlan intoned the required ritual.

"I'll be back," Angela said. "I promised my friend Eileen Gaughan that I'd come back to visit her."

"Detroit will be my Ireland," Annie Scanlan said bitterly. "Ireland has already killed most of my family."

"English Imperialism killed them," Angela said firmly, her Fenian convictions unchanged by the disappearing steeples.

She was already feeling woozy from the motion of the bay. The previous night she was shocked by the steerage quarters, raw and rough and noisy and smelly, but at least clean and no sickness. The English authorities, troubled by the stories of "coffin ships" maintained a cursory sanitary inspection at dockside.

Angela had presented her documentation from Dr. Gaughan, certifying that she had been inoculated against smallpox and diphtheria. The English doctor regarded her dubiously.

"You're a very tiny little one, aren't you, child?"

"We grow slowly in West Galway, but only because you Brits are after starving us to death."

He smiled and applied his stethoscope to her chest.

"But you have strong lungs, all the better to denounce us with, I suppose."

The doctor was a kind man.

"You're not Mr. Peel or Mr. Gladstone, Doctor, it's not your fault that me brothers and sisters and me ma and pa are dead and buried in Galway and our family home burned to the ground. I'm sorry I was rude to you."

"I don't say you're wrong in your judgments, child. But you are young and strong and you'll do well in the land beyond the sea. God bless you and protect you."

"Thank you, Doctor," she said, feeling very guilty, as she often did when her quick and biting voice made trouble.

Despite the promising beginning and the promise in the sea air, the passage was, according to the crew who checked on steerage periodically, terribly rough altogether. For Angie, as everyone called her, seasickness began while still in the bay at Kinsale and continued intermittently all the way to New York Harbor. Often she was afraid she might die of the continuing waves of nausea. Sometimes she was afraid that she *wouldn't* die.

She tried to weave her way out into the steerage deck, where she could vomit into the Atlantic, which richly deserved her wrath. Sometimes she considered throwing herself over the side of the boat. She would be so thin, if she finally made it to Chicago, that they would discard her at first sight. She would have to become a street beggar. God didn't approve of suicide, but the teacher had told them that God forgave suicides because they were mad with pain.

"God forgive you, Angie, for such terrible thoughts," a voice behind her on the deck warned.

"Ma!" she exclaimed. "Is it yourself?"

"Who else would it be, child?"

Angie whirled around. The woman was covered in a long, dark shawl. But her shape was Ma's shape. And her face was radiant as ma's had been when Angie was young.

"Do you still live, Ma?"

"We all do, child, and ourselves happy. We haven't collected our bodies yet, but we are still ourselves and all of us terrible proud of you altogether. Only don't go jumping into the sea. You'll be all right, and there's still many great things for you to do."

"Yes, Ma."

"And that's not meself who comes in the dreams. That's your own memories of what I was like. I come to tell you I'm sorry for what I did to spoil so much of your young life. I was envious because you had everything I had, only you would have a chance I would never have. It was wrong of me . . . I hope you'll forgive me."

"Ma, I love you and I forgive. It wasn't your fault."

"You were always the generous one, Angela Agnes."

Ma was crying. Did the holy ones in heaven really cry? Why not?

"Will I see you again, Ma?"

"You know what I'm like, Angie Agnes. Now that I have permission to haunt you, I might just be back on the odd occasion."

The figure in the dark faded away gradually, her radiant face the last part to disappear.

Did ma have to make things right with me to get out of purgatory, she wondered. Didn't she do it gracefully, still?

For a few moments her nausea ebbed. She staggered back to the streerage, wobbling on uncertain legs. A huge, mean boy waited inside the door for her.

"Looks like you need a little help," he said, seizing her right hand.

"Not from an overgrown lout like you, Tommy Fitzpatrick!" She shook her arm free.

Pete Scanlan glared at the Fitzpatrick lout, took her hand, and led her back to her little refuge in the far corner of steerage.

"The sea air help a little, small one?"

"Made me sleepy," she admitted and slipped into the little bed she had created with her tweed blanket.

And she did sleep peacefully for the first time on the terrible voyage, happy that ma and the others were still alive somewhere, even if they hadn't picked up their bodies yet, and that she and ma were friends again, like they'd been so many years before.

She awoke next morning to cheers! They had sighted New York at last. Immigrants would land at Castle Garden at noon. They should have their papers ready for examination and remember that not everyone who had crossed on the *Duke of Kent* would be admitted to Amerikay. Angela had heard that ten percent were rejected even if they had a letter guaranteeing that there was a job waiting for them. Why would this strange new country want to take a sickly little waif like her?

They were herded onto a ferry which was rocking in the surly waters of Upper New York Bay. Unsteady on her feet and feeling woozy, Angela found herself tilting toward the side of the ferry. A big New York policeman seemed perfectly willing to let her go over the side. She grabbed his thick uniform and hung on till Pete Scanlan steadied her.

"You almost lost this immigrant, Officer," Pete said.

"There are so many, what difference does one make more or less? What good will this sick little child bring to America anyway, especially since she's Irish?"

Pete controlled his Irish temper. Annie Scanlan hugged her.

"Someday you'll show them how wrong they are!"

Angela believed that, if she were given half a chance, she would indeed show them. Yet she knew they wouldn't let her in and if they did she wouldn't find the train to Chicago and the people in Chicago wouldn't want such a sick little child.

Castle Garden was a big gloomy fort which once had been a site for a battery of guns to fend off English invasion. Now it was nothing but a vast hall in which straggling lines of immigrant families, poor, disconsolate, beaten down, waited passively for America's decision whether to admit them or to send them back to countries that didn't want them either.

"Why are they letting us in?" she asked Pete Scanlan.

"Because they need us. They have more jobs than they have people. Your Yanks are no better than your Brits. They're not hiring us out of the goodness of their hearts."

"How long before we become Yanks?"

"The moment we leave this building, Angie," Ann Scanlan told her, "won't you be complaining about all the furriners coming into our country?"

It was a cold December day in New York City. Angela hated the city already. The city immigration officials were snobs who hated the Irish. She was convinced that they deliberately kept the process slow so that some of the immigrants would have to spend the night shivering in Castle Garden. She was still wobbly from seasickness, hungry and sleepy. But she reserved a little of her energy to hate the New York cops.

Finally, late in the afternoon as it was growing dark, they finally arrived at the head of their line.

"Is this older child yours?" asked the cop, a man with a thin face, long nose, and suspicious eyes.

"No, she's only holding one of our children."

"Carry your own children, please."

So Angela handed over poor little Chiara, who immediately began to scream.

Another inspector appeared.

"Are you waiting for admission?" he barked crossly.

"Yes, sir."

"Let me see your papers."

Now is the time I fail.

She gave him the correspondence from Chicago and her medical papers. He read them very carefully.

"Inoculated against smallpox and diphtheria? Isn't that unusual in Ireland?"

"I lived with the family of a physician."

"You don't look particularly healthy . . . skinny, undernourished."

"I suffered from seasickness on the way over and haven't eaten much in the last two weeks."

"Indeed . . . well, I'll have to call for a doctor for a physical exam."

The Scanlans were permitted to enter. They waved good-bye as they were ushered out.

"I'll write you," Angela shouted. "Thank you very much. God bless you!"

Then they were gone. Angela was alone again, as lost as she was at the railroad station in Cork. It was darker now in Castle Garden. The light was failing inside and outside. The immigration officers were folding up their tables, some of them donning thick overcoats. The lines remained in place, hopeful families assuming, wrongly Angela suspected, that they would have earned the place they had when the regular day of work had ended. They were worse than the Brits.

She started the rosary again.

"Are you waiting for someone, young woman?" a silver-haired policeman with gold stripes suggesting authority asked her.

"I am waiting for a medical examiner, sir. Since three o'clock, begging your pardon."

"I see . . . Might I look at your papers?"

Angela handed over her stack of papers. He glanced at them.

"Nothing incriminating . . . Why did the inspectors want a medical examiner?"

"They thought I looked unhealthy, weak, and skinny. I told them that I had seasickness through the whole voyage from Kinsale."

"Well, you're tiny all right . . . Let me look at your eyes . . . Bright enough, I'd say . . . now open your mouth and let me see your tongue . . . healthy enough . . . No fever . . ."

He placed his hand on her forehead.

"No, sir."

"Regular flow of blood?"

"Not for a long time, sir."

"Would you mind if I listened to your chest?"

He produced a stethoscope and listened very carefully, moving the instrument back and forth and then around the back of her neck.

"Good strong heart, good strong lungs, good strong young woman . . . Hard worker, I'd wager."

"I try, sir."

He removed an ink pad and a stamp from his overcoat pocket and briskly stamped all her documents.

"Angela Agnes Tierney," he read the name off the top document. "Welcome to the United States of America! May it be as generous to you as you are willing to be to it."

"Thank you, sir," she said. "And may the good Lord in heaven be as generous to you as you have been to me."

Ma would be proud of that response.

"Is someone waiting for you outside?" He tightened his white silk scarf.

"I don't know, sir."

The street was cold and dark, the gaslights cast

strange shadows—ghostly, Angela thought. The clatter of horses and the spin of wheels on the pavement grated on her skin. She clutched her rosary more strongly.

"Anyone waiting here for Angela Agnes Tierney? Bound for Chicago on the New York Central? Mrs. Sheehan, why did I have to ask?"

"Thank you, Colonel. Her friends in Chicago asked me to wait for her and transfer her to the New York Central. I think we can get her on the eight o'clock train."

"Angela, may I introduce you to Mrs. Cordelia Sheehan. She heads a group of women who take care of immigrants that might be lost when they come out of Castle Garden."

"How do you do, ma'am." Angela curtsied.

She shook hands with the Colonel and entered Mrs. Sheehan's private carriage.

"Are you hungry, Angie?"

"Yes, ma'am."

"Well let's see if we can get you a bite to eat."

"Yes, ma'am. What was the Colonel's name?"

"Harry Flannery. He's in there to make sure that Irish immigrants are not persecuted. It still happens, as much as it might surprise you."

So with her first good meal in three weeks warming her whole body—beef, mashed potatoes, and chocolate—Angela was delivered to Grand Central Station and Train 111 to Chicago. Mrs. Sheehan, who seemed to know everyone, introduced Angela to the conductor, who promised he would deliver her safely to Central Depot in Chicago, for which Mrs. Sheehan rewarded him with a bill of American currency. Then she gave Angela three one-dollar bills.

"A boy will come around offering food for sale. You give him these three bills and tell him that Mrs. Sheehan said that you could have any food that you want."

"Thank you, ma'am."

"And my love to your friends in Chicago. We'll meet again, I'm sure, Angela Agnes. God bless. Oh, there are few passengers today, so you'll have that seat all to yourself."

She kissed Angela firmly on the forehead and dashed off the train, whose engine was already beginning to huff and puff.

"This is the water-level route, Miss Tierney," the conductor informed her. "No big mountains. Just up the Hudson River to Albany and the Erie Canal to Buffalo and around the Great Lakes to Lake Michigan and right into Chicago. By now they'll have the tracks plowed from the snowstorm last night. More snow and ice than you'll ever see in the Old Country."

Angela watched the Hudson River go by under frozen moonlight, then curled up in her blanket. She was very tired and, though frightened about what might await her in Chicago, she slept while she still could. There would doubtless be many things for her to do as soon as she arrived at the house on Union Square. Before she permitted herself to sleep she finished the final decade of her rosary and prayed for the good people that had rescued her so far on her journey. "I'm sure you sent them," she murmured to the Lord.

She slept soundly enough because she was exhausted, but fears of the Gaughans haunted her dreams. There were five of them, Paddy and Mae, the parents, Timothy, a son, perhaps fifteen, Rosina, a daughter about her own age, and Vincent, perhaps nine or ten. They were wonderful folks according to Agatha, but none of them were likely to welcome a dirty, smelly, skinny little serving girl that they probably didn't need into their family. From the books she had read about life in the Big Houses of Ireland she knew that the poor serving girls were especially likely to be at the mercy of the young men of the family. She was already fashioning in both her dreams and waking moments how she would deal with this Timothy Gaughan should he become forward. Rosina, she decided, would be a spoiled brat, and Vincent an obnoxious brat. Dr. Paddy Gaughan would be an overweight and pompous fraud and his wife Mae a nervous perfectionist. Well, she could deal with them one way or another. They would be better than a crowd of nasty nuns. All she owed them was the cost of her journey. They would specify what that was and what her wages were and she would establish when she would feel free to leave. It should be possible to obtain another position where she would be treated justly.

It had not been generosity and concern for her to have sent the remarkable Mrs. Sheehan to meet her at the gate of Castle Garden. They were protecting their investment, that's all.

When she awoke in the morning and reviewed the decisions she had made during her hate-filled sleep, she felt a little guilty. She had tried them and found them guilty without giving them a chance to testify in their own defense. She would do her best to be fair to them. She would certainly work hard to earn her salary. No employer of hers could ever claim that she was a lazy worker. Maybe they were lonely people who needed an extra amount of love. She doubted that. Rich people were never lonely. "You should always judge new people gently," ma used to say. "They're entitled to that."

It was before those years when poor ma hated everyone.

"I think you should hate strangers," she had argued. "Then, when they're nice, you'll be pleasantly surprised."

"Aren't you're a terrible woman altogether, Angie Agnes, and yourself fixing to have an unhappy life."

Poor ma. Yet her life had not been unhappy, not at first anyway. If you have to die young, maybe it's good to die with the man you love and with the children you love.

Could ma read her dreams?

That thought troubled her. She'd better be careful.

She was awakened by bright sunlight. Snow-covered fields stretched in all directions and reflected a huge sun in a cloudless sky. Was this what Amerikay was like all the time in winter—snow, ice, and a sun without mercy?

"Good morning, Miss Angela," said the conductor. "I hope you slept well? The porter will be along shortly with your tea. Isn't it lovely outside? That's Lake Erie over there where the fields end. It is a shallow lake, so it often freezes over in the winter. Lake Michigan tends to be open, though they have icebreakers to let the ore ships get to port. We should be in Detroit in another hour and then in Chicago by five thirty in the afternoon. No more snow is foreseen in the immediate future."

"Thank you very much."

"There are soap and towels and water in the restroom at the head of the car. It's not like the Pullman cars, but we try to keep our restrooms clean."

"Thank you very much," she said again.

She was sure that she would always hate America with its drab and dull scenery, its endless distances, its gigantic lakes and its strange names—what was a Detroit? What was a Chicago? What was an Erie? How could people live in such horrid places?

Yet the people in the train car with her were not horrid. They were sympathetic and friendly, delighted by her youth and her quick tongue. They assured her that she would love America, and especially Chicago, which had burned down two years ago and restored itself like a phoenix from its own ashes.

"It's a dirty, noisy, smelly place, with too many people and not enough homes. Still, honey, it is alive, and we love it."

They all knew of Union Square, where she would live and work. It was a beautiful neighborhood with a lovely park and striking stone homes, one of the nicest places in the city. Very salubrious. She would certainly love it.

Well, she didn't want to live in a salubrious place with striking stone homes. She wanted to be back in West Galway where she belonged.

No, she admonished herself, not anymore. Now you belong in Union Square with its lovely park and its striking stone homes. These Chicagoans are a little crazy but Brits they are not.

"There's Lake Michigan," a woman cried out. "We're almost home!"

From what she could see of Lake Michigan it was the ugliest place in the world—a huge sea, surrounded by ice-covered trees, Galway without the bays and the little harbors and the farm houses.

"Great summer resort area," a man said proudly to her. "Wonderful weather, big beaches, lots of kids. Wonderful relaxation."

Angela flat out didn't believe him.

Eventually the train seemed to curve around the south end of the lake and turn into Chicago, mercifully perhaps covered by snow to protect its tawdry ugliness. The last run up to Central Depot was along the edge of the lake. The sun was setting behind a thick curtain of smoke and bathing the dark waters in an evil rusty gold. Hell, Angela thought, could not be more ugly.

"Central Depot," the conductor announced.

Home.

The train eased its way into the depot. The lake had frozen near the shore.

"Back there was a place called Camp Douglas," a young man told her. "Confederate prisoners during the war. A lot of them died of disease."

"War?" she said.

"Our Civil War. North and South fought over freeing slaves. North won. A lot of young men died, millions, more from disease than from bullets.

"The University of Chicago is down there too. It's very famous."

Angela shivered. What a strange, deadly, mysterious country. With such nice people.

She glanced out the window, wondering if she would be able to pick out the Gaughans in the light of the gas lamps. In the crowd of people waiting for passengers, they were easy to see—five very well-dressed, attractive people and, Lord save us all, they had brought their wolfhound!

Angela gulped and sat down.

She was dirty, smelly, messy, and tattered. Give her a wheel barrow and she was Molly Malone, disgusting, repulsive, an untouchable. She was going to invade their clean, beautiful home with her terrible smells. Once they saw her and smelled her, they would loathe her. Dear God, take me now. Let the lake come up and carry me away.

The car was empty. The crowd was thinning out on the platform. The Gaughans were growing uneasy.

"Help you with your luggage, Miss?" the porter asked.

"No, thank you. It's not all that much."

And, like me, it has the smell of steerage and of the sea and of human waste.

Darkness settling over the depot. The sun had given up its battle with this little section of Hades.

"Well, now, isn't it time to get out and face your new owners?"

A woman in a shawl at the back of the car.

"'Tis yourself," she said softly.

"'Tis."

"Don't worry, I'll face them."

"You've always been a brave one, first child of my womb."

She lifted her blanket and stumbled toward the door of the car. She almost tripped as she climbed down the stairs to the wooden platform. The Gaughans circled around her.

"I'm Angela," she said in a voice from another world.

And the wolfhound barked his approval.

— 6 —

 MY WIFE was in her studio, which, naturally, was bigger than my office. In an expensive gown and robe which suggested perhaps imperial Japan or a very high-glass Vegas bordello (an image I never advanced), she was stretched out on a chaise as though she were considering which one of her lovers she would summon for lunch. However, the meaning of the scene was quite different. She was thinking. Or, more precisely, she was communing with the various wisdoms of the ages that sometimes floated into this sacred place.

Usually the result was work for me.

"You're going off to the links, are you now?"

The words sounded as if they were a protest—irresponsible husband deserting his family responsibilities. In fact, they were an observation.

"Woman, I am!"

That sounded like a husband laying down the law when in fact he was agreeing to the obvious.

She sighed loudly.

"I don't like it, Dermot Michael, not at all, at all. What did Mr. Casey say about poor Finnbar?"

"That he's not poor at all. Son of a big and successful

construction company over there that has a reputation for honesty and responsibility. Rock Solid."

"I don't like it, Dermot Michael. There's evil at work."

"Does our young friend know about it?"

I sat on the edge of her chaise. She moved a bit to make me more comfortable.

"How could he and himself desperate in love? You'll win today?"

"I usually do."

Another sigh.

"Butterfield?"

Upper Middle Catholic.

"Ridgemoor."

Originally wealthy Protestant. Now Catholic. Traders who didn't have to work in the afternoon. Still in the city. Quick ride.

"Elite, he'll like that. He's a nice young man. Too bad there's so much evil."

"We'll take care of him, Nuala Anne."

"We will. There's new evil over across too."

That meant the parish.

"The rough ones are taking money from the others. Protection money."

"Parents uprising?"

"Those obese seventh-graders made the mistake of hitting on Peteyjack Murphy."

"They'll have the feds all over them."

Peteyjack was the younger child of Cindasue Lou McCloud Murphy and Peter Murphy. He was named for his father and his father's uncle, John Blackwood Ryan, Cardinal Archbishop of Chicago. Cindasue, from Stinkin' Crik, West Virginia and a Commander in the Yewnited States Coast Guard with some sort of gumshoe tie up to the Secret Service. She carried in her purse a .45-caliber service revolver and was definitely not the kind of person a stray polecat would want to be a-messin' around with.

"They took a quarter from poor Peteyjack and sent him home crying. Cindasue was at work, and she and Pete went over last night. She put her gun on the Pastor's desk and warned them that polecats attacking her children were taking a big chance. It scared the pastor a little, but I'm sure they won't stop. The place is Donnybrook old style."

Donnybrook is a fashionable suburb of Dublin now, but it was once the locale of the wildest annual fair in Ireland. Founded by King John, the Fair was a week of drunken violence in which the criminals who had poured in from all of Ireland took control of the event and as much of Dublin as they could manage.

"Thank heaven *you* don't pack a .45 in your purse."

She looked up at me and tilted her head.

"Sure, Dermot Michael, don't I still have me camogi stick below in the parlor and itself fading from not being used."

Camogi is a form of field hockey played by Irish women who are considered too delicate to play hurling, the national sport of Celtic Ireland. My wife at sixteen had been All-Ireland at camogi. Alas, I had never seen her play.

"You wouldn't do that."

"Wouldn't I now?"

"You have your taekwondo?"

"Not as good as cracking a couple of heads."

Pushed hard enough, me wife could become an Irish Tiger. The crowd across the street might push hard enough. We would have to take action soon.

"Don't do anything till I come home."

I brushed my lips against hers. As always there was an electric charge in those lips. The fire, whatever it was, never went out.

"Take good care, guys," I instructed the hounds. They dutifully walked me to the door and then returned to herself's lair.

I considered the camogi stick, slumped in the corner of the parlor.

"Never mess with *that* one," I issued a general warning.

Before I turned the ignition on in my battered old Benz, I called Mike Casey, former Superintendent of Police and President of Reliable Security, a shadow police force composed of off-duty cops earning a few extra dollars. Reliable and the "real" cops cooperated closely, since they were in fact the same people. The city was more secure, and the cops had a little more spending money and better insurance coverage. I had a permanent retainer on them because me wife—herself with the camogi stick—was a world-famous singer.

"Cindasue produced her .45?" Mike said. "Why am I not surprised?"

"She don't cotton to polecats a-robbin' her kids."

"That school yard is a tinderbox, Dermot. We have to watch it closely. Father Sauer and Dr. Fletcher are pushing the envelope. John Culhane should go in and arrest the lot of them."

"He can't until there's more complaints. I'm sure he's heard from Cindasue already . . . Your people are all around the place?"

"Sure, mothers pushing buggies, sewer workers checking manholes. It doesn't look like it's a situation which is likely to explode."

I thought about if for a moment.

"Mike, one of the things I've learned from herself is that once you have a situation in which a lot of little things are wrong, they can suddenly coalesce and you have a firestorm of evil. Like Germany in 1932. Or Iraq. Minor evils feed on one another and suddenly evil breaks out all over the place. We have a parish with Yuppies pouring in, stress with the old-timers, an unhealthy relationship between pastor and principal, disagreement about grades and athletics, the usual

crowd of bullies, resentments towards celebrities—
each of these problems edging towards the limit and
then suddenly they explode into something that is much
bigger than any of the individual conflicts and become
demons. So a very rational civil servant begins to revert
towards her Stinkin' Crik style of dealing with polecats."

Mike Casey was silent.

"From the beginning, Dermot, this situation has not
smelled right to me. I don't quite know what to do."

"I've told my brother that when it starts to burn we
have to put out the fire immediately."

"Tell him and Blackie I agree completely."

I did not add that I feared that my wife and daughter
would be at the center of the explosion. They were the
focus of the envy and the resentment which was corrod-
ing the parish and its school. No woman had the right to
all the talent Nuala Anne possessed, and no tween
should have such poise. Why not hate them?

As I drove downtown to pick up young Finnbar
Burke, my other voice, quiet for some time, intervened
to offer his opinion.

*That place is a loony bin. If you weren't afraid of
running away, you'd get your children out of there
now.*

*The kids want to stick it out. Herself thinks that it's
our parish and we ought to defend it.*

I thought you were the head of the family.

Whatever gave you that idea?

Finnbar Burke was waiting for me in front of an old
hotel just off the Magnificent Mile, which was being
rehabbed as a boutique hotel for business travelers. He
was wearing a dark green tweed hat, a buttoned tweed
vest, and a white shirt. Both his vest and his tweed cap
informed the world in gold letters reminiscent of the
Book of Kells that he was a member of OLD HEAD
LINKS/KINSALE/IRELAND. He was carrying the biggest

set of golf clubs I had ever seen, also in a dark green bag with the Old Head logo.

"Kinsale, is it?" I said, having learned from me wife how to express irony.

"And a vintage Benz," he replied. "Cool!"

I opened the trunk with a key, so old was the car.

"Not vintage, just old. I've had it longer than I've had me wife. She drives that red Lincoln Navigator parked in front of our house. She feels it makes a statement. I have to hide this in the alley. She wants to replace it with a Lexus, which means she'll have two cars and I won't have any."

He sighed the approved Kinsale sigh. "'Tis the way of it . . . You don't carry many clubs, do you now, Dermot?"

"I always have a hard time deciding between a three iron and a five iron. Since we're playing Ridgemoor, I'm bringing me five."

A driver, three irons, and a putter—more than enough for a golfer who knows his way around a course. Me wife claims I'm showing off.

Which you are.

"One of the great old Chicago courses," my guest informed me as we pulled away from the hotel. "It will be an honor to play it and itself inside the city limits."

Be careful, kid. Isn't your man a great one for gamesmanship?

"This is one of the hotels your firm is redoing, isn't it?"

"Slowly and carefully, Dermot. We bought it when the market was at bottom for such places. We're working on it now that the contractors are looking for something to do, and we'll open it when the business travel increases again and men and women will be looking for a comfortable, elegant hotel which is not run like a reform school."

"Low risk?"

"As low as we can make it. You see, our tradition back home, and now here, is to save things that should be saved—homes, hotels, even neighborhoods. We found that you can always make an honest profit that way, so long as you're quiet about what you're doing. We're astonished at how you Yanks let wonderful neighborhoods disappear."

"Some make it because, like ours, they luck out, mostly because of transportation."

"Yet others, like your old westside, had wonderful transportation and it disappeared almost overnight."

"Racial fear and corrupt real estate."

"And isn't there tension in your neighborhood between the new folks and the old folks?"

"Stirred up by the church?"

"We'd stay out of that neighborhood."

"A wise decision, though there's some old homes a block north that deserve to be saved."

"Not till you get rid of the amadons at the parish."

The kid was too smart by half.

"Me Julia tells me that you and herself can beat the amadons."

"We don't lose many times," I agreed.

"She wants me to buy one of those old homes so we can raise our kids in the parish. I tell her that sometimes the survival of a community is a damn fine thing, as the Duke of Wellington said."

Finnbar Burke was a very shrewd young man. He wanted to know how far we'd go for himself and his possible bride.

Pretty far, but now was not the time.

"We'll drive out on Chicago Avenue to Ridgeland, which becomes Narragansett when it crosses North Avenue. Isn't the course named after the third ridge of sand dunes that survived from the last ice age, the first being Clark Street, where you need a microscope to see the ridge. The second is the Vincennes Trail out in

Beverly, and the third is Ridgeland. The course was built for rich commodity brokers who have every afternoon off and figure they can get on the first tee by one thirty. Rich Protestants, now rich Irish Catholics . . . You let one in and the first thing you know the whole neighborhood is gone."

"And yourself one of those brokers?"

"Retired," I said sharply. "I made a lot of money one day because of a mistake. I now take the occasional position, but only when others wiser than me are taking it."

Like your wife.

"Ridgemoor is your official golf course?"

I had to think about that.

"Butterfield probably is, though we belong to Oak Park River Forest too, my family that is. My handicap is three at each of them. I got a four at Polerama this summer."

"I do about the same at home," Finnbar Burke said cautiously. "Maybe we should play each other even, and yourself with only five clubs."

"I should give you three strokes because you're new to the course."

"That wouldn't be proper at all, at all, would it now and yourself paying the green fees."

Finnbar Burke was testing me to see if he could properly pull my leg, which is fair enough between two sons of Erin.

"Well, you wouldn't expect me to pay them when I come down to Old Head from Polerama next summer?"

"Would you ever do that? It would be grand craic altogether and ourselves preparing for the World Irish Open?"

"I'd bring me wife along—you do let women play at Old Head, don't you now?"

He threw up his arms in dismay.

"How can we keep them out! The Brits and the Scots don't think we'll pull it off, but the prizes will be big, and isn't your man playing with us the year after next?"

"He's played the Old Head and yourself in the foursome?"

A stab in the dark.

"And didn't he beat the living shite out of me? A nice man, mind you, but not the world's greatest conversationalist, save you're talking about his golf game."

So Finnbar's family were among the movers and shakers in County Cork and the low-key imagement was probably part of the family's business style, membership in the Old Head by way of being an exception. They made money by saving whatever was worth saving and could be saved with a nice profit margin. The firm would be run by a tight family management with the shrewd oversight of a butcher shop or a bakery.

Finnbar was duly impressed with the old elegance of the clubhouse (a little less old than it pretended to be) and the easy style of the staff.

"And, sure we don't have this kind of autumn colors back home." He marveled at the late September symphony of leaves which was also carefully orchestrated by the staff. At Ridgemoor nothing was left to chance, especially the courtesy for the young man in the funny clothes who was the guest of Dermot Coyne who was also a nice young man—and always would be—with the world-famous wife.

"They have the same atmosphere here we want to cultivate in our boutique hotels," he whispered to me, "and it's meself who doesn't like that dogleg on the first hole—long par four is it now?"

"Long par five, actually, Finnbar. We try to separate the men from the boys here at the top of day."

"I may want some of those strokes I rejected."

The twosome which would play after us appeared

while we were teeing up on the first hole. Both were traders a little older than me and hence respected the Dermot Coyne legend more than it might have merited. They were friendly to my little guest with the odd clothes and the almost unintelligible Cork brogue.

"Rusty," I said, "this is my friend Finnbar Burke from Cork City."

I didn't know Rusty's last name and I had no idea who the other fella was. You learn to be a good faker if you're married to an Irish wife.

They shook hands and watched with some amusements as he drew a four wood.

Finnbar was a no-nonsense golfer. He glanced down the fairway, shoved the tee into the ground, addressed the ball briskly, and then, without any fooling around, bashed it towards the green. I was impressed with his first shot, which stopped about two hundred and fifty yards from the tee, right at the bend of the dogleg.

I heaved a sigh of relief. The kid was good, very good indeed, but not quite good enough to take Nuala Anne McGrail's aging young man. I drove over the trees, taking the short cut towards the green, and landed almost a hundred yards closer to the green.

"Brigid, Patrick, and Colmcille, aren't you a desperate man, Dermot Coyne, and meself wanting all of them three strokes you were after wanting to give me."

"Be careful, Finnbar Burke," one of my friends told him. "We say around here that Dermot Coyne is a charming young man, lots of fun and all that, but never play golf with him for money."

"And meself, nothing but a poor man with a hundred dollars riding on each hole!"

We weren't playing for money.

He was an excellent golfer and managed to get a par on the first hole against my birdie. And that was the way of it. Sometimes we were tied, but then I forged ahead on the next hole.

"This is great craic," he said, sweat pouring down his face, "but you're a desperate man altogether."

I almost blew it. He pulled even with me on the seventeenth, which I had planned to win but missed the putt for a bogey.

"Youthful vigor and healthy living will triumph in the end and I'll beat you by a hairsbreadth."

Eighteen at Ridgemoor is called "fool's gold" because the huge green is protected on three sides by a pond. Many a fool thinks he can hit his drive two hundred and ten yards and hit the green on his first shot. The psychological and physical obstacles are too many, however. When I get serious and concentrate, I can hit it every time. This round I drove to within three feet of the hole. Then I sunk the putt for an eagle.

Finnbar Burke of Cork City and the Old Head Links dissolved in laughter.

"Didn't I know all along you'd end it this way! Serves me right for trusting a frigging Yank!"

"And himself on his favorite course."

We sat down at the bar, ordered two shepherd pies and two Guinnesses, and settled down to talk about the game. Finnbar Burke was not only a good loser, he was a loser who celebrated the give and take of the game. Nice young man. Julie and he would do well.

"So what's the big project for you guys here in Chicago? What is your big save?"

He glanced around, smiled and said, "I know you're the kind of man who can keep a secret."

His light blue eyes sparkled with glee.

"A westside Irish Catholic like yourself knows about West End Parkway, doesn't he?"

"If he has any sense . . . You're going to restore it!"

"Why not?"

"From Central to Austin?"

"It never really was that long, but we're going to improve on the original. Some of the gracious old homes are still there . . ."

"But pretty much wrecks . . ."

"We hope to make it one of the great streets in Chicago. Ballrooms with parquet floors, indoor and outdoor pools, elegant gardens, stately homes, everything it once was and even more. It will continue south what your friends up at St. Lucy's did north of the L tracks and extend the redevelopment all the way to Jackson Park and the Expressway and then across Austin into South Oak Park and Forest Park."

"Your scheme?"

"With a good architect, yes."

"And your family buys in?"

"They like it, compare it with what they did in Donnybrook, only bigger potential. Mind you it's all done slowly. We never chew off too much. So we start with reviving two old homes at West End and Austin and see what happens."

"And the city is behind it?"

"Why wouldn't it be? Like I say, it's all transportation. You have two L lines—the Green and the Blue—and an expressway that runs out to the Mississippi River."

"At least."

"I don't see why Chicago let it all fade away so quickly."

"It happened so quickly out here that no one noticed. Panic pedaling and white flight."

"We'll have integration every step of the way, low-key, volunteers, all taken for granted."

"The people at St. Lucy's had a hard time at first," I said.

"They saved the whole area, an enormous achievement. We come along and stabilize it and extend it, with full cooperation. We know it won't be easy.

That'll be the fun of it. If something is easy, we won't be doing it."

I swore myself to secrecy and drove him back to the hotel, which was the company office and home for the personnel from Ireland. For a hundred years and more, American money had been flowing into Ireland; now some of it was flowing back, and not only for the big spire at the mouth of the river.

Finnbar Burke and I had become fast friends on the golf course, and in the conversation afterwards. I promised my help if it were ever needed. We promised that we'd play Butterfield next. He swore he'd be out practicing before the next match. Two guys enjoying great craic together.

Only it was not to be.

— 7 —

ME GOOD wife was still clad in her imperial gown and robe, still unprepared, it would seem, for the work of the day. She had arrayed herself on the antique couch in our parlor (living room to her), the two snow-white puppies deployed in protective modality at the foot of the couch, and the long inactive camogi stick on the floor next to her. She was so appealing that I experienced a strong impulse to fall on her and claim her as my own—which indeed she was.

Go for it!

Go away.

I settled for finding a place to sit next to her on the couch.

"You were on the links with Finnbar Burke? And you defeated the poor young fella on the last hole?"

"Woman, I did, and himself a grand young man."

I recited the history of our game and of his economic background and big plans. She nodded approvingly.

"Julie will never want for breakfast, will she? And in our neighborhood too? Dermot Michael Coyne, I don't need another pretty daughter and herself with pale gold hair like the poor thing in the story."

The phrase was pronounced the way it would be in Connemara: "Da pur ding in da story."

"You like Angela, do you now?"

"We Connemara women have to cling together, don't we?"

She sighed and readjusted her position on the couch. In the process, one of her marvelous breasts pressed against the fabric of her gown. Naturally, I rested my hand on it. She gasped and bit her lip. Sometimes I manage to surprise her.

"You battle a man on the links and then you come home and ravage your woman . . ."

"An interesting possibility, now that you mention it."

"I had a battle too," she said, "with your good friend Dr. Fletcher."

Dr. Fletcher was the former nun with a doctorate whom our pastor, Father Sauer, had appointed CEO of our parish school.

"What was the battle about?"

"Me doggies! Didn't she threaten me doggies?"

"The puppies!"

"She said that she couldn't promise that harm would not come to them from the attendant if I brought them on school property again."

"*What* attendant?"

"The escaped convict she had hired as her security guard . . . and didn't she say that in this time of global warming and food shortage that such dogs were a luxury of affluence which took food out of the mouths of poor people all over the world?"

"They knew she was talking about them?"

"Of course they did. Didn't I send them downstairs?"

She had a scary trick of signaling to the dogs by a kind of telepathy.

"And you responded by threatening to rearrange her physiognomy with your camogi stick if any harm came to them."

"I told her that she already had one of the ugliest faces in the world and that children and adults would run at the sight of her when I was finished. Didn't I chase her out of me house and warn her never to come back or I would turn the doggies loose on her."

I tightened my grip on her breast and felt her nipple rise to my hand. This one would be easy. An angry Nuala Anne was always a good lay, unless she were angry at me.

Predator.

A man takes what he can get.

"How do you know that the attendant is an ex-con?"

"Didn't Cindasue find out and wasn't he charged with assault and intent to kill?"

"I'll have to call my brother George . . ."

I began to rearrange her garments. The hounds withdrew.

"Didn't I talk to him already . . . He said Father Sauer was out of control . . . And now you'll be attacking me, poor defenseless woman that I am?"

"I had that thought in mind, but only when I saw you stretched out so invitingly. There's no point in having a mistress tucked away in an attic in Paris if I can't come in from the battlefield and fall all over her."

"And the poor woman with no choice at all, at all."

"None . . ."

"You won't let them kill me doggies, will you, Dermot Michael?"

"Woman, I will not!"

It turned out to be a very interesting late afternoon frolic.

That was excessive.

She's me wife.

All the worse.

I carried her upstairs and tucked her into bed.

"I think I'll need a nap before the brats come home. Sure, haven't I earned it!"

I had to take a nap too. It had been a long, hard day.

That evening after supper, we argued in my office about how to deal with the parish. My wife wanted to defy them and walk over to the school yard with the hounds every day. I argued that we should hold our cards close to our vests. The solution would have to come from elsewhere—the police or the Archdiocese. However, I suggested, we ought to pull our kids out of the school even if they wanted to stay. We didn't want to be part of the fight which was certainly in the wind. Enroll them in Chicago Latin for the rest of the year.

"They won't like it, Dermot Michael, they're their parents' children and they don't like the idea of running away."

"It's a fight they can't win. Not unless more families are willing to abandon the school."

Our eldest, flushed and sweaty from basketball at the little park around the corner—Mr. Flynn wouldn't let anyone play in the school yard—bounced upstairs, finger in place in her homework notebook.

"Da, Father Sourpuss is downstairs and wants to talk to you. He said explicitly it was you he wanted."

"How were the hoops?"

"Beat all the boys at twenty-one."

"Naturally."

Nuala and I went downstairs to see him. The hounds had both tried to shake hands with him and had been rebuffed.

Frank Sauer was a classmate of my brother George, hence in his late thirties. He was a thin, nervous man with rapidly blinking eyes and the dubious smile of a pre-owned car salesman at a Hyundai dealership. His thinning brown hair was arranged so as to protect as many bald spots as possible.

"Frank," I said, extending my hand. "Good to see you."

"Would you please dismiss your beasts. They make me nervous."

Nuala sent the signal. With some reluctance Maeve and Fiona trundled down the stairs, tails between their legs. They didn't like being rebuffed three times in one day.

"Sit down, Father," Nuala offered, the picture of pious Irish Catholic respect.

He ignored her.

"Dermot, I want to talk to you about those dogs. I don't want to argue with you. I want to ask you as a personal favor to keep them out of the school yard, indeed, off the street between your house and the yard."

Even though it was a warm September evening, he was shivering. His smile came and went as we talked, independently of what he said. What a shame that the Archdiocese didn't have stronger men to appoint as pastors in these tumultuous days when we were desperately short of vocations.

"Nuala?"

"Dermot, please. I've come here this evening to talk to you, man to man, as head of the family, and ask you to go along with this request before something unfortunate occurs."

"We won't get anywhere, Frank, if you insist on that context. I am not head of the family. We have a consensual democracy in this house. The actual head varies from issue to issue. On matters of the parish school I think the head is the young woman who opened the door for you, fresh from basketball down the street at the park because your Mr. Flynn won't let them play in the school yard. By the way, I'm sure you know that he's not a legitimate hire for a Catholic school."

He began to breathe heavily, perhaps to control his temper.

"Always a little unstable at the seminary," George had told me. "Probably shouldn't have ordained him."

"Dermot, please. We are trying to build a parish here that is socially aware. Arnie Flynn is indeed an ex-convict. Dr. Fletcher taught him in grammar school and believes he is totally reformed. His past mistakes should not be held against him. I will not discuss the matter further. We think you of all people should be on the side of the poor and the oppressed and not the oppressive laws that victimize them."

"You might start losing a lot of students, Frank."

"We want only those students who come from families that are willing to embrace the Catholic social principle of the preferential option for the poor."

"I guess, Frank, that I am committed to Mr. Joyce's social principle that Catholicism means 'here comes everyone.'"

Father Sauer turned on his heel and stormed out of the house. He was held together by shoelaces and rubber bands.

"OK," Nuala said, "Ms. Nosey Posey can come down the stairs."

"They're both 'round the bend," Mary Anne said glumly. "They'll ruin everything."

"You guys could go to Parker or Latin," I said.

Our eldest turned up her nose.

"We want a *Catholic* school."

"St. Clement's, FXW?" Nuala offered.

"We'd be on the waiting list."

"We have some clout . . ."

Mary Anne turned the idea over in her head.

"I'd like to think about it, Da. Maybe Cardinal Blackie or someone will work a miracle . . . I gotta do my homework, even if homework is capitalist oppression."

"Are they still stealing money from the little kids?" Nuala asked.

"Gena Finnerty still picks on second-graders. Dr. Lecher says it's all right."

"Lecher?" I said.

"As in Hannibal Lecher. The little kids believe that she was fired at her last school for eating first-graders alive."

She flounced upstairs with her homework notebook.

"I believe the man's name was Hannibal Lecter," I murmured.

"Little kids always get things wrong," Mary Anne shouted from the top of the stairs.

"Well?" asked my wife. "What does the head of the house think?"

"How would I know!"

The hounds appeared again, looking very dubious. We embraced both of them and assured them that we were about to take them down to the pub.

"I think just what you think, Dermot Michael—we keep the doggies out of trouble. We let our kids stay there as long as they want. We talk to our friends at FXW. And we wait and see. With all the trouble in this sad old world of ours, it seems a shame to be so upset about a brawl in our parish school."

"And yourself reading my mind. I suppose Blackie needs more to intervene."

"More, I should think, Dermot love, but not much more."

We assembled the dogs, left Julie in charge of the kids and walked hand in hand down the street to the pub where we had planned to sing.

"Me Finnbar tells me that you won today but you cheated!" Julie had said. "You had an eagle on the last hole."

"Dermot always does that, Julie."

"Actually he had a grand time altogether."

"So did I." And then I added sotto voce to me wife, "Especially after the golf."

"Shame on you, Dermot Michael Coyne, and yourself knowing that we behaved liked two animals."

"I thought we were animals."

She giggled.

"'Tis your fault altogether for being such a good lover."

Well, with a compliment like that, wasn't I willing to take on the whole parish, most of whom, it seemed, were at the pub. We sang the old-time songs and the hounds made friends with everyone and howled on signal. Everyone wanted to talk about the parish crisis. Both the newcomers and the old-timers thought that the leadership was crazy, that the bullying had to stop, and that Mr. Flynn had to go. Also the Finnerty family, which was new in the parish and strongly supported the Principal. Their kids were the prime bullies. They dismissed the support for Sourpuss and Dr. Lecher as a crazy minority. They were especially concerned that the teachers had lost the right to assign grades. They were to submit tentative grades to the Principal, who would then correct them from a "religious" point of view. Most of the teachers would leave at the end of the year.

"They never consult the school board," Josie Ostrowski, a VP in a data-gathering company, complained to me. "The parish council never meets. Fletcher has abolished the athletic committee and closed the gym. There's no one to complain to."

"The Archdiocese," I said, as though I were an expert, "is inundated by complaints from parishes, most of them ideological. They get concerned when they hear an enormous amount of static, which they *should* hear from our neighborhood. If the static gets loud enough and madcap enough, then they take action.

Under the present administration, that is likely to be sooner rather than later."

"Letters?" Josie asked.

"Letters, petitions, delegations, ads in the papers."

"We have better things to do in our lives," Marty Lyons protested, "than fight downtown. We don't want to look like malcontents."

"You all sound like malcontents," me wife said. She had been strumming on her guitar while the discussion continued.

"The athletic committee," said Larry Conor, a graduate of the dome, who was athletic director and coach of about everything, "has decided to ignore her. We use the park as our home-court gym and play with the players we have chosen instead of the geeks she assigns. The Finnertys raise hell because we won't play their Gena, whom the Principal has named captain of the team. We won't let her on the court because she wants to fight. It's a cuckoo's nest, not a Catholic school."

The talk continued. But no action came from it. They weren't offended enough to give up their passive attitudes towards the parish and devote some of their time to fighting back. Everyone had some experience with a crazy pastor or a tyrannical nun when they were growing up—which they described in great detail to much laughter. The Catholic church hadn't changed that much at all.

After Nuala had sung her final piece—always "Molly Malone"—we held hands as we walked home together.

"You're going to call His Riverence when we get home?"

She always referred to my brother with great respect, long before he became Blackie's Blackie.

"Woman, I will."

"Can I listen in?"

"Have I ever tried to stop you?"

"No, but don't you know it wouldn't do any good?"

George, the priest, listened carefully to our account of the evening at the pub.

"It isn't a battle between newcomers and old-timers?"

"Maybe a little, but the leaders of the bullies are all newcomers."

He was quiet for a moment.

"What should we do, Bro?"

"What you will have to do eventually would be better done now. Have someone do an impartial audit of the parish and suspend Pastor and Principal till it's over."

"They're doing some publicity about them in some Catholic journals—liberation theology in Chicago's gold coast. Trying to brand the boss as a conservative. One of the religion writers at a Chicago paper's about to do a partisan piece."

"You have to stop these people, Father George." Nuala was in her doomsday mentality. "They're evil. Terrible things will happen. People will get hurt. Maybe killed."

Silence.

"I know better than to argue with your instincts. We'll do what we can. The superintendent of schools is blocking everything. She's a classmate of Dr. Fletcher."

"And the new Vicar for Education?"

"Rick is fresh out of graduate school and greatly in awe of the superintendent . . ."

"You might want to look into Dr. Fletcher's degree," I pointed out. "And ask sister superintendents about it."

Silence.

"I'll do that, Dermot."

My turn for silence.

"George, you can pass this on to Himself and file it in your own memory. These clowns are going to go too far. Count on it. It's in their nature to do so. When they do, you and Blackie and everyone else must clamp down. Hard. Otherwise. I endorse my wife's analysis. All hell will break out."

Another silence between two brothers who always found it difficult to talk seriously with one another.

"Gotcha, Bro. We'll lay out our plans now."

Me wife nodded her approval.

"You did good, Dermot, you have the right of it."

On Friday afternoon we were invited to attend the basketball game between our parish and St. Clement's at the local park. Our firstborn admitted that she might play "a little bit" and that it was all right if we came and watched. We could even cheer for her. If we wanted to bring the Mick and the little kids that would be all right too. She was expecting to do well and wouldn't mind an audience.

We accepted the invitation, though Nuala and I admitted to one another that we were nervous.

"You'd better call your man."

This time I knew she meant Mike Casey. He would send Monica and Shareen, the two off-duty cops who did security protection for Nuala Anne on some public occasions—and for the family.

St. Joe's sports teams were for some reason called the Cardinals, and wore bright crimson uniforms. The young women came to the park in uniforms and sweat suits of cardinalatial red. Our own heroine looked smashing during the warm-up. She was having the time of her life, even to the extent of acknowledging our presence with a casual wave of her hand.

"She's really good, Dad," the Mick assured me. "Even the boys in seventh and eighth grade say so. Coach won't start her because she's only in seventh grade. Watch the game change when she gets in."

The stands at the park were pretty well filled.

"There are more people here than at the boy's football team outside. A lot of them will sneak in to watch Mary Anne."

"Those three young women over in the corner."

"Gross City—Kitty McGinnis, Sue Wozniak, and Gena Finnerty—biggest bullies in the school. Everyone who comes out for the team is entitled to uniforms and to sit on the bench. Coach ignores them because the Lecher mandated that he start them. He won't even put them in at the end of the game, because they would mess everything else up. All they can do is foul."

"Poor young women," Nuala sighed.

"Ba-aad," the Mick muttered.

Our firstborn was tall, lithe, and lovely. Her mother at thirteen, except more self-confident. She seemed to make most of her shots during the warm-up. Then she put on her crimson jacket and walked briskly to the bench.

The Cardinals did not play very well in the first quarter. They seemed listless and awkward. They missed shots and threw passes away. The Chicago Bulls on a (typical) bad night.

At the end of the quarter the coach sent our onetime baby into the game. Me wife gripped me hand. Our little one was all over the court, snatching rebounds, intercepting passes, feeding shooters. The team was lively, but it was still down six points.

The coach raised three fingers. Our point guard nodded and the game changed. Mary Anne drifted to the corner. The point guard whipped the ball to her. She rose with a jump shot that scarcely disturbed the net. The St. Joe crowd went wild. Their hero was at work.

She took five more shots before the half ended. Four of them were scores and the fifth earned her three free throws which made her total eighteen points. She laughed, spun around in pleasure and beat everyone down the court.

"She's not any taller than anyone else out there," her admiring brother informed me, "only she's got springs in her legs."

During the warm-up at the beginning of the second half, Gena Finnerty, without much effort at deception, charged into her and knocked her over. The crowd cried in protest. Mary Anne rose slowly to her feet, glared at her foe, and walked over to the bench. The coach whispered in her ear. Mary Anne nodded solemnly.

She didn't play in the third quarter, but rather sat contentedly on the bench and watched her teammates struggle to maintain their lead. With five minutes left in the game, the coach sent her back in. The ovation this time was indeed thunderous.

"I'm so nervous," me wife admitted.

"Get used to it," her older son advised. "It's always going to be this way."

She only hit four for six this time, plus four free throws. The coach pulled her with thirty seconds left in the game. More cheers. She waved at us and slipped into her crimson jacket and modestly accepted the congratulations of the losing team. She had won with such class that even those whom she had beaten loved her.

She joined us in the stands and hugged each of us, her mother last of all.

"Were you seeing yourself out there, Ma!"

"What I would like to have been?"

Of course they both cried, so did little Socra Marie who was dreaming her own dreams.

Then, as we were saying good-bye to the Coach, a bowling ball rolled across the floor and hit me—Maureen Finnerty in one of her famous attacks. Face purple, eyes wild, fingernails extended, she hit me with full force, screaming curses which I could not understand.

"She shouldn't be playing. My child is in eighth grade. She should have been out there. Why do you rich people take everything away from the poor kids? Your daughter is a selfish, stuck-up bitch! She'll pay for it, you just wait and see."

Her punches landed on my chest. I pushed her away. She came back at me again, filth pouring from her mouth. Monica emerged from the crowd and held her. Mrs. Finnerty tossed her away. Then Shareen appeared on the other side.

"Take your hands off me, you dirty nigger whore!"

"We're police officers, ma'am, and you're engaging in disorderly conduct."

I wondered where my wife was. Why hadn't she joined in the melee? I glanced around. Our young basketball star was firmly restraining her.

"Mo-*ther*, you'll only make it worse."

"Maybe I want to make it worse!"

Then the two top women in my life collapsed into each other's arms and the both of them laughing hysterically.

The Mick had been struggling to keep his two younger siblings from fighting to defend their poor da from the woman who Socra Marie dubbed "bitch-monster."

"Actually," our young star became loquacious, "poor Gena could play on the team if she lost some weight and practiced, but in her world it's only influence that matters. If she had as much influence as I did she would be sinking those three pointers. I challenged her to a match but she wouldn't play. Her poor father can't control any of them . . . you see that man over there with the stooped shoulders and the long hair, trying to talk to the cops? He's a hydrologist or something like that—he studies water levels. His big problem is that he's *not* crazy. Will they put Mrs. Finnerty in jail?"

"Overnight maybe. They won't bring her to trial this time."

Poor Maureen Finnerty. She was Nuala's age, maybe a little older. Too much food and too little impulse control. No matter how the contretemps at St. Joe's ended, she would suffer.

"She looks so fragile, Dermot Michael." My wife sighed as we were drifting into sleep.

"Maureen Finnerty?"

"Well, she too, but don't I mean poor little Mary Anne? She's just skin and bones and those bitches from St. Clement's were fouling her all the time."

"Whenever they could get close to her, which wasn't very often, but you have the right of it, Nuala love. She's graceful and lovely, but vulnerable."

"I don't want her to play professional basketball. Or even college."

"That will be up to her."

"I know."

"And yourself all-Ireland a few years older waving that awful hockey stick."

"Camogi, Dermot Michael."

We would perhaps have that discussion many times in the future.

The next morning one of the Chicago papers carried an interview with Dr. Lorraine Fletcher, CEO of St. Joe's school.

"We're trying to create a Catholic school that will de-emphasize grades and athletics and instead emphasize the preferential option of the poor. This parish is the people of God in West Lincoln Park. Our reforms have the support of the majority of the people. We are absolutely firm in our convictions that we are doing God's will. We are not afraid of Ryan. He is a nonentity. He is not the leader of the people of God. He was Cronin's shoe-shine boy."

The next day the other paper reported the CONTRO-VERSIAL PRINCIPAL'S DOCTORATE QUESTIONED. It seemed that the University of Illinois had no record of a Ph.D. being awarded to Dr. Lorraine Fletcher, the controversial Principal of St. Joe's Catholic school in the West Lincoln Park area of Chicago. Sister Mary Theodolinda, superintendent of Catholic schools, dismissed the controversy: "Lorraine is finishing her dissertation while working at St. Joe's. She will receive the degree in the spring."

A spokesperson for the Archdiocese of Chicago dismissed Fletcher's charge that John Cardinal Ryan had ever shined shoes, "for himself or anyone else."

Asked to comment on Fletcher's comment that he was a nonentity after a Confirmation service in River Forest, Cardinal Ryan replied, "Arguably that is true."

Typical Blackie.

At breakfast on Monday morning, before crossing Southport in the first big autumnal deluge, Mary Anne announced a career decision.

"That was a fun game. I love basketball. I'll play next year and at St. Ignatius College Prep if they let me, but no college or pro ball for me. That's not fun."

The decision would change many times. Mary Anne would often be in error but never in doubt.

"You mustn't be too hasty," her mother said, as any mother must, entering a qualification, a caveat, a hedge, "about turning down opportunities."

"You didn't play for Galway when you went to university."

"I fell in love with a frigging rich Yank!"

Laughter around the breakfast table.

"And you'd already decided you would be an accountant."

"But I really wanted to be an actress."

"And ended up a singer," Mary Anne ended her mother's biography, "because that's what the Yank wanted you to be."

"So he wouldn't have to work!"

The four kids and Julie and the hounds tumbled down the stairs, the kids struggling with rain capes and carrying their books. Mary Anne helped the always-flustered Socra Marie with her rain cape.

"Dermot Michael," me wife asked, "what in the world use is that cupola above your office?"

"With a telescope I can see the scoreboard at Wrigley?"

"Would you ever think of putting a TV camera there to monitor the school yard, like every time the childer are over there, even if we are not around to turn it on?"

"Woman of the house, I will think very seriously about that."

ANGELA DIDN'T want to open her eyes. The room was filled with light, the bed was soft, she had slept a long time, and a delightful aroma was all around her. She realized that the sweet perfume was herself. She had never smelled that way in all her life. It was a very pleasant dream. She didn't want it to end. She could not understand what exactly had happened at the Central Depot. There had been a lot of tears. She didn't think any of them were hers.

"I'm Angela," she had said. "I'm your new serving girl. I'm skinny and dirty and smelly and tattered and weak from motion sickness. But I'm a hard worker and I promise you'll be satisfied with me, if you'll give me just a couple of days."

A beautiful woman with a kind smile and a shapely body embraced her. Her dress was a kind of pale blue. Angela felt the corset stays under it.

"I'm Mae Gaughan, Angela. This is my husband, Doctor Paddy, and my daughter, Rosina, my older son, Timothy, and my younger son, Vinny. We welcome you to Chicago. We are happy you survived the trip. We don't need a serving girl. We have a couple of Negro servants who are wonderful. We need a little sister. We want you to come live with us and be our little sister."

"I'll work very hard," Angela insisted, "just give me some time. You'll see how hard I work."

"Please be my little sister." Rosina, a lovely young woman in a fawn-colored dress embraced her. "I've always wanted a little sister. We have a wonderful little brother. Don't leave us . . ."

She was wearing corset stays too. Why had they dressed up for her, a worthless, dirty little servant girl?

"Give over, ya eejit, can't you see that they've fallen in love with you and they want to adopt you into their family! You'll have to love them just the way you loved all of us. Mae will be a better mother than I could be . . ."

"Don't leave me, Ma!"

"I'll never leave you, dear one. Won't you have two mothers to love?"

Vinny, the little brother, grabbed her hand.

"Please stay with us. You're so pretty. We'll always love you!"

Tears, love . . . These people were mad! She'd better get on the train to New York.

Timothy, and himself with dancing blue eyes that took her breath away, tried to remove her battered old tweed blanket. She pulled it away from him.

"Just wanted to carry your luggage," he said, his face turning red. "I'm glad my new little sister is part Viking . . ."

"I'm not Viking. I'm a pre-Celtic aborigine. We've been trying to civilize the Celts since they invaded our nice little island. Their menfolk are as bad as ever."

She laughed when she said it, and they all laughed too. She handed her tweed bag to Timothy, who blushed again.

"You have a tongue in your mouth, little one." Dr. Gaughan shook hands with her. "And wit in your head. You'll fit in fine with the rest of the family. You're most welcome. Now we have our carriage out here and we'll take you home and get you a bite to eat." He glanced at her eyes. "And clear eyes and no hint of fever in your forehead."

"I'll work hard . . ."

"I'm sure you will, little one, I'm sure you will."

So it was concluded that she was a member of the family, the warm mother, the genial father, the sensitive sister, the adorable little boy—and Timmy with the blue eyes and the winning smile. She belonged to them and they all belonged to her. It would be a big responsibility. She would not let them down. And she would work hard.

The big Negro gentleman who drove the carriage bowed politely to her and welcomed her. His name was James Marshal, he said. Most folks just called him Mr. Marshal. His wife, who was the cook in the house, was Mrs. Marshal.

Angela would learn much later that polite speech to Negro servants was not typical. Also to Irish servants. Even by the Irish people for whom they worked.

She slept during the carriage ride and woke confused and uncertain, clinging to her rosary.

"You have a lot of sleep to catch up on, don't you, dear?" Mae Gaughan said soothingly. "Take your time, you have nothing but time."

Later, much later, Angela began to question the generosity and kindness of her new family. Weren't they just a little strange, morbid perhaps, about their new child? Then she came to understand that generosity and kindness *are* a little strange, and that she should strive to imitate her adopted family.

The Gaughans lived in a big stone house on the edge of a park they called Union Square. They had a large garden of roses in the backyard, which the women in the family carefully tended. She would see that later.

Mrs. Marshal fed her a "collation" of roast beef, warm bread, mashed potatoes, and steaming hot chocolate. She did her best with it, but she was almost too tired to eat.

"Timmy," she said to that young man who stared at her as one dazzled, "my, uh, Irish tweed luggage . . . There is nothing in it of any great value, except to me . . ."

"We'll take care of it, little sister!" he said, enveloping her in a big smile. Timmy was a nice, polite young man, but he could become a problem, especially because he made her heart leap a little. He was a man, and in general men were not to be trusted. But he *was* a nice man . . .

She was installed in the guest room which was big with windows that opened on the park and a big fireplace. The bathroom had not only "facilities" but a large tub filled with steaming water. Mae and Rosina helped her out of her clothes, wrapped her in towels, and led her to the tub. At first the water was too hot, then she reveled in it as someone might who was planning to rise from a tomb. This was all half-dream, half-vision by now. They washed her hair and then brushed it. Then they gave her a gown and a robe which must have been Rosina's, put her to bed and said the last decade of the rosary with her. She was sound asleep after the third Ave.

Finally, she opened her eyes. The Doctor, Mae, and Rosina hovered over her like three protective angels.

"How long have I been asleep?"

"Twelve hours or so," the Doctor said, glancing at his watch.

"I'm sorry."

"Nothing to be sorry about. Do you mind if I listen to your lungs?"

"That's what doctors do."

They all laughed again.

He listened very carefully.

"Breathe deeply."

She did.

"Strong heart and strong lungs . . . no flow of blood for a while?"

"Over a year."

"It will start again soon, and you'll grow a bit and put on some weight and catch up. You've been through a rough time, and we'll keep an eye on you."

"I'll try not to be a bother."

"When can she begin to go to school?" Rosina asked.

"Perhaps when the second semester starts. Mom can take you over to St. Mary's Academy during the Christmas vacation. I'm sure you'll be brilliant."

Rosina was in her second year at St. Mary's. She would go on for the full four years, though most of her classmates would leave in the spring to begin their careers as stenographers and machine operators. Timmy was in fourth year at St. Ignatius College and would graduate in two years and then go on to Rush Medical college.

"I want to go there too," Angela told herself, but kept the thought in her own head. "Not because Tim will be there—because I want to be a doctor."

And that was that.

The next day Mae and Rosina took her downtown to Marshall Field's to buy her some clothes of her own.

It was too much for poor Angela. She was overwhelmed by the size and the variety and quite incapable of making choices for herself. Moreover, her new family was far too lavish in its plans for outfitting her. She would absolutely not wear a corset, not with her skinny little body. It would be an affectation.

"I can't make these decisions," she said finally. "I don't know what I need or what I like. I'm sure I'll love your choices."

They were delighted at the proposal. Now they could have all their fun clothing this cute little doll that had washed up on the edge of Union Park. The doll didn't mind. They wanted to make her happy. She would make them happy.

She didn't even protest the second corset and the corset covers for her scarcely existing breasts. Later, of course, she would change her mind when she discovered that, suddenly, she had a figure that some men liked and some young women envied.

"I'm sure you're tired of hearing me say thank you," she whispered at the end of the day. "I am very grateful to you for making me part of your family. I'll never say thank you enough. Please imagine me saying it all the time."

Both the other women wept. So did Angela.

Later Angela would say that the Gaughans had given her a new life and she would always be grateful. Still later, when tensions arose, she wasn't so sure. And still later, fortunately when her foster parents were still alive and the final family ties were shaped, Angela realized that she had made a big contribution to her new family simply by being herself. That insight scared her for awhile. That she was capable of filling vacuums in the lives of others simply did not seem possible.

On Sunday night, when the Marshals enjoyed a day off, Mae cooked her famous pot roast dinner for the family and invited guests. Among the regulars were Peter Muldoon, the handsome young parish priest at St. Charles Borromeo, where Vinny went to school, and Dr. Calvin Crawford, the Dean of Rush Medical College. Angela resolved that she would keep her big Irish mouth shut tight, lest she embarrass her new family. Father Muldoon was a charmer, Dr. Crawford a pompous fool—and his wife Minerva a perfect match for him.

"So you came here expecting to be a serving girl," Father Muldoon began their conversation, "and find yourself a member of the family . . . Do you find this a welcome change?"

"A great surprise, Father. They must have been desperate for a new sister if they would settle for someone like me. They've been very kind and good. I am afraid that I'll say or do something stupid and they won't want me anymore."

"I doubt that, Angela. They seem to be very proud of you, as well they might be."

More compliments, and this one from a priest.

"They love me, Father, each of them in their own way. I cannot account for it, but I am very grateful."

He nodded wisely and smiled, a warm and gentle smile that set her at ease.

"Is it not the way God is with us. He does not consult with us but takes us unasked into his family and showers his exuberant love on us because of his generous spirit."

Angela thought very carefully about that.

"I suppose you are correct, Father Muldoon, the Gaughans are like God. That explains a lot, doesn't it?"

"They are indeed extraordinary people. You will attend St. Mary's Academy?"

"After Christmas, I will meet with the nuns to learn whether they want me. I hope they do, because Rosina will be there too, and that will be a help to me."

"I don't think there's much doubt about that. Mae Gaughan tells me that you play the piano and speak French."

"A little bit of both, and neither very well."

He smiled again.

"And after St. Mary's?"

"I will try to enroll in Rush Medical College. I want to be a doctor. I don't imagine Dr. Crawford would think that a good idea . . ."

"He and our host are arguing about the theory that disease is spread by miasmas, swamp-like areas which are thick with disease. We know, don't we, that inoculation prevents smallpox?"

"We do indeed."

"You have been inoculated, Angela?"

"By my doctor in Ireland."

"And as a doctor, you would not be afraid to be assigned to a pest-house of smallpox victims?"

"Sure I'd be afraid, but I'd do it because it was my duty and I wouldn't get sick."

"Because of God or your inoculation?"

Trick question.

"Is there a difference?"

He chuckled.

"You are a very interesting young woman, Angela Tierney. If I can assist you in your education, don't hesitate to call upon me. I do have a little influence in certain quarters."

"Thank you, Father."

Angela was not prepared to admit that she was an interesting young woman, not even on the testimony of a nice young priest. He had not, however, dismissed her plan to study to be a doctor. She shifted her attention to the discussion between Dr. Gaughan and Dr. Crawford.

"We have five major plagues here, Calvin: smallpox, diphtheria, malaria, cholera, and typhoid fever. The first two we can rout with more inoculations; malaria for some reason seems to be ebbing, and we have medications which seem to control it. Cholera is a matter of impurities in drinking water. If we should reverse the flow of the river, the water in the lake should be free of cholera. Only typhoid would remain."

"So you would advocate mass inoculations and the sanitary canal. And who, Patrick, would pay for these vast expenditures?"

"The same government which found a way to pay for the horrors of the recent war between North and South. The saving of so much human life would be well worth the cost."

"Would it, Patrick? How many of these immigrants who become sick so easily would ever become useful citizens? Are we not really better off without them?"

"I cannot accept such a view, Calvin. The immigrants are willing to work hard at back-breaking tasks. I see their contribution as essential to the well-being of the Republic. We could not have rebuilt this city so quickly after the fire without their work."

"And how would they remove the miasmas from our swampland? You cannot really believe so completely in this germ theory? No one has ever seen a germ, I might remind you. We might better spend what little money we have for public health funding by clearing away the lands which generate the miasma of disease. Your germ theory is not proven, and nothing will ever be able to prove it."

"Miasma is part of the same mythological folly," Dr. Gaughan insisted, "as bleeding patients into weakness from which they die before the germs finish them off."

"Paddy," Mae Gaughan intervened, "I wonder if you could interrupt your discussion to cut the roast for us."

Dr. Gaughan smiled slightly, grateful that his wife had cut off an argument which would grow more intense, yet sorry to yield the field of battle.

Timmy was sitting next to her at the table. He whispered a question:

"Who do you think has the better of the argument, pre-Celt little sister with the long silver-gold hair?"

Angela's face warmed at the compliment. He was a smooth one. Dangerous? Probably not too dangerous.

"Our father, of course. Dr. Crawford is a pompous fool!"

Timmy struggled to control the laughter that seemed always to lurk inside him, at least when Angela was around.

As they left the dining room to split into men and women, he touched Angela's arm.

"I'm happy that Dad is now your father too," he struggled in his embarrassment. "It means you are part of the family."

She scared the poor young man as much as he scared her. Interesting . . .

"Timothy, I have been absorbed into this family by an abundance of love which is almost godlike . . . I wasn't asked and I don't deserve it, but I'm happy to be your sister and Rosina's sister and Vinny's too."

She turned her back toward the drawing room, so she would see only the tiniest beginning of delight on his handsome face. She would keep Timmy at bay, but not too far away, by gentle teasing. Some day he might seek his revenge, but, she shivered slightly, that was beyond the boundaries of the distant future.

Minerva Crawford attacked her as soon as she was seated at the outer fringe of the women in the drawing room.

"Child! That surely isn't the natural color of your hair!"

"I'm afraid that it is, Mrs. Crawford. Out in the West of Ireland they say it is a sign of aborigine blood, pre-Celtic like the Indians are pre-American."

"It looks like straw . . . You simply must do something with it."

"In the West of Ireland they say it looks like a field of fresh wheat in the morning sun and is a sign of fertility and God's love."

"How disgusting!"

"I like it." Rosina, big sister, came to her rescue.

"You are not entitled to an opinion, young woman. Whatever they might say in the West of Ireland, a place which I haven't visited and hope never to, it simply won't do in the United States of America. Mae, you must do something about it if she is going to live in this house!"

"If I have to change the color of my hair to live in this wonderful house, I will leave it."

"Mae! Will you listen to her! You must send her to the Academy immediately. The nuns will teach her some respect! She is simply not acceptable in your family."

"She is new in this land, Minerva. We will see that she has time to adjust to American customs."

"Well, I certainly hope so. I suspect that hair is the result of some sickness, the bad airs which cause disease. Maybe that's why the rest of her family is dead."

"My family died because of the famine which the English imposed on Ireland," Angela replied. "Rather than starve they ate meat which was poisoned. It had nothing to do with the color of our hair."

"Mae, this child needs to learn some respect for her elders."

"Well, we'll see how she gets along with the nuns."

Minerva Crawford took that as agreement. Angela accepted it as approval from her new mom, whom she had begun to adore. Rosina grinned triumphantly.

Their interview with the Mother Superior at St. Mary's Academy did not begin any better.

"You have a strong Irish accent, young woman," Mother Superior observed.

"West of Ireland, Sister."

"You have Gaelic?"

"My parents spoke it at home, God be good to them, and I picked up a little. We studied it in school."

"English is not your first language."

"It is in the national schools, Sister."

"You can read English."

"Oh, yes, Sister."

"Would you read this piece of oratory, please."

She handed Angela a card. It was "Let no man write my epitaphs."

Angela began to read it and then, in the kind of bravado that she couldn't resist, she put the card aside and recited it from memory and with feeling.

Sister grinned.

She then fired questions about arithmetic and catechism, quite unrelated to one another, cutting off the answer to one question and shifting quickly to another. Angela enjoyed the challenge and fired back her answers briskly and confidently. Sister continued to grin.

"She plays the piano too, S'ter," Rosina said meekly.

"Ah, you took piano at school, did you?"

"No, S'ter, I play by ear."

"Do you now? Can you play something classical for me?"

"A little bit of Mozart's Night Music, maybe S'ter . . . Not very good, I'm afraid. Are you sure you don't want to go back to arithemetic?"

"You are a difficult child, Angela, but I do want to hear what you do with the Night Music."

Angela went to the upright piano in the corner of Mother Superior's office, ran her fingers over the keys to become familiar with them, paused at a key that needed tuning, sat for a moment to get in the right mood and, eyes closed, began to play. She made it very sad music, perhaps not what the composer intended. There were tears in her eyes when she finished. She looked up at the nun and thought she saw tears behind the thick lens.

"You are a very talented young woman, Angela

Tierney. Should we admit you, I'd be privileged to provide you with music lessons every week."

"Thank you, S'ter. But I want to be a doctor."

"All the more reason to play the piano: to keep your sanity. Mae?"

"I think it would be wonderful."

"Then it's settled, unless you protest too strongly, young woman."

"Oh, no, S'ter, I'd like to be able to read notes."

"She talks French too," Rosina insisted.

Angela blushed. The love of her new family was superabundant, but embarrassing. Why were they that way? Father Muldoon said they were like God.

She replied in French, saying that her accent was not from Paris but from *le petit ville* Carraroe in Connemara.

S'ter replied in French that she had the gold and silver hair of Carraroe too and Angela remarked that it was said to be like a new wheat field under the morning sun, but she thought it looked like newly harvested straw.

"Well, Mae, we can't be party to losing this gifted young woman to a public school, can we? I think next semester we will put her in some first-year courses and some second year, where she will have her sister to protect her against the young women who may yearn for hair like newly harvested straw. Then they will be able to do their third and fourth years together."

"Thank you, S'ter," Rosina and Angela said together.

"I see that Miss Tierney is the kind of child that works very hard. Normally I would praise that, but, Mae and Rosina, we may have to insist on some occasions that she should relax and perhaps play for family singing or take other kinds of recreation."

"I'll see to it, Sister," Mae promised. "And thank you very much."

As they left St. Mary's, Angela said in a soft voice, "Don't tell Mrs. Crawford. We don't want to break her heart."

"What should we tell her, darling?"

"Tell her that Mother Superior is taking me under her personal supervision."

The next three years were happy ones for Angela. She moved into Rosina's bedroom. "We can be real sisters," Rosina exclaimed. "We can talk about boys and fight with one another just like sisters do."

"I don't mind talking about boys, though they're a pretty boring subject. But I won't fight with you, Rosina. I'll never fight with you."

It was a promise Angela kept through the years to come, some difficult.

She bonded with the family wolfhound, Sir Charles, who also moved into the bedroom and made himself at home. She learned how to read notes. She improved her French accent. She had the highest grades in her class and graduated summa cum laude. Her body belatedly burst into full and enchanting womanhood. Her charm and wit won over most of her potential rivals in class. She kept Timmy at a distance, but not too great a distance. Indeed she was his date at the graduation dinner for the graduates of St. Ignatius College (a six-year school) and dazzled everyone at the Palmer House with her white classic dress and her gold and silver hair, which looked like a blooming wheat field under the rising sun.

The Gaughans urged their children to invite their classmates to songfests in their parlor several times a year, the first one at her first Christmastime in Chicago. Tim's friends from St. Ignatius were bemused by her even then. She was, as he put it, a mixture of sweet and tart, fun and serious, laughter and tears, sister and wife, that men his age found irresistible.

"Mistress and wife," Rosina murmured.

Angela fell in love with many of them, one after another, without ever speaking to them. Tim was another matter. She asked Father Muldoon if it were a sin of incest to fall in love with a foster brother.

"I haven't done it and I don't plan to do it. But I want to know if it's a temptation."

"Tim," said the wise young bishop as he was now, "is not a temptation to resist, Angela, but a temptation to love, which is a much more serious problem."

"I know that."

She was not sure, however, what it was that she knew or didn't know.

Dr. Gaughan was a rich man, but not because he was a doctor. His fees for intricate surgeries were small for ordinary people. He had made his money in real estate and construction when he came home after the war with dreams of suffering and death that, despite his amiability, he could never force out of his life. He was a gentle, sympathetic father, but one able to draw lines that you would not think of crossing. Angela was acutely sensitive to these lines and did not wander near them. She played a slightly different role in the family than did the other children. The doctor treated her more like an adult than the others, an adult he could be frank with.

He was careful with his investments, unwilling to expose his family to the various panics that wracked the country in the decades immediately after the war. He had, however, bought a "shack" on a small lake just north of the Illinois–Wisconsin border to which the family journeyed for the month of July. It was in fact more than a shack, but the plumbing was outside and the water came from the wells. Isolated from the city and its newspapers and the demands of their friends, the Gaughans were supposed to relax and refresh themselves. There was a small beach and a pier in front of the house and small rowboats. They often were in their swim garments from breakfast to supper. A small town with a soda fountain was in walking distance, and a decent-sized forest in which young and old could hike. Life was relaxed, informal and seemingly unregulated. Only as Angela realized the two adults kept it closely observed, aware as they were of the four young people who were guests. Seamus McGourty, a classmate of Tim's at St. Ignatius College, with fiery and unruly hair, was theoretically Tim's guest, but he was also Rosina's companion.

"Some of my colleagues would say, Angela, that I am taking quite a chance by inviting four young people who are in the early phases of attraction to the opposite sex into an environment that is seemingly unregulated."

"It is wise to keep that caution in mind," Angela had replied. "It would be a shame to ruin the vacation."

"To say nothing of some lives."

"I won't let that happen," she promised.

He seemed surprised by her response.

"I'm delighted to hear that. You are, I believe, the youngest of the four in years, but much older in experience and insight."

"I should think," she charged on, she hoped not being too candid, "that one very dark night of modest swimming Indian style would be quite enough, not that I would think that Rosina's virtue or mine would be at any great risk."

Dr. Gaughan laughed. "You are a very perceptive young woman, Angela Tierney."

"I'll be in charge, Doctor, which is what you're asking of me. I had similar thoughts myself. You have made my thoughts more clear."

"We cannot help but notice that there is a certain attraction between you and Timothy."

"Since that first day at Central Depot. His eyes are too magical altogether."

"As is your wheat-field hair."

She felt her face grow warm.

"We are very young, Dr. Gaughan, and we have many important things to do in our lives before we think of marriage, much less talk about it. In principle, however, I cannot exclude it as a possibility for discussion someday in the future."

"Mae and I certainly would not want to exclude it either. In some ways you are years older than Tim, and in some ways so much younger."

"That is exactly how he makes me feel!"

Angela was exhausted when the conversation ended. They had covered many matters and clarified her world. They had also made it more complicated. Her quick tongue and her "way with words," as the nuns called it, had caused her to be much more candid than she would have expected. Now she was safer but more vulnerable.

So the days at the Wisconsin shack were uneventful.

For Angela, however, there was one jarring moment that would haunt her for years. She and Tim Gaughan had taken a long and leisurely hike through the forest to the cornfields beyond. Then, instead of retracing their steps to the lake, they walked down a country road and then around to the road that merged with the trail to the shack.

The day, which had started out cool and pleasant, had become hot and humid. Tim said there would be a thunderstorm by nightfall.

"Why don't we sit down and rest for a few moments," she suggested. "We don't have weather like this in Ireland."

"Sure."

Perspiration had soaked the light blouse and the short skirt she was wearing.

"Hot," she complained.

"You're very beautiful, Angela."

"Why, thank you, Tim! You may need spectacles, but that's a nice compliment."

"Would you mind terribly if I kissed you?"

What do I say now?

"I don't suppose I'd fight you off . . ."

In fact, come to think of it, Angela wouldn't mind that, at all, at all.

He put an arm around her, led her face to his, and kissed her very gently. His salty lips rested on hers and she did not resist the sustained contact.

"Thank you, Angela. I liked that a lot."

Angela had yet to be kissed passionately. She knew that Tim's kiss was not passionate. It was something less and something more. It had jarred her to the depths of her soul.

"You're very good at this sort of thing, Timothy," she said, recovering her smooth, conversational voice. "Lots of practice, doubtless."

"I love you, Angela. I fell in love with you the day you came into our family. I will always love you."

He leaped to his feet and walked rapidly toward the shack, uncertain perhaps about what should happen next.

Her first thought was that she would not tell Rosina that night about the kiss. Her second thought was to wonder if Ma had been watching. Would Ma approve? She glanced around hastily. No shadowy or translucent shape. Why did she think of Ma? Because Ma was always watching. She was the only one who might have seen them. Then she wondered if she should have prolonged the kiss. She sighed deeply. They might both be in serious trouble if she had. She rose and, her body now sheathed in perspiration, walked unsteadily back to the shack, went to her room, put on her swimming costume and plunged off the end of the pier into the lake. She swam vigorously halfway across its narrow span and then turned around. Was it a mortal sin?

Nonsense. How could anything so tender possibly be a sin at all?

That night as they all sat on the screen porch watching the stars and she brought glasses of chilled lemonade to the others, she whispered to Tim, "Thank you, that was very nice."

Would he try to kiss her again? Angela found herself hoping he would.

Compared to the kiss in the sunlight, the naked swim in the starlight was boring. Splashing and giggling and nothing remotely like physical contact, made interesting only by Sir Charles's unexpected appearance.

And Ma's.

A woman was next to her in the lake at the edge of the band of four young people and one delighted dog, a woman spun out of starlight and barely there.

"Well now, ain't you the terrible sinful young woman?"

"I knew you'd be here and yourself hiding there in the lake when himself kissed me?"

"Och, sure, I didn't think you noticed . . . and isn't this lake comfortable compared to Galway Bay."

" 'Tis."

Sir Charles jabbed at her belly with his big snout and then sniffed for the other human he knew was there but couldn't quite see.

"Suspicious dog."

"Any special reason to be here tonight, Ma?"

"Only watching you having fun?"

"You like me fella?"

"And what do I know about matchmaking? Sure you could do worse."

"And the family, up there in heaven, do they like him?"

"Up isn't exactly the right word, chiara, but what wouldn't they like? Now I must be going . . . We love you . . . Always."

"Just like Timmy?"

"Like but different . . ."

And she was no longer outlined against the stars. Sir Charles barked furiously in protest.

"That was exciting, wasn't it?" Rosina asked. "What if there were moonlight?"

"Maybe we'll find out next year."

Timothy would kiss her again, not on the vacation but at such events as graduations and birthdays. Angela tried to dismiss such contacts as a family exchange of affection. But her lips still tasted his long after he touched them.

The song nights continued with their classmates and other St. Ignatius boys after Tim enrolled at Rush. They were not quite as much fun with Tim up in his room studying anatomy. Now Rosina's young man, Seamus McGourty, was at Rush too, so they were, as they told each other, temporary widows.

Tim, however, was her partner at the St. Mary's dinner at the Palmer House.

"I was afraid I might not be asked," he said ruefully.

"How could I not ask you, even if I wanted not to ask you," she replied. "I wouldn't have been able to live in the same house as you."

It was the kind of remark that made Tim dizzy. She couldn't keep him in his present position—close enough, but not too close—for much longer. He would graduate from Rush at the age of twenty-one, old enough to marry. She and Rosina planned to attend a "normal" school the nuns had established for their students who showed an interest in schoolteaching, a program that Bishop Muldoon had established. For Rosina it was a career decision, for Angela, a postponed decision. She needed more education before forcing her way into Rush—and before she made up her mind about becoming a doctor. In the latter decision there would be no room for Tim, whom she now loved dearly and in whose closeness to her when they danced quite paralyzed her thoughts.

She often thought about it at night. In three years she had become a happy, adored member of a generous and loving family, graduated from the Academy, led her class academically, learned to read notes, and made many friends—all accomplishments that would have seemed impossible dreams on that cold December evening at the Central Depot. The earlier years of her life had disappeared to the outer fringes of her memory. Soon they would be forgotten altogether, nightmares that had never happened, not really. Ma, Pa, the little kids, the canon, her teacher, Eileen—who were they? She was not better than they were, only more lucky. In two years she would graduate from "normal" school, ready to teach. She would be a good teacher, like her mentor back in Carraroe. Would that not be generous enough? She loved and was loved by a big, handsome, brilliant man with a wonderful smile and innocent blue eyes. They had never spoken of love, much less marriage. Yet, though she still kept him at a respectful distance, they were in fact very close.

Did she have any obligation to give back? She had asked Father Muldoon, who told her that everyone had to choose their own vocation or combination of vocations.

She still slept under her Irish tweed blanket which had become an icon, a reminder, a prayer rug. Timmy had brought it to her after he had it cleaned.

"I thought you might want this," he had said shyly.

"Thank you very much, Timothy," she had said, unable to hide her tears. "It reminds me of what I don't want never to forget."

"I thought it might."

That and the rosary which she carried with her everywhere, even to dances.

She patted the loyal Sir Charles.

"We have a lot to decide, don't we, Charlie?"

"THEY TRIED to drown me poor Finnbar!" Julie wailed as she burst into our bedroom.

Exhausted from the various strains and tensions in our lives, we had elected for sleep instead of play and were fortunately fully dressed when she appeared.

Me wife, always the first one to rise to a crisis, was the first to respond.

"What happened?" She enveloped Julie in a maternal hug.

"He was coming out of school downtown and a bunch of gangbangers beat him up and threw him into the Chicago River and the police had to come and fish him out and he's in the emergency room at Northwestern in critical condition."

"OK, dear, we'll take you down there right away. Get dressed.

"Dermot," she instructed me, "please call Mr. Casey and make arrangements. I'll call the Cardinal."

I woke Mike Casey and his wife in their love nest at the John Hancock Center.

"I'll get Monica and Shareen over to your house. The redhead will let them in?"

"And offer to play poker with them."

"I'll have one of the armored SUVs over to pick you folks up and get someone down to the ER to guard the young man. I'll be back to you on the phone in his car . . . He's your nanny's fella, what else is he?"

I gave him the full background including my golf match with himself as I dressed. Me wife handed me the clothes because she knew how disoriented I was when awakened in the middle of the night.

"Rich, bright, hardworking Irish kid," I said. "Nice guy. It might just be random violence."

"Maybe, but we don't assume such things. They must have known what time his class was over. Our car is outside."

"Let's go," I said to me wife, who was waiting for me. She handed me my raincoat. Was it raining? Of course it was.

Julie was there too, a slicker drawn around her body, terrified but now in control. Also our basketball star in her St. Ignatius College Prep sleep shirt, bleary-eyed like her father.

"Monica and Shareen are on their way. Let them in. And no one else. We'll say in touch by cell phone. You do too. Don't disturb the little kids or the Mick unless it's necessary."

"That one," she said, meaning her brother, "would sleep through an earthquake."

While we were cautiously easing our way down the slippery wooden stairs, myself supporting Julie and me wife supporting me, a second car pulled up—our two off-duty cops turned instant babysitters.

"Sorry to wake you kids up," Nuala apologized.

"It's OK, Nuala. It's our business."

"Besides, we love the little guys."

Still, they would get an excessive Christmas bonus.

Mike Casey was waiting for us and himself as bleary-eyed as meself and Mary Anne.

"Subject left the Gleacher Center shortly after the end of his class at nine thirty. Walked over to the River Walk to return to his hotel on the other side of the Mag Mile. Said good night to his classmates. They heard a commotion, his scream, and a splash. They ran after him just as three young men wearing ski masks ran away. They saw the subject flailing in the water and calling for help. Two of them, young women with lifeguard training experience, ran down the steps to the river's edge. One of them jumped in, and the other held on to both of them from the riverbank. The subject was in pain from an injury to his leg. The lifeguard reported that the water was very cold for this time of year. The young men called 911.

"A helicopter scrambled from the old Coast Guard station and a fireboat came up the river. Police squads, fire trucks, and ambulances arrived from their respective stations. It must have been a spectacular scene.

"The chopper had a hard time in the rain and the fog. It made several passes along the river between the Gleacher Center and the Sheraton. A Fire Department unit deployed from in front of the Center down to the riverside, introduced a ladder into the water, relieved the stalwart lifeguards, stabilized the subject, freed him from the restraints, and removed him to Northwestern Memorial Hospital's ER, where he received treatment for shock, hypothermia, a possible broken leg, abrasions from the restraints, and possible internal injuries. His condition was described as guarded but not life threatening. The police boat docked at the riverside and the chopper landed in front of the Gleacher Center. NBC News, needless to say, was all over the place. The elapsed time of the rescue operation was forty-five minutes."

"He'll be all right?"

"Yes, Julie, he'll be just fine."

"Thanks be to God."

She buried her face in me wife's rain jacket.

"Forty-five minutes?" I asked.

"It was not"—Mike Casey leaned back in his seat in the front of the car and sighed—"a classic operation that didn't quite follow the plan, mostly because of the fog and the rain and the wind and the absence of coordination of the various agencies involved."

"One of those."

"The police boat had the wrong location," he whispered. "It passed the drowning man three times at a high rate of speed and went up the river to the North Branch, thus endangering the lives of the subject and the young women who were keeping his head above water. The police helicopter got lost in the fog. Barely missed the Gleacher Center, according to complaints from the University and the NBC tower. According to pictures that appeared on TV earlier this evening they probably shouldn't have scrambled in such bad weather. But they're a can-do bunch over there. The whole 911 transcript will be considered by the police brass. There'll be some reprimands. We don't need this kind of mess just now."

We in this instance did not mean Reliable Security, it meant the Chicago Police Department, trying its best to make an impression on the International Olympic Committee.

Despite the rain and the fog, we arrived at the ER of Northwestern Memorial Hospital in less than fifteen minutes. We ducked into the place, nothing like the ones in the movies. A young woman, a nurse or nurse's aide perhaps, greeted us.

"Ms. McGrail? I'm Dr. Somerville. Cardinal Blackie said you'd be along. You must be Julie? The patient keeps talking about your hair. He's doing fine now. When he sees you, he'll be even better. He tells me that your hair is like fresh wheat in an early sunrise. He's right. Come this way please."

Julie, who at first glance was not disposed to smile at this young woman who had charge of her fella, smiled warmly and squeezed her arm.

"Thank you, Doctor, for taking such good care of him. He loves to talk."

"My mother is Irish, so I understand."

We turned the corner and saw the long line of emergency rooms, lights coming from only a couple of them. Quiet night at the ER. The doctor who appeared to be no older than our Mary Anne conducted us into one of the lighted rooms.

Young Finnbar Burke was trussed up in a leg apparatus with a large cast on his left thigh.

"I've brought some guests, Mr. Burke," she said brightly, as though she herself had produced the guests on demand.

Finnbar Burke's eyes focused. The look of confusion on his face was replaced by a huge Irish smile.

"Julie," he said reverently, "I'm so happy to see you. I thought I'd lost my mind completely. Why would anyone want to throw me in the Chicago River? I don't get it! I was just coming out of class when these guys jumped me, and put handcuffs on me"—he held up his bandaged wrists—"and threw me over the side of the railing into the river. I think. I bounced on the way down."

Julie sat on the side of his bed and caressed his face.

"You remember me boss, Nuala Anne McGrail, and her husband Dermot . . ."

"Nice man. Never play golf with him for money."

"And Mr. Casey, who is the Superintendent of Police."

"Retired, but President of Reliable Security. We're here to protect you from any further attacks."

Finnbar Burke frowned, still unable to figure it all out.

"You think they'll try again?"

"We have to find out who they were."

"You sure have clout, Ms. McGrail. The Cardinal has already been here to visit me and give me the sacraments."

"Cardinals sometimes do good things."

"I'm laying here wondering if I'm gonna die and dreaming of me Julie's golden hair, and this man comes in wearing an old Chicago Cubs poncho. I figure that he's a derelict who is escaping the rain."

" 'Finnbar Micheal,'—he calls me that, which is me real name in Irish—'I'm Blackie. Nuala Anne sent me.' Sure enough it's the Cardinal, because he's wearing the ring and the silver cross around his neck. So he tells me I'm not going to die and that I'll be playing golf again in a couple of months and gives me the last sacraments, and Dr. Somerville and the nurse come in and receive Holy Communion with me, and I know I'm going to be all right just so long as me Julie with the golden hair shows up."

Julie with the golden hair rested her head on his chest.

A gorgeously accoutered cop pushed his way into the room. World War II brown leather jacket, B-17 flight cap (without the frame, of course), CPD Air patch on his shoulder, .45-caliber gun in a holster next to a mobile phone next to a BlackBerry. He was only a tad overweight.

"All right, all right," he said in the preferred tones of a cop giving orders, "I'm in charge of this case. Everyone out of the room."

"I'm Michael Casey, Lieutenant . . ."

"I don't give a good fuck who you are. You're out of here. You too."

He shoved me, an unwise move. I didn't budge.

"This subject was the victim of a felonious attack. I assume you've been giving interviews to the people from NBC News explaining why there was no danger of you crashing the CPD's expensive helicopter into their tower while leaving the rescue of this subject to the CFD. You have neglected to establish security to protect the subject from a repeat attack. Officer McNamara and I represent Reliable Security. The subject's family has asked that we guard him."

The cop was still pushing me and I wasn't moving.

Mike Casey was on his cell phone.

"I don't give a fuck. I want all you motherfuckers out of here. I intend to interview the subject and continue my investigation."

"No one is going to interview my patient, Officer," Dr. Somerville insisted.

"No fucking nurse is giving me orders."

Me wife, unnaturally silent through all of this discussion, intervened.

"I think we have heard enough of your language, Lieutenant, to accept that you are one tough cop. I would advise you that if you want to continue wearing that silver bar you should moderate your language, follow Dr. Somerville's instructions, and remove your hands from my husband's person, lest you want to end up on the floor and face a visit from the professional practices board first thing tomorrow morning."

"Who are you, bitch?"

"The subject's prospective mother-in-law."

Julie and Finnbar Burke giggled.

The lieutenant's mobile phone rang.

"Quinn," he shouted into it, "what the fuck . . . It's my case . . . Yes sir, right away, sir. Yes sir. I was only trying to do my duty, sir . . . Yes sir . . . Yes sir. I'm out of here."

"Someday I'll get you, wise guy," he said, giving me a shove.

"My wife does the fighting for us," I said mildly. "When she'd be finished with you, the department would have to feed you to the fishes in the river."

Nuala Anne smothered a laugh.

I slipped out into the corridor while Finnbar Burke explained to everyone why I was a desperate golfer altogether. I dialed home base.

"Dermot Coyne's house, this is Mary Anne Coyne."

"Is it now?"

"Oh, hi, Da, the kids are all sleeping. I'm just chatting with Monica and Shareen."

"You don't have school tomorrow?"

"Oh, Da, you're so nineteen eighty . . . All right, I'll go to bed."

"Don't wake up Socra Marie."

"I never do, Da," she sighed with infinite patience.

"The kids?" Nuala asked.

"Your daughter said that I was so nineteen eighty when I told her to go to bed."

"I would have said nineteen seventy."

So it was arranged that Julie would stay with Finnbar Burke, as would one of Mike Casey's off-duty cops, and the rest of us would leave.

"How much money do you have in your purse?" I asked her before we left.

"About four dollars," she said, embarrassed.

I gave her five twenties. "You might need this . . ."

"I can't, Dermot."

"We can't have you walking home in the rain."

"I could take the bus."

"No way."

"Thank you, Dermot. It's nice to have a da like you."

"Tell that to me elder daughter."

"Oh, she knows it."

The next morning Nuala Anne and I were having

our morning planning session in my office. I had demonstrated how my television apparatus up in the cupola scanned the St. Joe's school yard. It caught one big boy terrorizing a little kid for his lunch money, and an overweight girl gratuitously pushing a frightened first-grader. "Dr." Fletcher and Mr. Flynn were watching with approval.

"Call His Riverence and tell him?"

"George?"

"Dermot? What good news from the Archdiocese do you bring?"

"You sound bitter."

"All the crazies out there are testing the boss to see how far they can go."

"And he is . . ."

"Keeping a little list."

"I'm doing the same thing here. I have a monitor on the school yard which records the beginning and the end of the day, recess and lunch time. Picked up two nasty extortions this morning."

"And you save them?"

"Automatically go on disks."

"I suspect that there are not a lot of bullies, just that it's more open."

"What will you do when you move in?"

"Turn them over to the cops."

"Music to my ears. We've got pictures of 'Dr.' Fletcher watching such extortion."

"She's crazy, Dermot."

"And dangerous."

"His Riverence is not very happy, is he, Dermot love?"

"He's not. I don't think they can move till there is actual violence in the school yard or massive rebellion."

The phone ran again.

"Dermot Coyne."

The sound of someone clearing his throat.

"I'm Finnton Burke, Mr. Coyne. I'm the Uncle of Finnbar Burke whom you were kind enough to visit in, ah, hospital last night. We're very grateful for your, ah, kindness."

"Finnbar is a fine young man, desperate on the links, of course."

A dry laugh.

"As you might imagine his family is greatly concerned about this seemingly unprovoked attack. We would like to think that it was merely random violence, but we are, ah, unsure. It has been suggested to us that it might be a matter you and your, ah, wife could assist us in . . . Our family firm does not particularly like public attention. We are very, ah, conservative and, ah, cautious."

"We are very fond of Finnbar," I said carefully.

"I am a lawyer and Vice President of the American firm as well as a director of the mother firm in Cork City."

"Would it be convenient for you to visit us this morning? My wife and I will both be available. Say half ten?"

Note that I said *my wife* and not *me wife*.

"That would be, ah, capital, Mr. Coyne."

"I should mention that we employ Ms. Julie Crean in our family. She may be in the house at that time, if she isn't in class at DePaul."

"Ah, yes, splendid young woman. We, ah, encountered her at the hospital this morning. Very intelligent. Hair like, ah, a budding wheat field . . ."

"In the early morning sun," I concluded the saying.

"Then we'll see you at half ten."

"Capital!"

Nuala waited for him to hang up.

"Typical Cork talk, pratie in his mouth."

"A very cautious lawyer," I observed. "Probably his masters in Cork City are in a state of great unease."

"He sounds like a head usher in Church, a finicky old man."

Finnton Burke did indeed look like a head usher— thin, graying hair, very proper manners and clothes, perpetually uneasy—but he was neither finicky nor old. Rather he was only a few years older than I am, and handsome in a pale, sickly Irish way. He might have said that he was not long for this world. But he didn't. Rather he sat down in our visitor's chair, rubbed his hands together, and spoke more confidently than he had on the phone—and more tersely.

"The Burke family was, as you may imagine, dismayed by the attack on Finnbar. We have never experienced anything like this in four generations. My cousins in Cork blame it on a violent city and are inclined to recall Finnbar from his assignment here. He is the heir to the company, the crown prince, one might say. Understandably we do not wish to lose him."

"I have a pretty clear idea of the kind of work your firm does," I answered. "Surely you don't make enemies with what is essentially an altruistic activity."

"We have many begrudgers in Ireland, Dermot, as I'm sure your wife would tell you."

"Don't they hide under every bush." Nuala Anne reverted to her thick Galway brogue.

"Would you have any enemies in Chicago?" I asked. "Men or women who might have long memories of old times in Cork?"

"The last troubles south of the Ulster border were in the early nineteen twenties—between the Free State and the Irregulars, if you know the history of the time. They cost Ireland the life of Michael Collins. Like most commercial firms in Cork City I believe we were on the side of the Free State. But that was ninety years ago . . ."

"Time passes more quickly for revolutionaries when they're on the scene of old battles," me wife said, "than it does for the irredentists who are thousands of miles away."

"True enough, ma'am. The rebel songs persist in American pubs, long after they have lost meaning for young people at home."

"And meself singing them and thinking that they were songs for eejits."

"We don't know of any families here from those days, though surely there were some. We would think, however, that if this were a revenge attack, they might claim credit for it."

"Is there any memory of someone being thrown in the river . . . what's the River in Cork? Is it the Corrib?"

"That's in Galway, you eejits. In Cork it is the Lee."

"We have thought of that, naturally. Our company has never been the kind that throws adversaries into any river."

Nuala returned from the kitchen with her teapot, her soda bread, and her tea service, all from Galway, including Nuala.

She ascertained that our guest wanted milk in his tea. She knew that I rejected such pollution of God's great gift.

I noted that our guest did not sample her soda bread.

"Thank you, Ms. McGrail, I was after needing a sip of hot tea."

"Your family has a tradition at the Old Head Links at Kinsale?"

"Indeed, though only young Finnbar is active there now. It is a very difficult course, but we know of no ill will in our family history associated with the links, other than the understandable fury of golfers at its challenges."

"The Royal Irish Yacht Club?"

"That's another matter. The family has a motor/sail craft moored there, which we use often and fight about. Young Finnbar's interests, however, are on the links and not on the harbor."

"As I remember my history," I said, "didn't the Free Staters have the audacity to land their troops, equipped by the English, while Regatta week was in progress?"

Finnton Burke permitted himself a smile.

"'Tis true, though I don't think that outside of Cork anyone remembers that . . ."

"Galwegians have long memories," Nuala remarked.

"As far as you know, your family had no special role in that event."

"I have never heard of one, Mr. Coyne, and I would very much doubt it. We are very conservative people. Restoration has always tried to stay out of politics during our hundred and fifty years of history. We've had our work to keep us busy and our faith to restrain us from military involvement. We were originally a Quaker firm. While we've been Catholic for over a century, there's perhaps still some of the Quaker left in us."

"You're asking us to supplement the investigations of the police, this of course with the permission of the police?"

"Commander Culhane recommended such a strategy. Begging your pardon, Ms. McGrail, we are dull folks with little in the way of mystical genes. On the other hand there is just enough superstition among us to want to make sure that we've excluded ancient curses."

"I have been worried about our Julie and young Finnbar. I don't think there are any ancient curses or Civil War feuds, but I do think there is evil, plain old unmystical evil, at work. We'll try to sort it out for you. But you should have more confidence in Commander Culhane's detective than in us."

"Yet didn't your man say to me that you've never failed to solve a mystery."

"John Culhane is a Cork man like yourself—as I'm sure he told you, Finnton Burke—and I think when he visited the old country, he may have swallowed the Blarney stone."

We made arrangements to visit their offices and talk with the staff. It was possible that Finnbar's parents would be flying over. They would certainly want to see us too.

"Your brother is the head of the firm?" Nuala asked.

"He is, Ms. McGrail, though you'd hardly notice. He is not one of your American CEOs."

"I hope they would like our Julie?"

He smiled broadly for the first time.

"My sister-in-law would consider her God's answers to our prayers."

"A plausible fella," Nuala observed when he had left. "Almost a Prot?"

"He didn't sample your soda bread, which no Irish Catholic would turn his back on."

"Cork folks are strange, aren't they now?"

"You don't think it's some blood feud."

"I didn't quite say that, Dermot love. I said it wasn't some ancient curse. There is evil swirling around, even in that emergency room. We're going to have to uncover it."

I called Bob Hurley, the husband of my sister Cynthia. A lawyer like his wife, his field was West Side real estate.

"Bob, my wife and I are working on a case that involves real estate on the West Side."

"Thinking of moving?"

"Not yet."

"We'd get you a really good deal, especially now."

"I'll keep that in mind ... You know anything

about a company that might be rebuilding West End Parkway?"

"Sure, it's a very shrewd idea. Irish firm. Used to be Abernathy and Sons. From Cork I believe. Doesn't sound very Irish, does it?"

"They were Quakers but became Catholics a hundred years ago."

"That's outside the statute. I noticed that one of their locals got beat up yesterday. In front of the UC Downtown Center. There goes the neighborhood . . . You and the good witch of the West involved?"

"He's keeping company, as she would put it, with our nanny. Great golfer . . . Anyone out there have reason to hate them?"

"Real estate everywhere these days involves a lot of hate. Great for lawyers. I haven't heard of anything. I'll poke around and get back to you."

"He wanted to sell you a house in the suburbs?" me wife asked.

"I declined. I like it here."

"Even with the trouble across the street?"

"That won't last till Thanksgiving. I think I'll ride the L down to Restoration Inc. and see what the people there look like."

She nodded.

"I'll do my exercise and my singing and get ready for tonight. First parent-teacher conference. Herself says that she'll get four failures."

"What!"

"The poor teacher submits guideline grades to Fletcher, who then establishes permanent grades. All the anger is heaped on the teacher."

"So what do we do if all our kids flunk?" I asked.

"Withdraw them from the school?"

"They won't want that, will they?"

"I'm not sure."

The offices of Restoration were a corner suite on the ninth floor of the "boutique hotel." The transformation was proceeding slowly and carefully. The workers were men and women of considerable skill. It was neither a cheap nor a hurry-up job.

There were four people in the office: Finnton Burke sitting behind an old table in the corner, working on an old and pokey computer; Josie Kieran, an American middle-aged accountant with an expensive wedding ring, poring over a double-entry account book; Nessa Malone, a young stenographer and receptionist from South County Dublin with a mouthful of gum and braces; and Sean McCaffery, a Yank in his middle twenties who was introduced to me as "our staff architect." Low-key, unimportant people who would work hard for generous salaries and Christmas bonuses and not stir up any trouble.

"Perhaps, Dermot, you could use our conference room for your interviews. I should note, my friends, that he does not work for the police, and that your answers will be held in strictest confidence. We want only to protect Finnbar from another senseless attack. Let me have a word with you first, Dermot."

The conference room was a card table surrounded by four hard chairs. On a second table of the same sort, a coffee and teapot, a few cups with no saucers, and a plate of oatmeal raisin cookies.

"Finnbar is much better this morning. In good spirits and thinking clearly again, thanks be to God. Julie was leaving to go back to school and then her duties with your wife."

"She will be instructed to get some sleep and then return during visiting hours this evening."

"She will have money to take a cab? I wouldn't want her to be in any jeopardy . . ."

"We're taking care of that."

"We didn't set any agreement on your fee . . ."

"We don't take fees. Nor so-called freewill offerings."

"You are very generous, Dermot."

"My wife is very generous."

"The doctors are quite hopeful about Finnbar's recovery. They're pleased with the way the break is healing and hope to have him on crutches in a couple of days. Off the crutches and out of the cast by Christmas. No golf till spring, I fear."

"You have passed this information on to his parents?"

"I have, of course. I'm sure, however, they'll fly over here to see him. You'll find them very interesting."

"I'm sure I will."

"GOLDEN DOME four years ago, Mr. Coyne. Fooled around in restorative architecture. Bumped into himself on the golf course. Got a job. Love it. Your name is legendary at the Dome. Walked away on a middle linebacker slot and a glorious career in the NFL afterwards. Made a lot of money on the CBOT and married a beautiful and talented singer. From Dublin. His girlfriend takes care of your kids and adores your wife."

"That about covers it, I guess."

"The Holy Cross Fathers would value you more if you had gone to some swampy banana republic and came back with a permanent case of malaria, but they point with pride just the same."

"You wait long enough, Sean McCaffery, and your vices all become virtues. I learned a hell of a lot at the Dome, some of it even in classrooms, only it wasn't what I would have had to learn not to flunk out. Same

at Marquette . . . You have any drawings of West End
Park?"

"Thought you'd ask."

He opened an outsized manila folder and spread out
the top drawing.

It was astonishingly good. The old parkway looked
brand new, elegant, and yet musty enough to be an 1898
reproduction.

"You are very good, Sean McCaffery, very good
indeed. All it needs is gaslights, carriages, and top
hats."

"Thanks, Mr. Coyne. I kind of thought it was neat
too. Finnbar fils and Finnbar pere really bought into
it. They're going to get construction contracts next
month. I'll be in charge. Well, me and Finnbar, if he
can get around on crutches . . . These folks are the
real thing, though they act like I don't know quite
what."

"Head ushers at the old parish!"

"Got it! Perfetto! Here's the details on the first two
homes. They'll be corner mansions right on Austin
Boulevard. Walking distance from the L. Inexpensive
compared to other such houses in the metropolitan
area . . . You want to put down an advance payment?
I can get it for you wholesale."

"No, thanks. I'll have to show you my house sometime."

"That's what Finnbar says."

"You work under severe constraints here?"

"No way. Uncle Finnton pretends to be an old fogey.
All he wants is quality work—or what he thinks is
quality work. He doesn't peer over our shoulders. He
sends my work to Cork and they go ape over it. Easiest
job in the world. Maybe the most fun. I'll miss himself,
though. That blond is a distraction, but those things are
inevitable, I guess. She'll be good for Finnbar?"

"Absolutely."

"That's what Uncle Finnton says. She sure is pretty. Can I have dibs on your next nanny?"

"Who would want to throw Finnbar into the Chicago River?"

"Business rivals from Ireland trying to break into the American market, real estate crooks out on the West Side, maybe River Forest types not wanting the competition, IRA dissidents in nursing homes."

He shrugged.

"The cops," I said, "are probably thinking the same things. Any talk here about these possibilities?"

"Uncle Finnton talks to Cork every day from the phone on his desk. Neither side has any suspicions. Me, I prefer Irish mafia, but I'm a romantic."

On the L platform I had called my friend Bernie, who has some friends who have friends, if you take my meaning.

"Hey, Dermot, how ya doin.'"

"Breathing in and out. Yourself?"

"Couldn't be better. Your wife and kids?"

"Flourishing. Yours?"

"Can't complain. Wouldn't do any good if I could."

"You read about the Irish immigrant kid that got himself thrown in the river?"

"Dumb cops almost drowned him and the babes jumped in to help him."

"The wife and I are interested in helping him out. There's some West Side real estate involved. The kid and his company are foreigners, innocents. I wondered if you'd have heard anything . . ."

"I'm with you all the way, Dermot. There are some real assholes out here, same guys that blockbusted the old West Side. The friends of my friends won't have anything to do with them. They won't take 'em out, but sometimes they send signals, you know. Some of these assholes are so dumb that they don't get the signals, know what I mean?"

Bernie and I went to grammar school and high school together. I used to sit in the basement with his grandfather and watch the Bears games on giant screens. I did a big favor for the old man once, so he owes me. Bernie does too. I never hear any complaints that I'm picking up too many markers.

"Yeah, too many people never get the signals these days, even in the church."

I was thinking of the crazies across the street in St. Joe's.

"Tell me about it, Dermot. Tell me about it. Hey, you want me to ask my friends to check with their friends and see if they know what went down? They don't like anybody messing around. Attracts attention, know what I mean?"

Like everyone else in their line of work, Bernie was heavily influenced by *The Sopranos*. Fiction shaping the style of fact.

Actually, Bernie was mostly straight—maybe completely straight. He had to maintain the illusion that he wasn't. He kept up our friendship because you could never tell when some of the friends of his friends wanted to have a channel into the Archdiocese.

"Yeah!"

If that should occur, I'd have to decide what to do. He did know, however, that I was, as he said, "painfully straight."

"Hey, Dermot, tell you what I'll do. I'll find out whatever I can and be back to you by the close of business today. My best to the lovely songbird."

"And to Rita and the kids."

"Thanks, I appreciate that."

So we were covering that angle.

I had told Mike Casey about him once.

"Keep up the connection, Dermot. He'd never ask anything of you that he knew you couldn't do. He's harmless. I'll look him up."

Later he said to me, "Your friend out on the West Side?"

"Yeah?"

"Harmless but very useful. Don't push him too hard because he respects you so much he might become reckless."

"Right!"

"Any suggestions among that crowd of unsavories?" I asked my friend Sean McCaffery.

"This firm is utterly transparent, Mr. Coyne. Not by policy, but by habit. They never seem to have anything that they need to keep secret. If anyone made threats to Uncle Finnton he'd be on the phone to Cork City five minutes later, and all of us would be listening to the phone."

Much of the limited attention in the mind of Nessa Malone was diverted to the contest in her mouth between her bubble gum and her braces. She was perhaps a little less than eighteen, had not been to University, though her "leaving certs" would have made that possible. Instead she had applied for the job at Restoration/America because she wanted to get away from her "stupid family" in Taighat town and see the world. Uncle Finnton had been impressed by her ability to take dictation, her courtesy on the phone, and her skill in keeping schedules straight.

The firm had appreciated her talents, given her raises, and even paid for her orthodontia, which would transform her completely. She liked everyone in the firm, especially Finnbar, who was so friendly and helpful to everyone. Sean was OK, though sometimes she couldn't understand what he was talking about. She didn't like Josie Kiernan very much because she acted so superior all the time, stuck up because of her college degree and because of her husband's job as an inspector for Internal Revenue. Nessa couldn't understand why Uncle Finnton had hired her, because everyone else in the office was so nice. Nessa had no idea what an accountant did except "play with numbers," nor did she want to know what an accountant did because it was all so stupid. Finnbar wanted her to enroll in a junior college in the Loop but she'd had enough school for a while and wouldn't do anything before her orthodontia was complete. Nessa sometimes showed flashes of intelligence that her leaving cert must have caught. She could become a first-class office manager if her stupid family had not made her somewhat stupid. Maybe Uncle Finnton saw possibilities for Restoration, like he had seen perhaps with Sean McCaffery.

As best Nessa could recall there had been no strange or threatening phone calls. Lots of idiots attracted by the name of the firm and the Cork background, but nothing that seemed unusual. "Of course, Mr. Coyne, every company gets all kind of eejits on their phone these days." Some people even wondered if they were a Muslim group or a Christian one. To which she protested that it was a *Catholic* firm from Ireland.

She had no idea why someone had wanted to throw poor Finnbar into the River. No one could possibly dislike such a fine young man. She would pray for him every night until he was back in the office.

"These days we all need as many prayers as we can get," I responded, sincerely enough.

"God will take care of us no matter what happens, so long as we have enough faith."

I almost quoted Cardinal Ryan and the late and lamented Bishop Peter Muldoon about the superabundance of God's love, but didn't think this was the time for an effort at theological education.

Josie Kieran treated me with the same contempt that Nessa had reported.

"Really, Mr. Coyne, I have so much work to do that I shouldn't be taking time answering your questions, which I'm sure are foolish. It is clear as day who the criminals are. It was a gang of blacks, the same kinds of people that are shooting one another down on the streets. They are all on drugs and they have become impossible now that there is a darky running for president."

"Mixed race," I said automatically, "half black, half white, background in Kenya and Kansas."

"A darky is a darky, Mr. Coyne. He isn't even a Christian. He went to an Islamic school."

I didn't say that the school was named in honor of St. Francis.

She paid no attention to what went on in the office. Her job was to pay the bills and keep the accounts reconciled. She was very good at those jobs and minded her own business. She didn't care what kind of work the company did, though it was involved with real estate and saving old homes. Mr. Burke was a very nice man, very fair, and very intelligent. The others were all children, spending the firm's money foolishly. She simply tuned them out and went home at four thirty every night on the Illinois Central. She was sorry to learn about young Mr. Burke's accident, but he was so lightweight that you had to put a heavy book on him or he'd fly away. No, she had no more suggestions, and now she had to get back to her work.

I was glad to get out of the place.

"I told you there was nothing to be found here. We pay our workers very well and take good care of them. They are all very loyal," Finnton Burke said.

I made a sound indicating some agreement and slipped over to the subway to catch a train up to Southport.

Julie was back in the house, exhausted and subdued.

"Are you going to figure it out, Dermot?" she asked me.

"Nuala Anne and I have never missed one, Julie . . . How's your fella?"

"Obnoxious. He wants to get into rehab so he can be back on the links by Christmas, as if you could play golf in this country at Christmas."

Nuala was in her studio (thus distinguished from my office), reading about Angela Tierney.

"Tough little kid, isn't she?"

"How does it feel to be the father of a child who has four F's on her first report card?"

"WHAT!"

"My daughter had four F's."

That was a good sign. If it was *my* daughter, it was somehow my fault.

"What happened?"

"Read this note from Dr. Fletcher."

Some parents will note that their child's grades are much lower than they were last year. This results from our new policy of compassion. It is not fair that young people who are fortunate to have intelligent parents should receive the highest grades while those not so blessed should have lower grades, though they work much harder. The staff at your school has evaluated the efforts as well as test scores of our students and distributed high and low grades in more equitable fashion. Do not complain to the teachers when you meet with them tonight. These decisions were made collectively to reflect the purpose of Catholic education. They are definitive. They are not subject to revocation or revision. If it seems to you that their grades will preclude their admission to certain high schools, we would remind you that the purpose of Catholic

*education is to produce compassionate Christians,
not academic success stories. If you are not satisfied with our decisions, you are perfectly free to
enroll your children in other schools.*

> *Rev. Frank T. Sauer*
> *Pastor*
> *Dr. Lorraine Fletcher*
> *CEO*

"Did you fax it to my brother?"

"Certainly."

"And he said?"

"That the policy will not stand. I gather that the
Superintendent of Schools has approved it. She might
not stand either."

"Your other children?"

"All abysmal failures . . . I gather from my friends
that the Lecher has left at least half of the report cards
unchanged. The outcry will come only from those
who have been moved from top to bottom. Poor little
Socra Marie is inconsolable."

"And Mary Anne?"

"Quietly furious. She was especially good at martial arts this afternoon."

"Should we take them out of the school?"

"Let's see what Blackie does first."

The atmosphere at the parent-teacher meetings, always charged with emotions, was prerevolutionary.
Women as well as men were using curse words to
express their rage. The teachers, who were innocent,
became the targets of parental rage, though they
pleaded that they had nothing to do with the grades.

Mary Anne's teacher, just a year out of DePaul and
almost indistinguishable from her students, was weeping when we entered.

"Those are not my grades. I gave Mary Anne A's in

everything. I'm going to resign tomorrow morning, even if it means I can't pay for the condo I just bought. The other women can't afford to quit . . ."

"Don't do anything impulsive," Nuala Anne warned. "They've gone too far this time."

Our four kids and Julie Crean were waiting in the parlor for our return, under the watchful patronage of the two hounds.

"Well?" Mary Anne demanded as soon as we entered the room and before we hung up our raincoats.

"They all claim no responsibility for the revolution. They are embarrassed, troubled, scared."

"Why are they scared?" Socra Marie asked.

"Afraid that they will lose their jobs and other schools will not hire them because everyone knows what's going on here."

"What did you tell them?" the Mick inquired, his jaw resting on folded fingers.

"To be patient. This inanity would not stand."

"Uncle George and Cardinal Blackie will shoot them down?"

"That's an unduly pugnacious description, Mary Anne. I would prefer to say that they will restore the status quo."

"And get rid of Hannibal and Sourpuss?"

"People always make the same mistake about the Cardinal, dear," my wife explained. "Like Father Brown in Mister Chesterton's funny little books, he only seems harmless."

"Gotcha!"

The five of them and the two dogs retired to their respective homework.

"Let's go look at the fax," Nuala suggested.

There were two faxes waiting for us, both from Father Rick Neal, Vicar for Education. The first was a brief press release to the faculty and St. Joe's Catholic school.

The change of grades at St. Joe's Catholic school would appear to be inconsistent with the philosophy of Catholic education. Therefore the grades distributed today are nullified. Teachers will mail their original grades to me at this office in the enclosed stamped envelopes by the end of business tomorrow. The next set of grades in December will be based on the usual criteria with which both parents and students are familiar.

The second release was a statement from the Cardinal in praise of Sister Mary Theodolinda who, after thirty-five years of work in the apostolate of Catholic Schools, was retiring.

Sister hopes to devote her time and energy to a book about her experiences in Catholic education. Father Richard Neal, Vicar for Education, will lead a search committee to seek a replacement for Sister, a replacement who will continue our historic quest for innovation and excellence in Catholic schools.

"You guys are really cool." Mary Anne, accompanied by Fiona, appeared at the door of our office.

"And we are as angry as you are, dear," Nuala answered for both of us.

She raised an eyebrow to me. I nodded.

"In strictest confidence—you don't tell your brothers or sister, or even Julie, about these faxes from Uncle George."

She frowned as she began to read them, then she smiled and her smile turned into a grin. "I'll never underestimate Cardinal Blackie."

"This does not mean the troubles are over, it means only that we know who is going to win."

Both statements appeared as single paragraph articles in the next day's *Tribune*.

"Do you think this is the end of it?" my wife asked as she poured my morning cup of tea with all the elaborate grace of a papal liturgy.

"Father Sauer is smart enough to be able to read the handwriting on the wall. The Catholic bureaucracy is closing in on him, and his protection there—the good Sister Theodolinda—is out of a job. He's next. He may not be ready to sacrifice his parish to Fletcher's cause. Blackie sends clear signals. Things may quiet down for awhile."

"She'll never quit, Dermot."

"You're right. Too bad for her own good and the parish's she can't back off."

"She wants to get our kids because she hates me. I'm the celebrity she's always talking about. I represent all that is wrong with American capitalism."

— 10 —

THE NEXT day I ate lunch at the Bar Association with Bob Hurley and two denizens of the West Side real estate market, which now stretched out almost to Rockford. Both of them were in the non-shady crowd. Their firms had not been involved in the blockbusting thirty years ago. Roy Morningstar (English for Morgenstern) specialized in Oak Brook, the huge DuPage county residential and commercial area out beyond the Cook County line. Five feet eight at most with dark brown eyes that oozed sincerity, he was the grandson of a Holocaust survivor, active in Jewish community affairs, and a specialist in shopping malls. His favorite gesture was a slight shrug of the shoulders which said, in effect, "What can I tell you?"

"You want to buy a mall, Mr. Coyne? What can I tell you? I have a bunch of them for sale, not the big ones, of course, though there are a lot of properties inside the bag that are worthless now for all the interest they would stir up. A mansion with housing for your thoroughbreds? I could get it for you cheap, even below wholesale. Nothing is moving out here. I mean nothing. Maybe next year, if we are all alive?"

Johnny Bowler, an overweight Irish-American with a bald head and sad blue eyes who specialized on the close-in suburbs—Oak Park, River Forest, Elmwood Park, Forest Park, LaGrange—was equally pessimistic. "An upturn? Not next year. Maybe the year after. Worst I've seen, absolute worst. My dad says go back to the Great Depression to see it."

"I didn't vote for him," I said, my standard response to those who complained about the economy.

Everyone talked about the Great Depression these days, but none of them had been there. I'd read the books. We were not in something like the Great Depression, even the housing bust. We weren't throwing people out on the streets yet, not that we could exclude the possibility.

"What about this crowd that's trying to redo West End Park?"

Johnny Bowler answered.

"The Irish firm . . . What do they call themselves, Restoration? They're really part of the market. Hey, they build up that neighborhood again? It will be a big deal, but it's long term at best. No help to us, no threat either . . . I don't like the Irish butting into our business, though. Why should they be building that idiot spire down at the River? That's rubbing it in. When things get better here, Americans ought not prop up their economy with tourism."

"Better their money," I said, "than Russian or Chinese."

"You know anything about Ireland?"

"A little," I said, waiving off Bob Hurley.

"Is that not the company whose young man was thrown in the Chicago River the other night?" Roy Morningstar asked.

"Yeah, I read about that. Probably just some gangbangers. They're not big enough to be a problem. Allied Irish Bank? That's another question."

"The West Side Irish," Bob observed, "have taken a real beating the last thirty years. They might resent foreigners intruding."

"Hell," Johnny Bowler insisted, "the Irish aren't foreigners."

"Any kind of Irish Republican resentments out here?" I asked innocently. "They have long memories."

"The Greenhorns, maybe, but most Irish Americans don't give a shit about the Irish Republicans. Probably think they are the conservative party over there."

"There was once a man"—Roy Morningstar frowned as he struggled for a memory—"who owned a big gasoline station at Harlem and Lake. I don't remember his name. He was active in some kind of group which was sending money to Northern Ireland for the fighting over there. A little obsessed with it, people say. An immigrant himself, judging by the way he talked. Northaid, I think he called it."

"Noraid," I said.

"Yes, Dermot, I think that was what he called it. He's probably long since dead by now—Freistaters he called the people in charge of things. Really hated them."

"Free Staters?"

"Yes, that's it. They are the ones in charge of Northern Ireland?"

"No, that's the English government . . . The Free Staters are the recognized government of Ireland, duly elected by their own people. They are called Free Staters by those who lost to them in the Irish Civil War."

"So . . . But wasn't that settled recently?"

"It was, Roy, but the extremists would regard that as another sellout to England and the Northern Protestants."

"Stupid bastards, why fight over something that happened fifty years ago?"

"A hundred years ago, Johnny. Or maybe seven hundred, depending on how you count."

"Why the fuck are they messing around in our business?"

"Because the administration believes in a weak dollar to help American business."

We walked back to the law offices of Warner, Werner, Wanzer, Hurley, and Hurley. I wanted to greet my sister Cyndi and see what mischief she and my wife were spinning for the Archdiocese.

"It looks like the Archdiocese backed down," she said as soon as I walked into her office.

She was clearly disappointed by this apparent retreat.

"I don't think that the people in charge at St. Joe's have backed down."

"That idiot ex-nun doesn't know what we can do to them. Is she sleeping with the priest?"

"I don't think so. I suspect rather that she's a substitute for a domineering mother."

"Doesn't matter! We could get an injunction against them tomorrow on the grounds that their grading system is doing grave harm to many of the students and violates the implicit contract the school makes to the parents. Extend the injunction to include the Church. I assume your friend Blackie knows what we did out in Joliet?"

"I'm sure he does. That's why he issued the releases that were in the *Trib* this morning."

"If the school doesn't reply and the Church does not take action, then the Church is certainly liable. People spend a lot of money for that school so they can get their kids into a good high school like St. Ignatius or Fenwick."

"Keep your powder dry," I warned her.

"Tell the Cardinal that I love him even if I have to sue him."

"I was the youngest," I said, "and didn't pay much attention to such things. Did Ma and Pa have anything to do with the Irish nationalists when they were still alive?"

She thought a moment.

"A bell kind of rings in the back of my head, Dermot. As you remember, they had to get out in the early nineteen twenties. I think that maybe some strange people came through the house when I was a kid.

"Ma and Pa were our maternal grandparents, deeply adored by all of us. Our own mother worshipped them too, but she wanted them to concentrate on being good Americans. And they weren't much interested in the old country. They had left it behind with little regret. Too bad neither of them lived to know your wife. They would have totally adored her . . . Let me see, there was some local leader who represented the Irregulars. Owned a gas station somewhere . . . That was a long time ago, Dermot. I'll ask Mom, she might remember."

— 11 —

"WE ARE certainly grateful," Finnbar Burke Sr. told us, "for your good care of our son. He was much impressed that the Cardinal himself came to visit him. And comes back."

"The Cardinal," Lilianna Burke agreed, "is a charming man, so much like a parish priest."

"He *is* a parish priest," me good wife insisted. "That's why he's such a good Cardinal."

"'Tis the twinkle in his eyes," Finnbar Sr. said. "You can tell he's four steps ahead of you."

We were having supper at the Everest, one of the best of Chicago restaurants, with a view of the West Side at night as far out as Glen Ellyn and beyond. Finnbar Sr. was the opposite of his brother. It was easy to believe that this big, grinning man raced motorboats, sailboats, horses, and automobiles, and was the father of our Julie's young man.

His mother was a trim woman in her middle forties with shrewd green eyes and hair the same color as Julie's.

"And we're especially grateful for Julie," she said,

adjusting one of her many rings. "She's the answer to our prayers. And smart as a whip too."

"And quite good with children, as you tell us, Ms. McGrail."

"That's me ma over across in Connemara. I'm Nuala Anne."

"In our family," Finnbar Sr. said, "we worry about heirs—foolishly, I tell me wife, because God provides. Our young man is very much interested in golf and in business. It's reassuring to see that he's interested in women, and a beautiful woman at that."

"Sure didn't your son make her beautiful?"

"And how exactly did he do that, uh, Nuala Anne?"

"He looked at her with desire in his eyes. Nothing like that to make a young woman feel that she is attractive after all."

"True enough," Finnbar Sr. said, "true enough . . . I don't want to ask inappropriate questions, but would you say they have an agreement?"

"Absolutely," me wife responded before I could say something more cautious. "My daughter agrees with me, and she's Julie's confidant."

"And how old is this wise young woman?"

"Several hundred years sometimes and going on thirteen other times," I replied. "In matters of the heart, like her mother, she is never wrong."

"She also is a potential all-state power forward at basketball," Nuala asserted.

"Capital," Finnbar Sr. said. "Well, Lord knows we won't oppose the match, not that it would do us much good if we wanted to."

"You're making progress," Lilianna asked nervously.

"We're getting there," I said, which did not answer her question but did not stretch the truth. "Tell me, has anything like this happened in the past, with the family or the firm perhaps? Your brother had no recollection of such an event. We wonder if it might be some kind of symbolic revenge."

Our new friends were both silent.

"There was something a long time ago. Finnbar would not necessarily have known about it . . . You have some clues?"

"It seems that there was a cell of Irregulars out in the Western Suburbs several decades ago. I use 'Irregulars' advisedly because they saw themselves as opposed to the Free State. I suppose they would have been more Official IRA as opposed to Provincial."

Finnbar Sr. lost his verve and enthusiasm. He looked at his wife. She lifted her shoulders in imitation of Roy Morningstar's favorite gesture.

"I can't believe it, Dermot, Nuala. It's been almost ninety years. Blood feuds don't last that long."

"In Ireland that's only a short time," my wife observed.

"'Tis true . . . I'll try to tell you about it. I wasn't there. It was my great-grandfather that was responsible, another Finnbar Burke. He was not a young man in 1921, but he was powerful, a big fella, overweight, drank too much, smoked too much, whored too much, lived too long probably. You know the story of the Cork Regatta of 1922? Most people don't . . . The Free State troops were trained, equipped and directed by English officers. Or so it was said. Maybe it wasn't true. They decided to land in Cork Harbor in the middle of the Regatta, which was the big social and sports event in our city at the time—still is for that matter, every other year. Well, the Free State transport ship steers right into the harbor in the midst of all the different races. They begin to off-load their soldiers, dressed in dark green uniforms, into lighters to go ashore.

"The Cork IRA had made a lot of noise and probably was responsible for the start of the Civil War even though Michael Collins, Cork's greatest hero, after

whom my father, my son, and myself are named, was
the leader of the Free State. They probably knew that
the Free Staters were coming because they marched
down the Parade earlier in the day and then went
home for tea and a sip of the creature. When the Free
Staters were coming ashore, a squad of the Irregulars
marched down to the harbor and commandeered our
yacht, the St. Finbar. My great-grandfather, himself a
Finnbar, Michael Finnbar, refused to cooperate, so a
sixteen-year-old kid put a revolver to his head and ordered him to bring the yacht up the harbor to where
the Free Staters were landing. The Irregulars now had
a navy for the first and last time, only they didn't know
what to do with it. Then on a beautiful summer day
under a clear blue sky, the Battle of Cork Harbor took
place. The Irregulars started to fire their weapons at the
soldiers. They didn't hit anyone. Most of their weapons
didn't work. The Free Staters were hardly professional
soldiers yet, but they knew how to fire weapons. The
Irregulars were a bunch of kids with guns they had
never operated. They fell off the edge of the yacht into
the bay, the first and only casualties of the capture of
Cork by the Irish Free State. The three that were still
alive threw away their weapons and raised their hands
in surrender. My great-grandfather went into the bridge
of the yacht and came out with his Lee-Enfield and shot
all three of them in the back. He ordered his crew to
throw the bodies into the harbor. Then he sailed out
into the lower harbor for the race of the large yachts,
which he won."

His wife shivered. A thick raincloud rolled down
the Congress Expressway (only Republicans and traf-
fic reporters call it the Eisenhower) towards our building and enveloped it.

Nuala glared at the rain as though it were evil.

"We're supposed to have been cursed ever since.
One member of each generation drowned. Killed in

the war serving with the Royal Navy. Shot down over Korea. Boating accidents. Caught in undertows. When this story gets to Cork the *Examiner* will carry it and ask whether the curse continues."

My wife spoke in her solemn Irish-witch tone. "Can't you tell them that it does not because two brave young women lifeguards who were his classmates kept him alive and the Chicago Fire Department rescued him? And isn't the curse broken now? And here on the shore of Lake Michigan?"

"I'll write a letter to the *Examiner* saying that. It would help if we knew who the attackers were."

"Did any of the Irregulars actually speak the curse?" I asked.

"It is said that the last one, Joey McGowan, who was only sixteen, turned and screamed the curse at great-grandfather, who then shot his face away."

"We don't know for sure if any of this really happened," Lilianna said. "Yet when we heard that young Finnbar had been thrown into the river, we were terrified . . ."

"Understandably," I said.

On our way back to Southport Avenue Nuala Anne said, "I don't believe in the curse, Dermot Michael, but I do believe there's something evil out there that is trying to bring back its memory."

"Why?"

"Maybe just for the fun of it. Can't Mr. Casey find out about that cell of former Irregulars out on your West Side?"

I called him on my mobile phone, since we were in her Lincoln Navigator and she was driving.

"Dermot, that was thirty years ago!"

"There must be someone who remembers the activist who owned the gasoline station."

"I'll see what I can find out. Does herself think it's

a curse really dooming someone after almost a century?"

"She thinks someone is trying to pretend that, for purposes of their own."

"Well we can begin with a list of names of men who owned that gasoline station on Harlem Avenue and Lake Street. Maybe we'll come up with a name that means something."

"Try McGowan for starters."

Back home we found Julie in tears again. Finnbar's parents were stuck up and didn't like her at all. What was she to do about it?

"Didn't herself say you were the answer to all the family's prayers for Finnbar and yourself an eejit for not believing they could possibly like a nerd like you?"

"And," I jumped in, "didn't they say that you were beautiful and thoughtful and that they couldn't understand how their son could possibly appeal to such a lovely and intelligent young woman!"

"They never said those things!"

"And ourselves lying to you too!"

The conversation was now between Julie and Nuala.

"You'll be having dinner with them tomorrow night?"

"They want to vet me?"

"They want to know you better."

"They are biased against me."

"Woman, they are not. Isn't their bias in the other direction?"

"Why?"

"Because, onchuck, they love you!"

An onchuck is a female amadon, got it?

"And yourself knowing that I resist being loved?"

"Tell me about it!"

A rare use of her daughter's slang.

"But I do give over . . . Eventually . . ."

The poor child was frightened. Me wife, however, did not back off.

"Eventually, in this context, is tomorrow night."

"What do I have to do?"

"You have to walk into that restaurant like you owned the whole city of Cork and everyone in the city wanting you for their daughter-in-law!"

"Like you walk into the pub down below," I said, "and Finnbar on your arm!"

Sometimes in that house dominated by Irish syntax, I talk like them. And being a poet in my spare time, when I'm not a spear-carrier, I occasionally manage to carry it off.

Anyway, both the women had to weep over the image of the couple entering the pub and the conversation was over. Sometimes, very rarely, it's useful to have a poet around.

But a poet was no use at all when Mary Anne informed us after school that Hannibal Lecter had ordered the faculty to ignore the letters from the Vicar for Education. He was a young punk with no authority. Only the superintendent of schools could issue such an order. Someone, the kids had learned, said that he had a valid doctorate from Notre Dame. Hannibal Lecter had replied with a tirade against "your alma mater, Da" on the grounds that it was a phony university.

"My half-alma mater, dear," I replied. "A cheer and a half for Old Notre Dame."

"The kids say she's losing her cool more often as the Church closes in. One of my classmates who hates her even more than I do says that she should be burned at the stake with a silver bullet in her heart."

"Mary Anne!" Her mother insisted, "We shouldn't hate anyone. We should forgive them with an abundance of love, just like God forgives us."

"Yes, Ma . . . I really don't want to see her burned at the stake."

"I do," Patjo said. "She is mean to little kids."

I left it to Nuala and Julie to argue for God's love, which of course, one must do.

I sneaked off to my TV monitor system and noted down the names of the bullies who had extorted money from the little ones that day or beat up on the nerds. Same ones every day.

Then I called Finnbar Burke Jr. at the rehab institute.

"How you doing?"

"Getting there, Dermot . . . Looking forward to the first tee at Ridgemoor sometime in April."

"Already have several days booked."

"I tried to get angry at the guys who attacked me. Just can't do it. Never much into the revenge thing."

"That's so first-century Christian, Finnbar!"

"I suppose so . . . My pa and ma really like Julie! I think if they had a choice they'd take her instead of me."

"My family are the same way about Nuala."

"She's kind of shy until she starts being funny. She lives off people's laughter."

"A rare grace . . . The guys who beat up on you . . . Who were they?"

"No one I knew."

"Did the cops ask you about their racial background?"

"They just seemed to assume that they were gangbangers, which means they were African-American, I guess."

"Were they?"

"They were Irish, Dermot, just like me."

"You could tell?"

"Irish curses—who else uses the word gobshite?"

"And with a bit of the drink taken?"

"The smell of Guinness all over them. Right out of a pub."

"You didn't tell the cops?"

"They didn't ask."

Friggin' eejits!

I called Mike Casey.

"That changes everything, Dermot."

"Tell me about it."

"The agents that are guarding him should be on the lookout for drunken Irishmen."

"There can't be too many of them in town."

"And most of them illegals. I'll see what I can find out."

I had a gnawing feeling that there was something very important that I had missed.

— 12 —

ANGELA KNEW after her first year of "normal" school that she would not be a schoolteacher, as much as she loved being in a classroom with little children. She took all the biology courses that she could and began to read Papa Paddy's anatomy books.

"I think I know what's on your mind, small one."

"You don't think I should try to become a doctor?"

"I would be very proud of you. It won't be easy. I can protect you to some extent and so can your brother and Seamus. But most doctors don't want women to break their monopoly on the profession. Your professors and your fellow students will haze you every inch of the way. You are tough enough and certainly smart enough to beat them, but it will be unpleasant. We've had a few women graduates from Rush, one or two of them do all right in the profession. They weren't as attractive as you . . . I see by the look on your face that you're thinking you can take care of yourself. They'll find that out and try even harder to break you . . . If you need any help let me know."

"I'm sure I'll need help and I will let you know."

"Rosina and Seamus will, I suspect, marry one another after their graduations."

"They will be very happy together," Angela said.

"You have no such plans, I presume?"

"Not at the moment. I have other things I want to do first."

She knew this was a delicate area. Both Papa Paddy and Mama Mae had paired her with Timothy in their minds, especially since their mutual attraction was obvious enough. Yet Timmy was sensitive to her decision making about medical school and did not raise the issue of marriage.

Seamus and Rosina did marry in June, just after their graduations. Angela was the maid of honor and Timmy the best man. They danced together at the wedding dinner at the new Palmer House. All eyes were on them, expecting and hoping that they would be the next happily married couple. Angela found herself drawn in that direction, not strongly enough to change her mind (which she did not often do) but strongly enough to feel the pain.

"Do you remember what I said when I kissed you up at the lake, Angela?"

"Did you kiss me at the lake, Timothy? I don't remember. Was it last year?"

"Year before."

"Oh, that . . . Yes, I vaguely remember. I believe I said something about your being reasonably skillful . . ."

"And I said that I had always loved you and always would."

Her heart jumped. Twice.

"Yes, I do recall that, Timmy."

"I renew it now."

He drew her very close, pressing his body against hers. She felt dizzy.

"Thank you, Timothy. I respect that pledge. I will not hold you to it, however."

And that was it. She almost surrendered to him then and there. Later that night, alone for the first time in the bedroom which had once belonged to her and Rosina, she felt woefully alone. Even Sir Charles had climbed into Rosina's bed.

"Well," her ma said, from the doorway, "you know what you're doing. You may have other chances with that young man. But eventually there won't be any more."

"I know that, Ma. Am I making a mistake?"

"We don't know the future, Angie, only the present. I am proud of your stubbornness . . ."

"I know where it comes from."

Ma laughed. Sir Charles had raised his head and sniffed suspiciously. Then he gave up and went back to sleep.

American medical education was a mess at that time. There were few rules and regulations about matriculation and graduation. Almost anyone could matriculate and there were few requirements for graduation. One could put in some time—a year at the beginning of Rush—observing surgeries and attending lectures, perhaps even working in hospitals. But medical licenses were easy to get and there were no quality standards for the practice of medicine. The Flexner report, which would revolutionize medical education and to some extent medical practice, was in preparation. There were rumors about it that frightened most faculties and licensed physicians. But it was generally assumed that pressure from the profession would be so strong that it would never be released. Rush was proud that it required a two-year course with entrance examinations at the beginning and license tests at the end. However, the requirements were not stringent and no one did roll calls at the lectures. Whether the students signed up for residencies was left entirely to them.

The board which interviewed Angela was hostile, though the influence of her foster father and of her foster brother and brother-in-law, already important physicians, practically guaranteed that she would be admitted.

Two of the examiners in the cavernous operating theater were elderly, one with a hearing horn, poor man. One was young and nasty.

"Why do you want to be a doctor, young woman?" demanded the deaf. "Don't you know that women doctors never find a husband? Most men feel that they're perverts anyway!"

She recited her reasons, standard answers about taking care of sick people. Then she added, "I'm not a pervert, Doctor, and I do hope to marry, please God, not to another doctor."

The younger doctor leered.

"You realize that you will be subject to sexual aggression in this school. You will be very fortunate if you escape rape."

"I will take my chances, Doctor, as those doctors who try to molest me must take their chances."

"It won't be that easy, my dear," he said with another leer.

"I believe that in the State of Illinois there are laws against rape."

The third examiner was a glum, unsmiling man.

"Your gumption is admirable, young woman. I'm afraid that won't be enough. Let's see how much you know about anatomy."

He fired up a barrage of difficult questions to which she responded with a barrage of answers.

"You've done your homework, young woman, I hope it does you some good. Doctors are very difficult men, however."

"So I'm told."

Angela's strategy was to match tough words with tough words. She would not show any signs of fear or weakness. She would respond in kind to any harsh words and indeed take the initiative in being tough. The students who were her own age, just two years younger than Tim and Seamus, were the most difficult of all because they were the most stupid. She responded to each attempted grope with a knee in the groin. When a group of them blocked a corridor and announced that they were going to teach her a lesson, she produced a scalpel from her skirt pocket, flipped it open, and said, "Which one of you wants to be cut first?"

They backed off.

She was horrified at the dissection of dead bodies which was supposed to teach her about anatomy. Most of the bodies were stolen, it was said, by grave robbers and delivered to the school late at night. Angela was assigned the corpse of a young but wasted prostitute who was pregnant when she died.

Angela ignored the nasty remarks from her colleagues and recited the rosary for the repose of the poor girl's soul. She was sure that God loved her just as he loved everyone. Loved her more than he loved Angela, perhaps.

The most horrible experiences of her first year, however, were the surgeries conducted in the operating theater, surgeries which were designed to demonstrate the great skill of the surgeon for future imitation.

The first one featured the most famous surgeon on the faculty, Hezikiah Dalton. He was going to demonstrate how to remove a large growth from the abdominal cavity of a woman, a youngish person in her late twenties who had already produced "four useless children" to contribute to the decline of the world's food supplies. She had believed that this growth was another child, which she had admitted to the doctor would bring her great joy. He commented that it would not bring joy to a country which already had too many useless immigrants. The woman was Italian and could not understand what the doctor was saying, but knew that he was being nasty.

The doctors and nurses in long gowns and caps looked like a group of priests huddling around an altar and the young woman like a sacrament they were going to create.

"Now, madam, would you be so good as to tell those who will watch this surgery why you seek it?"

"So I can go home and take care of my husband and my bambini!" she said in a loud, clear, and confident voice.

"You might well ask why we should operate on this woman?" he said as an assistant poured chloroform on a crude mask over her mouth. "The answer is that she is here and seeks surgery and it provides an opportunity to demonstrate how a skilled surgeon deals with a difficult problem. Will she survive? Her prognosis is poor whether we remove the growth or not. We may prolong her life briefly, but that is hardly our primary intent. We will not lament her departure. She will not in any case bear any more children, we will see to that."

Angela used the skills at shorthand she had learned at St. Mary's to take down Dr. Dalton's comments. Her stomach, which had resisted all the horrors of Rush, revolted as she watched and listened as this poor woman was sliced up by a surgeon demonstrating his great skill. There were four children waiting at home for their mother. Doubtless they loved her and she loved them. Also a husband, probably a semiliterate immigrant. They surely loved one another, even if his demands on her may have been cruel.

"Now we see the cause of her distress, a large growth, probably cancerous, which we must remove with as much elegance as possible without damaging any of the nearby organs. Of course we will remove her womb before we proceed. In a few quick moves of the blade, we will eliminate the possibility of any more bambini. So it is done. We will insert sutures later. Now to the major work at hand."

Deftly he removed the growth, disentangling it from her intestines. Angela had to admit to herself that he was good at what he did. Yet there was no concern over the life of the woman who had submitted herself to his skills so she could return to the care of her husband and children.

"That doesn't look like cancer to me," a gray-haired doctor next to Angela muttered. "He's taking too many chances."

Angela wrote that comment down in her notes.

Suddenly, a fountain of blood rose from the woman's abdomen.

"Ah," said the surgeon calmly, "we have an artery problem near the womb, or near where it was. We must suture it immediately."

With hurried and still-elegant gestures he managed to close the bleeding artery. The audience was silent. Blood was everywhere on the stage. The nurse whispered in his ears.

"Alas, despite our heroic efforts, it seems that the patient has died. The strain was too great on her heart. We will now cover her lifeless body and consign her soul to the God who made her."

"Bull shite," Angela said.

The doctor next to her smiled and whispered, "Right you are."

"We of course regret the death of any patient, even if there was no fault in the loss. But it is clear that this unfortunate woman had little time left to her life. A provident deity has spared further suffering."

The body was carried off the stage. Negro attendants began to scrub up the bloody mess.

"I will be happy to answer any questions you might have or respond to any comments," Dr. Dalton said as he washed the blood off his hands.

"Yes?"

There were a number of technical questions.

Then the man next to Angela raised his hand.

"Hez, you'll autopsy that growth and let us know the findings. From this distance it didn't look malignant."

"I assure you, Dr. Fredericks, that from up here there was no doubt. But I will of course report the autopsy findings to you.

"The young person next to Dr. Fredericks."

"I have a comment to make, Dr. Dalton," Angela said.

"I am ready to learn from everyone."

"You killed that woman. If you hadn't been so eager to do your hysterectomy and get to the main event, you would have sutured the womb immediately and the artery might not have burst. Her husband has no wife, her children no mother, because you wanted to prevent any more Italian children and to exhibit your great skills as a surgeon. You may be a great surgeon, but you also are a murderer."

"You are a hysterical woman," Dr. Dalton screamed. "I will end this lecture now."

He stalked off the stage.

"You're Paddy Gaughan's foster daughter, aren't you?" Dr. Fredericks asked.

"Angela, sir."

"You're a remarkable young woman, Angela. Tell Paddy that Dr. Fredericks said so."

"Thank you, Doctor."

No one looked Angela in the eye as they left the operating theater.

One of the first-year students did whisper to her, "Well done."

"I was at a surgery this afternoon at the operating theater."

"The surgeon was?" Papa Paddy looked up from his copy of the *Chicago Daily News*.

"Hezikiah Dalton."

Her foster father winced.

"Did he kill anyone?"

"Yes. An Italian woman with four children. He cut out her womb but did not suture because he was too busy showing his skills in removing a large, probably not cancerous tumor. She bled to death."

"Who said it was not cancerous?"

"Dr. Fredericks, who was sitting next to me."

"Lenny? A good man . . . Undoubtedly he is right. Did you chat with him? I suppose he knew who you were?"

"Everyone does . . . He said to tell you that I am a remarkable young woman."

"That was very nice, not that it comes as a surprise to me. What led to that comment?"

"I accused Dr. Dalton of killing the woman. I recorded the whole event in shorthand. This is what I said:

" 'You killed that woman. If you hadn't been so eager to do your hysterectomy and get to the main event, you would have sutured the womb immediately and the artery might not have burst. Her husband has no wife, her children no mother, because you wanted to prevent any more Italian children being born and to exhibit your great skills as a surgeon. You may be a great surgeon, but you also are a murderer.' "

Papa Paddy did not even try to restrain his smile.

"And my good friend Hez?"

"He accused me of being a hysterical woman and stormed out of the theater."

"You won't have any more trouble at Rush, small one."

"Why not?"

"Because they will know they have a demon on their hands, an intelligent demon who speaks the truth. Dr. Fredericks is quite correct. When you see him again— and he has become your friend this afternoon—tell him I said that he didn't know the half of it."

"He noticed I was there when I said, 'bull shite!' I'm a terrible woman altogether."

"Indeed you are. May I have those notes? I'll have them transcribed."

Then Seamus and Timothy tumbled into the room.

"Dad, you'd never guess what happened at Rush this afternoon. We just heard it from two friends that were there . . . But you've heard about it already . . ."

"Little sister, will you translate the relevant passage of your notes for these uncouth young men?"

Angela read it again.

"Dear God in Heaven!" Seamus exclaimed.

"They all must be terrified over there," Timothy agreed.

"And Len Fredericks sent her home with a message to me which confirmed our impression that little sister is a remarkable young woman."

"No one will bother you any more over there, Angela. You'll own Rush from now on."

"I don't understand why. I just lost my temper and said what I thought."

"I wish I had been there," Shay said.

"Me too."

Mama Mae came in.

"What's all the excitement about?"

So they retold the story again.

Exhausted now and drained, Angela sank into an easy chair.

"I'm so proud of you, Angela, so proud. He's such a terrible man."

"He won't give any of those shows of his again."

"If only we could have saved that poor young woman's life."

"We are still struggling to take advantage of all our knowledge," Dr. Paddy murmured. "The Flexner report can't appear soon enough."

"There was a time"—Angela was now experiencing some pangs of guilt—"when Dr. Dalton was a young man with good intentions."

"Very brave man during the war. Now believes in his own excellence. Can happen to any of us."

The next day some of her classmates at Rush congratulated her for her courage. As one of them said to her ruefully, "None of us are going to make trouble for you, Angela. Now we just hope you're on our side."

She didn't understand that either.

— 13 —

AT THE end of her first year at Rush, Angela applied for residency at Mercy Hospital, which was administered by the Sisters of Mercy but was also the municipal hospital for the city. Sister Mary John of the Cross considered her suspiciously.

"How old are you, young woman?"

"Nineteen, S'ter. Going on twenty."

"And you're from Galway?"

"Carraroe in Connemara, Sister."

"Rather wild country over there."

"Yes, S'ter."

"And you live with Dr. Gaughan's family, but your name is Tierney."

"Yes, S'ter."

"I know where I heard about you. You're the one who took on Hezikiah Dalton. Either you were very dumb or very brave."

"I'm not at all brave, S'ter."

"My friend Dr. Fredricks thinks so . . . Well, I don't think you're dumb. You want to work in the obstetrics ward. You think you'll like delivering babies?"

"I helped in the delivery of two of my brothers back in Ireland."

"They both lived?"

"For a time. Later they died with the rest of my family."

"You're a good young woman, Angela Tierney. We will be delighted to have you at Mercy. I hope you will be pleased with us. We try hard. Hospitals are better than they used to be, God knows. But we have a long way to go."

Angela had read articles which suggested that those who deliver babies should wash their hands in chlorinated water every day to prevent the spread of puerperal fever among new members. Since she was, for all practical purpose, the head of the obstetrics department at Mercy, she posted orders for this practice and provided the chlorinated water. The nurses and midwives were skeptical until the cases of puerperal fever disappeared from the ward. She began to prepare a handbook of hygiene for mothers with new babies. It insisted on cleanliness for both mother and midwife.

She also had to do Cesareans, since there was no one else in the hospital who had done it. She had dashed over to Rush and seen her patron, Lenny Fredericks, who gave her some quick instructions. The first time, Angela was more frightened than the young woman. When the firstborn son appeared, happy and healthy, they both wept. Mother and child were promptly cleansed in chlorinated water, which some of the nuns claimed was Dr. Tierney's Holy Water. She began free workshops for midwives, called "Keeping Mother and Child Alive: Childbirth and Sanitation." Her fundamental assumption was that everything *had* to be clean.

When Angela graduated from Rush—her two years there had passed like two weeks—her family had a party for her. Bishop Muldoon came, as did Dr.

Fredericks and nuns from both St. Mary's and Mercy. She had the impression that the orders were competing for her. She had swept through her medical education in record time and was appointed to the Chicago Board of Health, an institution which had some real power. It was all very heady, she told herself, for an orphan from Connemara.

The day after the party, a week of torrential rain hit Chicago, the river flooded into the lake and cholera came to Chicago again. Contaminated drinking water, Angela told everyone on the Board of Health. They were inclined to agree. Sister John of the Cross asked Angela if she would take charge of a ward of nine Mercy nuns who would almost certainly die. Of course she would. She asked her father to send a shipment of a hundred five-gallon bottles of the spring water they had drunk at the lake—pure Wisconsin water. Then she insisted that each of the young women drink a half pint of the water after every bowel movement.

"It's foul water that made you sick," she told them confidently. "It will be this sweet water from the north woods that will keep you alive."

An article in a French journal had argued, with a little evidence, that cholera victims died of dehydration. If *le médicin* could keep the patient hydrated with uncontaminated water, they would survive until the *résistance naturel* in their bodies rid them of the infection.

Angela was about the same age as the young nuns. There was no reason why they should trust her, save that she was Dr. Tierney. On the third day of the "water torture," as they called it, they came close to outright revolt. Angela led them in the recitation of the rosary and the singing of hymns, and they fell asleep. She remained awake, watching them closely.

"Dear God, grant life to these young brides of yours.

They are brave, vital young women, and Irish at that, if I may remind you. Bring them back to health so that they may serve you in this strange new land which I share with them. Please, please please, I beg you."

She fell asleep in her chair, and they woke her up at dawn.

"Angie, wake up, we want more of your magic water!"

"And right away!"

She led them in singing the Lourdes Hymn.

"Is this Lourdes water?"

"'Tis Holy Water from the north woods, and hasn't his Lordship Bishop Muldoon blessed it for youse."

They cheered for Bishop Muldoon.

Angela sent one of the nurses to bring Sister John of the Cross.

"Glory be to God!" she exclaimed as she came into the room. "You've saved them, Angela child, God bless you and keep you, didn't you save them all!"

The good Bishop came to the hospital to bless them. They were convinced that the Bishop had worked a miracle for them.

"I think, Sisters, we ought to give thanks to God and to Dr. Tierney, who made a very wise decision."

"And ourselves hating her because she made us drink all your water."

"I didn't bless that water, did I, Angela?"

"You did without noticing it, me Lord. I asked Jesus to bless it in your name and then I said a prayer over all the bottles."

"You're unstoppable."

"Sister," she said later to the administrator, "ask this man from the Board of Health to inspect the water supply at your little novitiate and replace the pipes that bring in sewer water. That's what almost killed your wonderful young women. Make them drink the

Bishop's water until it's fixed. If they run out, tell me and I'll get more."

Later Sister John told her that it was another miracle. How could she possibly have known about the pipes in the basement of the novitiate?

"I'm a witch, S'ter."

"No, you're a great scientist and a living saint."

She later learned that Mother General Sister Mary of the Holy Innocents refused to replace the pipes in the novitiate, so she sent people from the Board of Health over to the building with orders to demolish it.

Angela had kept careful records of each of the young nuns—age, weight, temperature, number of bowel movements, and traced-out charts showing how many pints of pure water were required.

"Angela, this is brilliant." Timmy went exuberant, as he often did when he was excited. "You must write it up for the American Medical Association News and send it off to them by telegraph tonight."

"I don't want to write anything. It will just call attention to myself."

"Let's see what Pa says."

Pa said that Timmy was right. He should write the bulletin and send it to the AMA, giving full credit to Angela Tierney, MD, of Rush Medical College and Mercy Hospital in Chicago.

"I'm going to bed," Angela pleaded. "I haven't had any sleep for a week."

Timmy was back in a half hour with a draft.

"Looks good," Papa Paddy said. "They're going to want verification. So add my name to it, and yours too."

"It's her finding!"

"Timmy, I don't care."

"We're there only for their verification. They'll want to get it out right away. Here, you read it."

Angela glanced at it.

"Looks fine to me. Are the numbers right, Timmy?"

"I have your notes."

"Put them in Dad's safe with the other stuff."

She wasn't sure what the other stuff was.

The AMA wanted to see her notes. Papa Paddy sent them by courier and requested a receipt. A one-word telegram came for Angela.

CONGRATULATIONS. STOP. JAMA.

Thus did Angela Tierney, MD, become famous all over the medical world at the age of twenty-two, eight years after she had arrived at the Central Depot on Chicago's Lake Shore.

She would have two more encounters with serious illness in the next year: smallpox and pneumonia. Her dedication to fighting infectious diseases was sealed by these experiences.

"WHY DON'T we look at your calendar?" Nuala Anne in her exercise clothes entered my office as I finished my census of extortions on the St. Joe's school yard. The rain that had drenched the city again last night, had left the yard a muck of mud and standing water.

My wife in a state of relative undress is enough to wipe any distractions out of my mind. She knows it, of course and likes sometimes to wipe away the distractions. This time, however, an insight had come in the process of fighting off extra ounces. I was disappointed.

"Same guilty parties. The population of extortionists is limited to nine bullies, three of them members of the Finnerty family and four more of them hangers-on. We get rid of them, we change the atmosphere of the school yard."

"Or make room for a new crowd of hellions . . . Let's look at your calendar."

"See," she said triumphantly, "you're responsible for the attack on your man."

"What are you talking about?"

"Weren't you after taking him out to Ridgemoor on

September 16 and September 18 didn't them shite hawks thrum him in the River?"

"Coincidence," I said.

"There are no coincidences, Dermot Michael Coyne. How many times do I have to tell you that! Your man is living a quiet life for his creepy little firm, going to school two nights a week, sleeping in that morbid little hotel and nothing happens to him. No one knows he's in town. His only amusement is kissing Julie and the odd fantasy of taking off her clothes. Then you bring him out there to that swamp of half-drunk Irish traders, and two nights later don't they thrum him into the River? Sure, isn't it all as plain as the nose on your face? A nose which I kind of like?"

She kissed the nose and pressed her breasts, imprisoned in a stern exercise bra, against my chest.

"Woman, you're trying to seduce me as yourself well knows."

"Spur-of-the-moment fantasy. 'Tis all your fault and meself loving you so much . . ."

She climbed into me lap and kissed me repeatedly and enthusiastically.

"I'll go take me shower and anoint meself appropriately and then maybe come back here and torment you some more."

"I'll wait patiently."

My brain was a jumbled mess as the hormones raced through it and then to the rest of my body.

Some of the literature said that women become more sexually aggressive as they grow older. The data didn't suspect such a contention, but some men I knew, older than me, reported that their wives were driving them crazy.

"Better me than someone else," one of them said, "though it can be exhausting . . . She's pretty clever about it too."

Middle-age male fantasy, I told myself.

Me wife was merely celebrating the fact that she might have solved the mystery.

While I was trying to reactivate my mind, the phone rang. Mike Casey.

"It was a long time ago," he said, sounding skeptical, "but there was an IRA gunman living in Elmwood Park in the sixties and the seventies, on the run from even his own if you believed him, one Martin McGurn. He did own a gas station on Harlem south of Lake Street and then a popular bar on North Avenue at Narragansett. He talked a big line and some of it may be true. But the worst he did was collect money for Noraid, which was not against the law. He had a reputation for being a hard man, a ruthless alley fighter. No arrests, however. We have no indication that the Irish government was the least interested in him. The provos were busy with the Prots up North. On occasion he may have hid other people on the run, but we weren't interested in illegal aliens in those days . . . He died six or seven years ago, at a ripe old age for a gunman, if that's what he was."

"Marty McGurn . . ."

"No, he was always Martin."

"I grew up out there and never heard of him."

"I don't imagine your kind hung around at an Irish bar in those days. More likely you were hanging at Ridgemoor Country Club."

"Or on Rush Street."

I put a sheet of output paper on my desk with the intent of working on a list of names. But my office was flooded with erotic perfume, followed by me wife in black lace.

"I haven't seen that one before."

"I was saving it for something special."

"Why is today special?"

"Because, Dermot Michael Coyne, you're such a special husband and I love you so much."

I couldn't argue with that assumption.

At noontime, worn out from my morning exertions but exhilarated by the complexities of my wife's love for me, I listened to the latest reports from the battlefield across the street.

Three couples, all of them veteran and affluent parishioners, waited the previous evening upon the Pastor with a lawyer, and a police juvenile officer and charges against all the Finnerty children for their depredations against the weak and infirm. The Pastor flatly denied the charges against the students. We have nothing but good children in our school. He summoned the Principal, who adjusted her rhetoric to the situation, though she said that the Finnertys were poor people out of place in the affluence of the neighborhood.

"Let them move out of the neighborhood."

"Or get them out of the school."

"We are prepared to go into court and seek relief against the bullies, the school, and the Catholic Church."

"We hope that these matters can be settled amicably, but if necessary we may have to take the children into custody on juvenile charges."

The Pastor promised that they would talk to the Finnertys. The Principal insisted that such bullies which might exist were acting only in self defense.

Well that very morning Mr. and Mrs. Finnerty appeared in the rectory with their three children to meet with the juvenile officer and the lawyer. Mr. Finnerty was a skilled and well-paid hydrological engineer and had little to say. His wife, according to Mick, who had absorbed all this from his teacher, was, like everyone said, nuttier than all the Christmas fruitcakes, went postal. The rich celebrities in the parish were picking on her children because they were standing on their rights. Go ahead and sue us. We want our day in court. She swore and cursed them all. The juvenile officer and the lawyer, not used to such abuse from a woman, did not back down, but did not repeat their threats. The Pastor said nothing. The Principal renewed her commitment to the Catholicism of the school and the support of the "ordinary people" of the parish. There were other schools . . .

At recess time, the Finnertys and their respective gangs continued their terrorist tactics.

"What's the solution, Mick?" I asked my firstborn son.

"Turn the wolfhounds loose on them. Get rid of Sourpuss and Hannibal Lecter. Shoot all the Finnertys."

I called George.

"This report is based on the account of my son Mick, the one who is supposed to look like you."

"Not good news?"

"Nope."

"Our sister Cyndi called to warn us that she will shortly file a suit like the one she did in Joliet. Blackie seems delighted at the prospect. That way he'll be able to close the school down and order an investigation."

"He shouldn't wait too long. It is Mick's impression that the bullies will increase their efforts."

"Is Frank sleeping with her?"

"I doubt it, George. But she's in charge. My son advises that we get rid of them both."

"Intelligent young man. Tell him it will be soon."

I turned on our TV monitor.

"Great picture," my wife said, sitting on the edge of the desk. "Hey, there's a lot of people in the yard."

"Parents come to protect their children from extortionists. Observe that the excellent Mr. Flynn is back."

"Those two female cops?"

"Juvenile officers, I suppose."

"Mike Casey's people."

"Invisible like those two people in the Comcast

truck and the good matron walking her baby and the man mowing the lawn down the street."

As we watched, Kevin Finnerty and his two regular coconspirators approached a second-grade boy, whom they had extorted many times before, and began to push the poor little kid around. He fought back and they knocked him down. The boy's parents were on them immediately, as were the juvenile officers, who endeavored without much success to take the extortionists into custody. One of the officers reached for her mobile and called for backup.

The door of an SUV swung open and Maureen Finnerty emerged from it, an angry bowling ball aimed right at the cop with the mobile, a tiny Asian-American woman who tumbled over into the muck of the parkway like a tenpin. The Comcast crew blew their cover and rushed to defend a fellow cop (as they should have). It took both of them to subdue Maureen and cuff her. She continued to struggle and presumably swear at them. The other juvenile cop lifted her fallen Asian-American colleague from the mud. The parents of the intended victim continued to fight to hold off the bullies. The other parents gathered around the melee, probably shouting encouragement. The student body, doubtless screaming, "Fight! Fight!" converged on the scene of the fight. Mr. Flynn tried to chase them away. Dr. Fletcher charged into the fray, pushing people around, including the juvenile cop. Then four squad cars appeared, their sirens providing a soundtrack for our silent movie. Cops ran in all directions. Kids ran for the sanctuary of the school. The little Asian-American woman, definitely Chinese-American, I thought, took charge and by sheer force of character formed the police into an organized unit. The still-struggling bullies, Maureen Finnerty, and Dr. Fletcher were arrested and handcuffed. The cops seized the mother of the victim, a pretty matron of some twenty-five summers. The Asian cop waved the others off her. The matron picked up her battered son and hugged him. Her husband, perhaps a graduate student, confused by the riot, was telling the story to a cop—pointing at Maureen Finnerty, who was still kicking and struggling as she was forced into the back of the squad car.

"Brigid, Patrick, and Colmcille!" my wife exclaimed, more prayer I thought than curse. "Never in the West of Ireland did I see anything like that! I'm glad I wasn't there! Wouldn't I have exploded altogether if those monsters were picking on my sweet little Patjo."

That youngest of our children would have given a much better account of himself, I thought.

And himself an alley fighter like you are.

Better believe it.

The Pastor in his full clericals appeared. Befuddled, he walked over to the lead police car. The eejits released Dr. Fletcher, but not Mrs. Finnerty.

"Eejits!" Nuala Anne exclaimed.

"It's the end, regardless," I said confidently.

However, what I did not anticipate was that three black high school students would be gunned down that afternoon on the South Side and that there would a huge protest, led by local clergy and politicians. It was never clear to me whom the protests were against—the street gangs who couldn't care less or the police and the city who couldn't do more. Yet angry and frightened people had to do something. Anyway, those events preempted the news cycle for that afternoon. There would have to be one more explosion—sometime soon, I hoped.

The three Finnerty gang kids were released to their families though charges against them were still pending. The next morning they strode into the school yard as arrogantly as ever. Maureen Finnerty was accused of disorderly conduct, assault on a police officer, and resisting arrest. She was released on her own recognizance at noon the next day. James Flynn was duly reported to his parole officer. Brief accounts appeared in small articles in both papers. I didn't call George. He could read as well as I could. Petitions for peace bonds were filed against Maureen Finnerty. And the ultimate war in Heaven was postponed.

The battlefield was drenched again by the autumn rains, and even the extortionists fled the school yard. I resolved that we should avoid the fight. Nuala did not need the publicity of a school yard fight. I would accomplish nothing by cracking a few junior high school heads.

Mike Casey called me to report that one of Martin McGurn's sons had married a woman named McGowan back in the nineteen sixties. They had moved out of Chicago and no one knew where they were. Could she have been a descendant of Joey McGowan? And would some other descendant have seen Finnbar Burke at Ridgemoor and plotted revenge? Unlikely and irrational, but the First Battle of St. Joe's had been the same thing. Please God, none of our kids would be involved in the second battle, to say nothing of my wife.

— 15 —

THE SMALLPOX epidemic that hit Chicago shortly after the cholera epidemic was not the worst in the city's history. To some extent it was controlled by the gradual increase in inoculations, though most Chicagoans were not inoculated. Also those who had survived earlier epidemics of both variola major and variola minor (60 percent of the former and 90 percent of the latter) were likely to be immune.

At the meetings of the Board of Health, Angela had spoken strongly in favor of universal inoculation, which would destroy the disease before it could wreak its havoc. The enormous cost of inoculating everyone in Chicago made that strategy "impracticable," as one of the businessmen on the board argued. "Where would we get the money?"

"Inoculate the schoolchildren," Angela argued. "That way we would gradually eliminate it from the population."

"Taxes are too high as it is."

"What is the cost to the city of the deaths of tens of thousands of people?"

"Most of the people who will die are not productive citizens."

"Many of them work very hard."

"Immigrants can always be replaced by other immigrants. There is a constant supply of Eastern and Southern Europeans."

"You didn't say Irish. I thank you for the restraint."

Silence around the table.

"What are we to do then?"

"We could quarantine them in a pesthouse."

"Lock them up in a prison?"

"Angela, what choice do we have?"

"It would certainly save many lives."

"And cost some too, as the police herd into quarantine those who were not infected."

"It's done in other places. We quarantined many at Camp Douglas. I was the doctor there. We saved a lot of Confederate lives, more than the Rebs did at Andersonville."

"How would we staff it?"

"Hire men and women who have had it or are inoculated," Angela said briskly.

"Wouldn't there be a risk to their lives? The inoculations don't always work."

"Generally they prevent death . . . We would have to pay them for their work . . ."

"Who would direct it?"

"I will," Angela said. "It is one way to prove that inoculation works. I will donate my salary—which had better be large—to pay for the inoculation of schoolchildren . . ."

"Not all parents will want that."

"They don't have to take it. I'll give the money to Catholic schools. The parents won't resist it if the church is doing it."

Her family was not pleased with her for this decision.

"Angela," Mama Mae said, "you can't go on risking your life like this."

"It's not a risk, Mama Mae. I'm immune."

"You won't be living here, will you?" Rosina asked, worried about her baby.

"Certainly not. I'll live at the pesthouse until the epidemic is over. I'm not going to run away from my responsibility."

"I take your point," Papa Paddy murmured. "And respect your courage. Yet . . . Well, we haven't had you very long and we don't want to lose you."

"You know very well that you won't lose me."

"The doctor knows it, small one, the foster father doesn't. However, I will not resist your conscience."

Vinny, now studying for the priesthood at the College of St. Mary of the Lake, a day school preparatory seminary behind the Cathedral, cast his vote. "I admire you more than ever, big sister."

Timmy's handsome face was unreadable.

"And I agree with you, little brother. Our sister shows us what faith is all about, that . . ."

She was grateful for the admiration. Someday . . . But she wouldn't think about someday.

"Pray for me."

The pesthouse was a small orphanage just off the grounds of the municipal cemetery on North Avenue, where many of those who did not survive the Camp Douglas horror were buried. She ordered that the building be scrubbed with chlorinated water and that a hundred large bottles of her Wisconsin spring water be brought. She fixed up a small chapel for the young immigrant priest who had volunteered to be chaplain and used her own money to order the delivery of flowers every day. There was no way to pretend, however, that a pesthouse was not a pesthouse.

"Do you think you're being very brave?" a reporter from the *Daily News* asked her.

"It requires no bravery at all," she said confidently. "I have been inoculated and am immune to the disease."

No one came voluntarily to the pesthouse. They had either been arrested on the streets by the police or sent, often under guard, from hospitals that wanted to be rid of them as quickly as possible.

Half of them, she told herself, would survive. Maybe more.

Angela used all her charm on the patients.

"I know you don't want to be here," she said. "I don't want you to be here either. However, more than half of you will leave alive, maybe even three-quarters, and we will have good doctors to take care of you and who will make you as comfortable as is humanly possible . . . We will not willingly give up a single one of you to this horrible death."

She sang for them, prayed for and with them, brought in Bishop Muldoon to give confirmation, knelt at their bedside when they were dying. Some of the women began to say that Angela was an angel.

These behaviors were not planned. Angela was being herself. She hated the pesthouse with its dead and dying, with its violated faces and burned-out eyes, its constant stench. She had published her sanitation handbook for midwives after she was elected to the Board of Health. Now she kept a diary—*Life in a Pesthouse*—which would later become a big success and be translated into many languages. She used the money for the inoculation of schoolchildren. Angela was becoming a legend, a lonely legend with an aching heart.

Her dreams in the pesthouse were terrible. The ma of her previous dreams came back, more ugly and hateful; the smells of the cholera ward combined with the smells of the pesthouse and permeated her body so that when she got off the train at Central Depot her new family ran away in horror. "She smells like death!" Timmy had yelled. Her own, dear, beloved Timmy.

"Timmy would never say that," her own ma said. "He still loves you, even if you are an eejit. And don't pay any attention to that skeleton of me that claims to speak for me. You know that as well as I do."

"Yes, Ma."

Four out of five patients in her pesthouse survived, some badly scarred, others relatively untouched. It was later argued that quarantine was good even for the people quarantined. Angela was outspoken on the subject: "They survive only if the medical care in the quarantine is excellent, and the personal care kind and reassuring."

When the sores and the scabs disappeared, the patients were eager to return to their families, their work, their lives. Angela kept them till a week after the end of symptoms and ordered the police to hunt those who had left without leave. She did not punish them, however.

If I were here and thought I had recovered, I might have run away.

The worst kind of pox, almost always fatal, was the "black pox" in which the disease spread to tissues inside the body; black blood poured from every orifice, and the eyes turned red.

She held the hands of those dying so horribly and promised that God would transform them. Sometimes she wondered about God. However, the guilty ones were the people who would not spend money on inoculation. When the last patients left the pesthouse, she thanked the young doctors—most of them right behind her at Rush—and nurses for their heroic work and sponsored a party for them at the Palmer House, to which she did not come because she was suffering from the onslaught of pneumonia.

Smallpox does not cause pneumonia, but months of exertion and weakness caused by weight loss and overwork can, though. Angela, true to her convictions, was convinced that the weakness in both her lungs resulted from invasion by some kind of microbe.

"You are one very sick child, little sister," said her father, "but we will pull you through, never fear."

Her hospital room—the guest room where she had spent her first nights in the family—was filled with wonderful aromas to ease her breathing. Eucalyptus, pine, lavender. They also eased her soul. This time Angela was convinced that she was going to die. She didn't mind dying. It had been a good life. She had been loved by two wonderful families. She had helped a few people to live a little longer. She wished that the doctors in her family would let her die peacefully.

But no, they had to make her suffer. She was to lean over the side of her bed, her face just above a hospital pan, and they would pound her on the back to force the liquid out of her lungs. It usually worked, but why bother, since she was going to die?

She heard Tim and Papa talk about a crisis. In some pneumonia cases, the temperature of the patient rose precipitously and then either the patient died, which would happen to her, or the fever broke and the patient recovered. Since she was going to die, the crisis would be the end of her and it would all be over. She could finally get some sleep. Wasn't that what they called it— eternal rest? She really needed eternal rest. Then she dove into a deep black pit and sighed quietly.

Much later she woke up. She was still in the guest room and the sunlight was pouring in through the windows. Sir Charles was in the room, sleeping next to her bed. Timothy was sitting next to the bed, his head nodding.

"Hi there, little sister. Still with us, huh? You sure had us scared last night. You're OK now, no fever and finally good sounds in your lungs. You are even getting back some of your color. We were all praying very hard for you. Rosina and Shay came over with Barry, and they prayed too. Well, Barry fell asleep. Everyone is sleeping now. I'm here just in case you go hysterical on us again."

"I was hysterical?"

"Talking to your ma again. She was apparently telling you that you weren't going to die and you accused her of lying to you. But she was correct, wasn't she? Do you mind if I listen to your lungs?"

"Not at all, Doctor."

He listened carefully, moving the stethoscope gently around her chest.

"The back?"

"Certainly."

"Sounds great . . . a shame you couldn't take notes on your trip to the far edge of death. It would make a great book."

"Timmy," she said, "I'm convinced that some day we will have medications that will wipe out diseases like this—kill all the germs."

He folded the stethoscope.

"You've been right so far. I'm sure you'll be right again . . . I'll go wake up Da and tell him the good news. The reporters are outside waiting. Bishop Muldoon is waiting for word."

"Thank you, Timmy, for taking such good care of me."

"It was my pleasure," he said and winked.

She felt her face turn warm. After all these years, Tim could still do that to her.

Her convalescence was long and easy . . . She ached in every inch of her body, she slept away most of the days, read novels, and even played on her guitar and sung lullabies to herself. Yet while her strength returned and her appetite was almost normal, she still felt like she was carrying a heavy burden. She was alive, yes. In a while she could go back to her OB practice and her arguments on the Board of Health. She was receiving lecture invitations, but she asked her mom to write letters politely declining "for the present." But life didn't seem quite as sweet and exciting as it had been.

One day she was sitting in her chair, looking out at the snow in Union Square and reading at a languid pace a new novel by Mr. Thackeray, whom she loathed because he was so English. Timmy came into the room in a thick sweater.

"You've been outside?"

"Walking, thinking . . . It's not as cold as it looks. Pretty soon we'll have to let you go for a little walk."

"Not for a long time," she said. "Not till I get my strength back."

Timmy made her irritable these days. Everyone else did too. Especially Rosina with her obnoxious little baby.

"Mind if I talk seriously for a minute or two?"

"I don't think I'm ready for really serious talk yet, but if you wish . . ."

"I'm thinking of taking a leave from Rush and from Mercy and going on a trip to Europe, a long one, several years anyway."

He sat down uneasily on the couch next to her chair.

"Why would you do that, Tim? There's so much to do here in Chicago."

"And there will be more to do. I've seen an advance copy of the Flexner report. It's devastating. We're going to have to change everything. I know I'm going to be deeply involved in the new ways. I reckoned I ought to prepare myself by observing what went on in other countries . . ."

"That's a very interesting perspective . . . You must do whatever you think best."

She realized from the expression on Tim's face that her responses were troubling him.

"Well, I was wondering if you would consider accompanying me on this exploration?"

"What!" she cried. "Whatever in the world are you talking about!"

"I mean as my wife, of course. I mean . . . Well, we could both learn a lot more together than either of us could by ourselves . . ."

"Timothy Gaughan, you're impossible. You're not only crude. You are cruel. I am recovering from a very serious illness and you come blundering in here with crazy ideas about a tour of Europe and marriage! You never stopped to think how that might upset me. You should be ashamed of yourself."

"I'm sorry if you're offended, Angela. I didn't mean to be offensive."

"Well, I don't know how you could expect anything else from me. Let me be blunt so this issue never arises again. I may well never marry. It has very little attraction for me just now. I am certainly not prepared to make any decisions about marriage, much less about a marriage partner. But I do know that neither now or ever would I consider marrying you. Is that clear?"

She couldn't believe those damning words had poured out of her mouth. If Tim had not blundered about time and place, she would not have lost her temper. It was all his fault.

His poor face looked so sad.

"Very clear, Angela. I'm sorry I've made a mess of it, but I must make plans for the journey."

"Find yourself another woman to share your bed on this cockamamie pilgrimage."

She knew that she would always regret those harsh and terrible words. But they were said and could never be unsaid.

Timmy rose from the couch.

"I'm sorry, Angela. I obviously chose the wrong time and the wrong place."

"And the wrong woman!" she shouted at him.

He paused at the door and turned, his face twisted with grief and humiliation.

"I still meant what I said at the lake so long ago, Angela. I've always loved you and I always will."

Even the demon inside her could not find something mean to say in response.

Much later, when she learned from Dr. Lenny Fredericks about the "emotional letdown" after pneumonia, did she understand what had happened. She was angry at Timmy because he was such an idiot to propose to her when she was depressed. And she was angry at herself for her tirade. If she had shut off her demon she might be floating down the Danube with him this very week.

Did she want to do that? She wasn't sure. She should have asked for more time to think about it. Too late now.

She realized that she could not continue living in the Gaughan house. They might not know all the details, but they would certainly surmise that she had given their son and brother a dishonorable discharge. She rented a small two-room suite in a residential hotel for women farther out on Washington Boulevard near Garfield park, close to the L which would bring her to and from work every day. To add to her sorrow, her pal Sir Charles had died at an honorable old age. There were many tears when she said good-bye after a Sunday afternoon dinner, in June, just before Tim was to sail to Europe. She was as lonely in her tiny bedroom as she had been on the train to Chicago ten years before.

She realized that she was still dependent on the Gaughan family. The trust fund that her father had established for her on her eighteenth birthday continued to earn money and had become a source of income for her so generous that she did not need to work for the rest of her life. Most of it was unspent at the end of the year and she put the money back into her account. After she moved out of the house on Union Square, she lived most of the time from her salaries at Rush and Mercy and the Board of Health. She used her lecture fees and royalties on her books for the inoculation of children in Catholic schools. She spent little on herself and limited her budget for new clothes. She had become a socially important person in the city and was invited to many events, especially those connected with the approaching World's Columbian Exhibition. She understood that men and women found her attractive, especially in the simple unadorned gowns she always wore. Thus she felt no embarrassment when she wore the same dress to two or three events.

She always attended such events unattended. Hostesses came to understand that it was necessary to find an attractive dinner partner for Dr. Tierney. Occasionally the partner became obnoxious. Angela promptly froze him out. Some of them were interesting, one or two of them very interesting.

But not as interesting as Timmy.

She insisted that she might marry some day, but not right now. However, she knew that she never would. She hoped that she would not grow into a mean, ill-tempered spinster, but knew that her character and disposition inclined her in that direction. So she tried to keep her tart tongue under control. It was, she discovered to her surprise, easier to keep the world at a distance with a charming smile and a gentle laugh than to attack it with a rapier.

"Won't the next step be to stand for Parliament."

Ma was walking behind her in Garfield Park with a dog accompanying her, both fading in and out of the sunlight.

"They call it Congress here, and I don't think so . . . Is that Charlie you have with you?"

"Well, who else would it be?"

"There are dogs in Heaven?"

"Where else would they be . . . and himself agreeing with me that you were an eejit for rejecting that nice young man and now you living in that spinster house!"

"He asked me at the wrong time!"

"There is no wrong time to love, darlin' . . . I hope you've learned that."

And they were gone.

"Thank you, God, for sending me that guardian angel. I'm sorry about Tim. I hope I get another chance."

The "spinster house" was even more lonely that night. Angela cried and wept herself to sleep.

She avoided her foster family. They must hate her because of what she had done to Timmy. She hated herself.

"Timmy was a fool!" Rosina exclaimed one day when they were having lunch in the women's tea room at Marshall Field's. "We all know that. We are angry at him for making such a mess and forcing you out of the house. My parents miss you so desperately, dear little sister, and so do I. Vinny is in the seminary on Pacca Street in Baltimore. Timmy is wandering around Europe like a lost soul. I'm busy with my child and will soon have another one, which is wonderful, but they're not getting any younger. Besides, little sister, you were always the favorite since that day at Central Depot. None of us minded because you were our favorite too . . . I wish you and Timmy were married. I really do . . ."

"It was not to be, big sister."

"Well, not then anyway . . . Timmy will be home . . . Next time I hope he won't be such an idiot."

"He was in love, Rosina."

"So were you. So *are* you. So is he. He asks about you in every letter, indirectly and clumsily."

Angela's heart was beating faster.

"I killed it, Rosina. Permanently."

"Well, we'll see . . . But I don't want to talk about him anymore. I want to invite you to Mom's pot roast on next Sunday. They'll be so happy to see you! I beg you, little sister, *please!*"

Angela desperately wanted to see the family again.

"I'll try," she admitted.

She actually bought a new flowery spring dress with matching sun umbrella. When Mrs. Marshal answered the door on Sunday afternoon, she spun the umbrella and said, "I was wandering through the park and thought I smelled pot roast!"

Mrs. Marshal embraced her.

"Honey, sure good to have you back and don't you sure enough look like the goddess of spring.

"Look who I found at the door," Mrs. Marshal introduced her to those in the parlor. "A flower just walked in from the park."

The first reactions were from Angela's nephew, who toddled over with a large smile on his Irish face. Just like his father's. Just like Tim's. Then a silly new wolf-hound bitch called Joan who had to slobber all over her. Then her mother and father, both weeping, Rosina and Shay smiling proudly, and her little brother Vinny home from Baltimore, handsome in his clericals and so much smoother than his big brother. Finally, Bishop Muldoon, as gentle and genial as ever.

"Such a handsome family, madam." She bowed to her mother. "They have matured so nicely . . . well, some of them."

They fell into each other's arms. More tears and yet more tears. Everyone in the room was weeping, except her adorable nephew and the irrepressible Joanie, who repeatedly nudged Angela's thigh, wanting more attention.

"Stop it, you silly puppy. I have to hug my dad before you."

"Well, little sister, we have a lot of vitality here, but you're the first one who has brought spring."

Yet more tears.

At first there was no mention of Timmy. Knowing they wanted to talk about him, she introduced the subject at the dinner table.

"How is Tim enjoying his trip to Europe? Learning a lot, I hope?"

"He's terrible homesick, dear. Sometimes he writes short, sad letters and other times long, interesting letters. He's never been away from home during his life. He didn't think he'd miss it as much as he does. He asks for you often."

Poor dear man. He wanted to bring part of home along with him. Not a good idea.

"He didn't like London or Paris," her father said. "Loved Cologne and Berlin and Heidelberg, especially the beer gardens, I think. Now he's in Vienna and goes to the opera very often and paddles some weird kind of boat on the Danube."

"He's working hard," Vinny picked up the story. "Says we can learn a lot from the Europeans, but they could learn a few things from us."

"The French asked him if he knew this formidable American woman," Bishop Muldoon said, well aware what he was doing, "Angela Tierney, MD, and asked what she looks like—you know how the French are. He says he described her, and the French rolled their eyes and said *tres formidable*—that means very formidable."

"I know what it means, Bishop."

Much laughter.

She came to most of the Sunday dinners after that.

She needed the family more than they needed her. There were always news notes about Tim, who reported that Venice smelled and that Angela would not have remained in the city for more than a day because the water was so filthy.

She even spent a long weekend every July, trapped in bittersweet memories. At the place on the lake where Tim had declared his love and kissed her, she did not weep but prayed for him.

"Come home quickly, my beloved. I will always love you."

She said the words aloud, hoping that they would cross time and space and find her beloved wherever he might be.

That night she tried to write him a letter, but did not progress beyond the first sentence . . .

"Writing to Tim?" Rosina said, carrying her precious little daughter who, unlike her brother, slept quietly through the night.

"Trying to . . . I just can't . . ."

"Find the right voice?"

"Something like that."

"You will . . . Soon enough."

"When I stop being afraid."

"Of what are you afraid?"

"I don't know."

— 16 —

THE RAIN was as thick as a curtain in a museum or a funeral parlor, both of which hid something that no one should see. Or a curtain in a woman's dressing room in a store.

Erotic fantasies?

I'm too old to have them.

And your wife sitting right next to you?

The morning television had reported that the Des Plaines and Fox Rivers were at flood stage and that some of the viaducts on the Kennedy expressway were closed.

The curtains of rain obscured the St. Joe's playground across the street. There were few children in the school yard. The cement basketball courts were a river transferring the flood, which rushed down the alley behind the school to Southport Avenue, whose dubious drains tended to clog up, perhaps to protect the ancient sewers beneath the streets. The excess water would eventually be drained into the Deep Tunnel beneath and dumped into the giant reservoirs northwest and southwest of the city. No more flooded basements, save when the reservoirs were at capacity. Some water might be released into Lake Michigan and folks in certain neighborhoods might be advised to boil their water, though that happened rarely. The Sanitary and Ship Canal, which had reversed the flow of the Chicago River and whose construction Angela Tierney had so strongly supported, ended the cholera epidemics, as she had confidently predicted. It did not, however, clear the viaducts they would have to pass through to reach St. Wenceslas gym for another war in heaven inside the North Side Catholic league. The Kings were heavy favorites over the Cardinals because St. W was a much bigger school and its team is always well coached and very physical. I flipped on the cupola TV monitor. Nothing. If anything happened at recess, there'd be no record.

Angela Tierney, MD was a strange one—smart, confident, and fragile beyond words. Her courtship, thus far, was the reverse of the story of Dermot Michael and Nuala Anne. She had made the first move, which I pretended not to notice. Then she had come to Chicago, moved in with me family (all of whom adored her) and I was a captive, though hardly unwilling . . .

"If it is meant to be," Ma (me grandmother) would have said, "then it will be."

"She's a frigging eejit," Nuala announced. "He didn't really want her and maybe a baby cluttering up his *wanderjahr*. No reason she should feel guilty."

"Except to claim the moral high ground."

"And yourself knowing too much altogether about women, Dermot Michael Coyne . . . I haven't claimed it lately, have I?"

"You don't have to. You already own it."

She slapped my hand and then picked it up and kissed it.

The latest "Be nice to Dermot" campaign might last longer than some of the others.

Then Mike Casey was on the phone.

"Nothing yet on the marriage between Martin McGurn's son to someone name McGowan. The puzzle is, which one might be the hard-liner. Both names could have a connection to the shoot-out in Cork Harbor."

"Let's say," me wife had picked up the phone, "that the McGurn child hated the Free State, and the McGowan daughter had the memories of the death of an uncle, perhaps. Perhaps the two of them met in the McGurn pub and found love in a common cause, a common hate. It wouldn't be the first time. The one who might have recognized Julie's fella could be a maternal grandson of such a union whose mother was a McGurn and whose father's name we don't know. So you wouldn't know his name, Dermot love, if you had introduced him to our Finnbar at the links. He could have gone home and mentioned it in the presence of his grandmother that he had met someone from Cork with the same name of the man that killed the member of the family."

Mike Casey and I listened, trying to keep straight the relationships which might be involved.

"The grandparents would be in their late seventies by now," Mike said.

"No one is too old for revenge, and no crime too old not to demand revenge." Me wife pronounced this truth solemnly.

"I've been replaying the time in the clubhouse. I don't think I introduced him to anyone in the clubhouse."

"Sure, couldn't you have met them on the links—in your foursome or just behind you? Finnbar's togs would interest some folks in introducing themselves."

"Come to think of it, I did. But I don't remember who they were. I don't think I knew their names."

"And yourself introducing people whose names you don't know?"

"Easiest thing in the world, if you're Irish."

"And themselves not having a caddy manager at Ridgemoor?"

That's why she's the detective and yourself the spear-carrier.

Tell me about it.

"You want me to call him, Dermot?"

"He's more likely to tell me than you."

"Well, Dermot, there's your solution to the mystery. As easy as cherry pie, isn't it now?"

Why cherry pie should be a metaphor for something that is easy, I don't know. However, it could be a solution. We'd know who had sent the thugs, but we wouldn't be able to prove it.

"Well," me wife said, taking off her robe and disclosing light blue lingerie, doubtless to match the aura or halo that surrounded me, "I must face my weekly session with Madam. She'll be upset that I haven't practiced all week and meself with a Christmas show to lead next month."

Christmas shows came 'round a lot more frequently, it seemed to me, than Christmas came 'round.

"Well, it's nice of you to provide a preview of coming attractions."

I touched the smooth skin of her belly.

"They call them trailers these days—and they become boring if you replay them often enough."

She swept up her robe and disappeared down the corridor.

I called the caddy master, but he wasn't working today because of the rain. Then Julie, the kids, and the dogs came in for lunch—salami and swiss cheese on rye with skim milk. I helped myself to a can of Guinness.

"How's your fella keeping?" I asked Julie.

"Och, isn't the poor dear man busy feeling sorry for himself, and himself hurting bad?"

I defy anyone to parse that typical example of Irish double-talk to know whether it is an expression of sympathy or a complaint. You would have to see the sad look on Julie's face to know it was the former.

"You had a nice dinner with his parents last night?"

"Sure, don't they act like I'm already their perfect long-dreamed-of daughter-in-law and ourselves not even talking about engagement yet?"

That might have been a complaint or an expression of satisfaction.

Again the joy on her face strongly suggested the latter.

"But I thought he's your fella?" Mary Anne said, tongue in cheek I was sure.

"Well, he thinks he is anyway."

If you were Erin born, you knew all these codes.

"Da, it looks like the rain is going to stop."

Our eldest was building up to something.

"It does indeed. All the better for driving out to St.W."

"Well, it will probably go down in the yard when school gets out."

"What will go down, hon?"

"Gena Finnerty and friends will try to injure me so I can't play tomorrow. It'll be a totally excellent opportunity to practice my martial arts in real life."

"I don't like this, Mary Anne, not one bit."

"I know you don't, Da. But we can handle it ourselves. Anyway, if worse comes to worst I can run faster than those fat-ass sluts."

"Mary Anne'll kick the shite out of them," Socra Marie announced.

"Socra Marie!" Julie, Mary Anne, and myself shouted our protest.

"Besides, with all those cops you and Mr. Casey have all around, there won't be any danger. The bad guys are really stupid. They don't even watch cop programs on TV."

"Don't bring the doggies," I warned Julie. "We don't want any fat-ass sluts to get their throats torn open."

"Might not be a bad idea," Mary Anne said, a warrior psyching herself up for battle.

Upstairs I climbed into the cupola and wiped the lens and leaned against the outside window. I adjusted the sound system to its highest level so we might be able to record the sounds of battle—now the second and last battle of St. Joe's yard, please God.

Then I called Mike Casey.

"Mike, I hear it's going down this afternoon."

"What is?"

"The attempt to injure my older daughter so that she can't play in the St. Wenceslas game tomorrow afternoon."

"Dermot, what is wrong with the world?"

"Evil," I said.

"I'll get a half dozen people over there in unmarked cars, Sergeant Wan-Ho in charge."

"I'm recording it all live on my secret television system, so tell your guys to go easy with the batons, as much as they might want to use them."

"Any rockets or automatic weapons involved?"

"I doubt that. However, the media might show up, so no batons on them either."

Then I thought about another move which both Blackie and my sister Cyndi might want. I called our friend Mary Alice Quinn at WTB.

"I got something for you, MAQ."

"You always do, Derm. What's happening?"

"You've been reading about the contretemps at St. Joe's?"

"Yeah, what the hell's going on out there?"

"A little experiment in Catholic education. They're letting the bullies run the school."

"Yeah that's what it sounds like . . . So this afternoon . . ."

"This afternoon it is scheduled that three eighth-grade girls are going to beat up on a seventh-grade girl so she can't play in a basketball game against St. Wenceslas tomorrow afternoon."

"No shit!"

"It may not happen. They may lose their nerve. Someone with some sense, like the Pastor and the Principal, might see that there are cops all around and stop it."

"They're involved?"

"It's called liberation theology Catholic education."

"No shit!"

"And MAQ, it is altogether possible that I know someone who will have the whole thing on tape, maybe with sound."

"We'll be there."

We were on the road to Armageddon.

And me wife wasn't there.

Thank God.

Promptly at 2:45 the kids began pouring out of the school, my daughter in her crimson jacket in the center of the scene. Gena and two of her thugs were right behind. Filth poured out of their mouths, language Mary Alice could not possibly use on TV.

The she-demons grabbed her, one of them pulling on her arm. My daughter twisted away from them, assumed the standard martial arts defense, and began cutting at them with her hands. They continued to shout foul words. Mary Anne, true to the dicta of her revered teacher, ignored the verbal attacks and concentrated on self-defense.

— 17 —

 SEAMUS MCGOURTY was the first one to report to Angela in her office at Rush that charges were being brought against her before the ethics review committee of the Chicago Medical Society, with recommendations that she be expelled.

"Let them expel me, I don't care."

"The problem is that the Trustees of Rush College of Medicine, terrified by the newly released Flexner report, have appointed your brother as Dean of the School with a mandate to bring it in full compliance with the report. If his sister is expelled from the Chicago Medical Society, he may have to resign."

"OK, we fight . . . Who is behind it?"

"We don't know for sure. Someone who doesn't like you. The charges are that you fabricated your report to the American Medical Association about the nuns you cured of cholera, that there is not and never were data and records to support your brief report of the cures. The argument is that it should have been vetted by the Chicago Medical Society before it was submitted to the national journal."

"Where is the rule that says that?"

"There isn't one. They're making up their rules as they go along. I will be your medical advocate. Clayton Lyndon, one of the best lawyers in town, will represent you legally and will warn anyone who gives false testimony under oath in this hearing that they will be liable to perjury charges in civil courts and slander charges from you. A three-man panel will hear the charges. The head of Chicago Medical will appoint one, you may appoint another, and they will together choose a third. Three votes are necessary for conviction, two for motions. Whom do you want?"

"Not much time to think about it, Shay?"

"I know. They're striking quickly so they can hinder Tim before he assumes his deanship."

"Certainly I want Dr. Len Fredericks to be on the panel. He's a good friend."

"Dr. Lorenz Schultz will present the case for the CMS. Your father wants me to defend you because I am such a tenacious arguer. You can ask for someone else."

"You'll do just fine. The nuns?"

"Their mother general, Mother Mary of the Holy Innocents has forbidden them to appear."

"It looks like the fix is in, Shay."

"Someone has engineered this whole thing. We'll find out who it is before this is over."

The good news, she told herself that night, *is that Tim is coming home. The bad news is, I'm being used to harm him.*

The next morning she went to Mass at St. Charles Borromeo, hoping to catch Bishop Muldoon.

"Mother Mary won't let the nuns testify?" he said with untypical impatience. "What is the matter with the woman?"

"She doesn't like me, Bishop."

"Why ever not?"

"I told Sister John of the Cross that the reason the

Sisters were infected by cholera was that the sewers leaked into the basement of the novitiate building and into the water pipes. The building should be repaired. I found out later that Holy Innocents wouldn't let John of the Cross repair the building because she didn't trust me. I was an ambitious and immoral young woman who was singularizing herself. So I reported the building to the Board of Health and they gave the Sisters the option of repairing the building or the board would order it destroyed. They chose the latter."

"Those poor young women were sent back to that contaminated building!"

"I'm afraid so."

"The Archbishop and I have had a lot of trouble with Holy Innocents recently. She comes from a very wealthy family and thinks she is superior to everyone else. This time she has gone too far. I will speak to the Archbishop directly."

"Thank you, Bishop."

She whispered this good news into Shay's ear. His red face grew brighter, as it always did when he was happy.

"We will save them until the end, well, almost the end. Timothy will be here by then."

"I don't want him to testify."

"You are even worse than your foster sister. She will listen to reason sometimes. You never do. I'll resign as your counsel if you don't let me call him. Whatever problems you and Tim have—and I don't pretend to understand them—are irrelevant to this issue."

"Yes, Shay," she said meekly, and then added, "of course."

The hearing began the next morning in the vast operating theater of Rush Medical. The Judge, Arnold Thurman, was the chief justice of the Federal District Appellate Panel. "No fairer man has ever sat on the federal bench in this state," her father had said.

The Judge, a portly man with long white hair and a long red face, introduced himself and the "spokesman for the CMS and the spokesman for the defendant, Angela Tierney." He also introduced the panel of doctors, who would act as jury.

"A point of order, Your Honor."

"Yes, ah, Dr. McGourty."

"I ask that the defendant appear in the record as Angela Agnes Tierney, MD. She is a licensed physician and a graduate of this school. She has every bit as much right to these letters as anyone in the room. As I will demonstrate, the basic issue in this complaint against Dr. Tierney is whether a woman has the right to be a doctor, and even a doctor with an emerging world reputation."

There was applause from the young medical students who had crowded into the theater. They adored Angie, as they all called her.

The judge then introduced again the three panelists who would act as jury, remarked that the defense had picked one of them, the CMS the second, and the two of them had picked the third. Unanimous consent was required for expulsion. The agreement of two of the panel sufficed to sustain a ruling of the presiding judge.

Angela was astonished that her own choice was her classmate Edgar Portman-Johnson, a slick, handsome young man from Peoria who had sung at the Gaughan singing parties and added a powerful baritone voice to the group. Len Fredericks, her closest friend among the senior doctors at Rush, was the "neutral" juror.

How had Shay done that?

It was Chicago, was it not, and his father an alderman.

Lorenz Schultz, a man with courtly manners, a strong German accent, and a tedious voice began making the case against her. He wore a greatcoat and a vast beige vest which covered, however inadequately, a large stomach. From her earliest days in the school, this girl had engaged in self-promotion, she was rude, *ja, ja*, and lacked the docility, *ja, ja*, that a good medical student ought to display. He then wandered into a long autobiographical account of the docility which was required in Frankfurt am Main, where he had learned not only the required skills of a doctor, but the character necessary in a doctor. This young woman had demonstrated very few skills and no character at all.

Clayton Lyndon, a dark Irishman like Timmy, whispered something in Shay's ear.

"Your Honor, I am sure we all appreciated Dr. Schultz's fascinating memoirs of Frankfurt am Main, which incidentally is not to be confused with Frankfurt an Oder. I would remark only that it has not brought us any closer to the establishment of the charges against Dr. Tierney. Is she charged with fraud in the treatment of the eight nuns who are still alive today, even if prevented by ecclesiastical authority from appearing in this courtroom? Surely it is incumbent on the prosecution to establish this fraud. Or is she charged with reporting a medical finding of considerable importance to a professional journal? Or is the charge that subsequent research has refuted these findings, though the available literature suggests just the opposite? Or is she charged with not keeping proper records? These are different charges and there seems to be proof adduced for each one if they are all part of her indictment. I may be hasty, Your Honor, but it does seem that a clique in the Chicago Medical Society decided to get rid of Dr. Tierney and has yet to have time to prepare detailed charges . . . I would add that the comments of some members in the press that her crime is not to have sent it to the publication of the CMS first. I have searched in vain in the rules and bylaws for evidence that there is such a regulation and evidence that many members have violated it. Moreover it is most unlikely that her notes would have ever seen the light of day if it had been submitted to JCMA. One wonders how many cholera victims would have died if her findings had been suppressed."

The judge signaled for Arthur Hastings-Hudson, MD, the longtime president of the CMS, to join him at the podium which had become the bench for the trial. Hastings-Hudson moved his large bulk ponderously to the bench. They chatted for some time, the Judge's long red face becoming even longer.

After several minutes of discussion, the Judge waved Arthur back to his Presidential chair.

"I have informed the CMS that the only charge which I feel capable of adjudicating is the final one. There would be, I should think, an obligation to send one's supportive notes to a journal before publication. Otherwise I will adjourn this hearing sine die. Is that acceptable, Dr. Hastings-Hudson?"

"*Ja, ja,* I object! There are more important philosophical charges against Tierney, which I discussed in my opening remarks. She is simply not the kind of person that a doctor should be."

"The failure to attach appropriate notes to an article would seem to be some evidence of that. However, it is this failure I am prepared to adjudicate. I repeat, Dr. Hastings-Hudson, is that acceptable?"

The president of the CMS, his dignity affronted by the clarity of Anglo-Saxon juridical procedure, nodded heavily.

"Good . . . Dr. McGourty?"

"Your Honor, defense is prepared to stipulate that there was a solemn obligation that Dr. Tierney submit her notes from the experimental site to the journal, along with the description of her treatment. I would also suggest that the JAMA had the obligation to demand those notes before publication and that the very publication itself of the article suggests that the JAMA did in fact have the notes even if it no longer does. I argue that the defendant has no obligation to prove that the JAMA may have lost the notes after they were submitted."

The Judge smiled.

"Your forensic style may well be wasted in the medical profession. Therefore we will continue with the agreement that there is but one matter at issue before this hearing: whether Dr. Tierney did in fact submit notes along with the article."

This agreement, however, was not satisfactory to many of the senior doctors in the audience who wanted to expel Angela. One by one, filled with their self-importance as practitioners of "medical science," they rose to denounce her personally as a hysterical woman and as a heretic who did not respect established science.

"Everyone in our profession knows that disease is not spread by microbes and not cured by magical waters, but rather lurks in miasmic airs that we need to extirpate from the regions where they have settled. Swamps near lakes and rivers are especially dangerous to our patients."

"And not sewage in our basements!" Shay scoffed.

"Every good doctor knows a balanced and properly conservative drawing of blood from the bodies of victims would have been much more beneficial for the patients than this magical water from the holy forests of Wisconsin."

"Let the record show," Shay demanded, "that the article in the JAMA did not claim curative powers for the waters. Rather they were used as an antidote to dehydration."

Angie's young allies hooted and hollered. The judge demanded order.

Angela could not help but feel sorry for the old

men, some of them feeble, who had risen to defend the medical wisdom which had shaped their lives. Their worlds were crumbling around them. The stentorian tones which had impressed patients and one another for all their lives now earned them ridicule from the students.

Shay was on his feet again.

"If the CMS will stipulate that bloodletting and miasmic airs are the orthodoxy of their profession, we will stipulate that Dr. Angela Tierney is indeed a heretic—just like Joan of Arc. However, I did not think this was a heresy trial."

The doctors, some of whom were still in their thirties, continued their rants, most of which had been written out and were recited in frail voices.

"Your Honor," said one tiny graybeard with a high, nasal voice, "I wonder if a habeas corpus writ might be appropriate."

"What body do you want, Doctor?"

"The bodies of the nuns who were cured by the magical miracle waters that Dr. Tierney imported to keep them alive. Would it not be useful to see that they were still alive and well?"

"Dr. McGourty?"

"It would be, Your Honor, but unfortunately their religious superiors have forbidden those young women from appearing at this hearing."

"Do you know why, Doctor?"

"I am trying to ascertain the reason, Your Honor, but have been unable."

The day droned on. The cold December air was miasmic enough, Angela thought, to qualify for extirpation from the swamps. She wrapped her Irish tweed blanket around her shoulders. She did not want to have another attack of pneumonia and the resulting emotional trauma. Not again.

Finally the Judge called for a recess.

"We will gather here tomorrow at nine thirty to hear Dr. Tierney's defense team present their case. I note that all they have to do to carry the day is to prove that Dr. Tierney did send her notes to the journal which published her brief article. The defendant does not have to adduce the notes themselves or a copy thereof."

More cheers from her supporters and murmurs of displeasure from the core members of the Chicago Medical Society.

"I don't know why anyone would want to associate with those phantoms," Shay said as he and Rosina took her home to Garfield Park.

"I feel sorry for them."

"Someone has organized this attack on you, Angela," Shay said. "They have not organized it very well, save for removing your notes from the AMA files. Did you see those reporters in back? The CMS will be the laughingstock of the city by tomorrow evening . . . You're totally safe, Angela. Two of the three members of the panel are on your side."

"The fix is in."

"Fight a fix with a fix, Angela. That's the Chicago way. Our friend Hastings-Hudson didn't want to do this, so he arranged for the Judge and the panel so that it wouldn't be complete comedy. He appointed Len Fredericks to it because Len has the reputation of being a fair and intelligent man. Then I appointed our classmate and they decided on Edgar Portman-Johnson, who is as much a heretic as you are. The other side didn't have a single vote even before the trial began."

"I hope so. I would so much like to resign after it's over."

"Not till Tim is announced as Dean of Rush."

"All right."

She shivered as she walked up the two flights of stairs to her room. Garfield Park, grim and ugly in its late autumn clothes, made her shiver even more. She poured herself a stiff dose of brandy to fight off the cold, wrapped herself in her Irish tweed blanket, and fell promptly to sleep.

Only occasionally and for purely medicinal purposes, she told God as she fell asleep, her rosary still curved around her fingers.

Will Tim come tomorrow? I hope not. I'll have to face him sometime, but not tomorrow.

If he were in bed with me, I wouldn't need the brandy!

The fog and the rain clouds had lifted in the morning and the sun had appeared in the sky. Samhain at home, Halloween in this Protestant country.

The operating theater was filled when she entered and began to walk down the steps to the stage. Cutting Angela's soul open was a strong attraction. She hoped that she did not have to testify. The demon who controlled her tongue would surely take charge.

As it was the reporters tormented her with questions.

"Why do you put up with these senile fogies?"

"I am proud of my membership in CMS and I will not willingly give it up."

"Do you think there is a plot against you?"

"It would certainly seem so. I have no idea why anyone would want to go to all that trouble."

"Is it true that Mother Mary forbade the young nuns from testifying?"

"So I am told."

And struggling with the reporters to talk to her, even to touch her arm, were swarms of young doctors and medical students.

"We'll riot if they expel you! We really will!"

"I don't think that will be necessary."

Joan of Arc, she thought, *didn't have supporters like this . . . A riot? . . . That might be fun . . . You should be ashamed of yourself.*

The Judge called the hearing to order and was ignored. He banged his gavel furiously in vain. Dr. Len Fredericks rose from the jury table and signaled for quiet. The crowd reluctantly settled down.

"Dr. McGourty, whom do you call as your first witness?"

"I call multiple witnesses: Sister Mary Grace, RSM, RN, a member of the Holy Innocents, and her band of seven survivors!"

Cheers from the audience.

The eight nuns, shadowed by Bishop Peter Muldoon, PP, entered the theater stage from the room in which the patients usually waited.

Angela stood up to recognize their courage.

Sister Mary Grace walked to the stand but stopped at the defendant's chair to embrace Angela. The others followed, one by one.

Attendants scurried to find seven other chairs. The Judge, not used to the silliness of young nuns on the loose, seemed stunned.

"Can we get on with the testimony, Dr. McGourty?"

"Certainly, Your Honor. Sister, am I correct that you and your band were patients in Dr. Tierney's ward during the cholera epidemic?"

"Yes, Doctor," Mary Grace said demurely, though she was the least demure of the crowd.

"What was she like?"

"Oh, she was like a novice mistress, stricter even. Whenever we had a bowel movement—and that was almost all the time—she made us drink that horrible spring water. We all hated her, though she was kind and sweet and pretty. We were going to die, couldn't she just leave us alone?"

"Indeed!"

"And she made us pray and sing and she brought her guitar to lead us in the singing. So we said we hated her, but that wasn't true, because we loved her.

She was the angel that was going to lead us to heaven, even if we were bloated all the time with her spring water."

"And what did you sing?"

"Mostly religious songs, but some popular. I guess we sang the Lourdes Hymn, because it was about miracles."

The nuns began the hymn. The judge didn't stop them.

"Great theater," Shay muttered.

"Hush," Angela whispered.

"Then what happened?" Shay asked.

"Well, we got better, all of a sudden. One night we went to sleep early, worn out, feeling utterly empty. We slept peacefully for the first time. We woke up feeling better, much better. Angela was at the top of the ward, smiling down on us.

" 'Young ladies, you are rehydrating. Keep drinking your magic water!' "

" 'I'm hungry,' one of us said.

" 'I thought you might be. I have some good Irish oatmeal for you.' "

"And you all recovered and are alive and well."

"Yes, Doctor. We're once again what Dr. Tierney, God love her, liked to call silly young Irish nuns."

Lorenz Schultz wanted to cross-examine.

"*Ja, ja*, Schwester, did you notice whether Dr. Tierney was taking notes during your stay in her ward?"

"Oh, yes, Doctor, all the time. Temperature, number of bowel movements, quality of bowel movements, pints of water consumed. You could never get away from the water, which, tell the truth, was quite sweet and had a lovely aroma."

"Ah."

"As she wept over our survival, like she is weeping now, we realized she was one of us, a young woman from the West of Ireland, and we all wanted her to be our superior, but she didn't seem to have a vocation."

"*Ja.*"

"She told us that she had to take the notes to persuade other doctors around the world that dehydration was what killed people infected with cholera."

"One more question, Sister. Why did Mother Mary of the Holy Innocents forbid you to testify in this hearing?"

"Oh, she doesn't like Dr. Tierney at all, at all."

"And why not?"

"Well, there was a big argument about our novitiate house. Dr. Tierney said that sewer water leaked into the basement during a storm and into our water pipes. We were drinking sewage every day during the flood. Mother said that was nonsense and ordered us back into the building. The flood, she said, was over—which it was."

"Then what happened?"

"One of us told Dr. Tierney, and she told the Board of Health, and they tore the house down when Mother refused to install new pipes."

"Which one of you reported Mother to Dr. Tierney?"

"Ain't saying," she said with a wicked West of Ireland grin.

"Why are you testifying now against Mother Mary's will?"

"Bishop Muldoon said that Archbishop Feehan had released us from holy obedience on this subject."

"Thank you, Sister, you have been most helpful, as have been your colleagues. You may leave now. You are to be congratulated on your courage."

Angela stood up again as they left. She may well have been the one who began the singing of the Lourdes Hymn as they left.

"Well," the presiding judge remarked, "that testimony provides all the evidence that is needed on the question of whether Dr. Tierney kept an accurate record of her experiment and that it was successful. Do you have any more witnesses, Dr. McGourty?"

"Call Dean Timothy Patrick Gaughan, please."

Angela instinctively sank into her chair to acquire as much invisibility as possible. Timothy walked onto the stage, in a cutaway morning suit and a ridiculous top hat. Same old Timmy—unruly black hair when he took off the hat, disarming smile, mischievous blue eyes, tall, strong, and defiant. Not quite as uneasy as she had always found him.

He paused at the witness chair and kissed her forehead, briefly and respectfully, though she didn't think his smile was the least bit respectful. She kept her head high and her back straight so that no one knew she was, as they would say out in Galway, destroyed altogether.

He was a big, strong man who in bed at night would be more than an adequate substitute for brandy—even the best brandy.

Her amadon supporters cheered, whooped, and whistled.

"Your name, sir?"

"Timothy Patrick Gaughan."

"Your occupation."

"Medical doctor."

"Your affiliation?"

"As of this morning, sir, I am Dean of Rush Medical College, charged with implementing the recommendations of the Flexner report."

The applause for this nicely timed announcement was loud and extended.

Poor Timmy blushed in embarrassment. It would be a very difficult task.

"I see. Congratulations, sir."

"Thank you."

"What is your relationship with Dr. Tierney?"

"She is my foster sister. She entered our family when she was about fourteen."

"I must ask you, sir, only for the record, if there is any, ah, romantic relationship between you and Dr. Tierney?"

"No sir, unfortunately for me perhaps."

Yet another ovation.

"Now, Doctor, did you happen to be present when Dr. Tierney returned from Mercy Hospital after the end of her experiment?"

"My father and I were present and we were both very interested in the success of her experiment. She was too tired to talk about it and simply gave me her notes. She sank into an easy chair in our apartment, and seemed to be sleeping. I became astonished at the findings. Similar reports had come from other countries, but this was the first one in America and was extremely important. It had to be communicated to the rest of the medical world immediately. I gave the notes to Dr. Gaughan, my father. He was dazzled too.

" 'This is monumental, Timmy,' he said. 'We must see that it is published immediately. Little sister . . .' That's our affectionate name for Dr. Tierney . . . 'you must write it up and send it to the AMA.'

" 'Too tired.'

" 'I'll write it up for you, just put your notes into shape for a research note. I'll let you see it.'

" 'Whatever you want, Timmy,' she said. I knew she was very tired because this was not the rhetorical style in our family life. So I went upstairs to my room and wrote out the article, which merely was an incorporation of her notes . . . You want to know what was in the notes, reread the article . . . I woke her up. She read the piece very carefully and made several changes, thanked me, and fell back to sleep."

Since you're telling him everything, Tim, why don't

you tell them how you forced a kiss on me up at the lake.

"I promptly went over to the Western Union office on Harrison Street and sent it off to the AMA."

"Do you have a dated copy of that telegram?"

"Of course I do. Here it is."

He waved the copy for everyone to see and passed it over to the Judge, who gave it to the panel. Lenny Fredericks winked at Angela.

"Then what happened?"

"The AMA replied by telegraph. 'Send notes. Stop.' "

"You have a copy of that telegraph?"

"Of course I do. I would have been a very poor brother if I did not keep it in the safe in my room. I went back to the telegraph office and sent the notes by courier to New York. I then telegraphed them to say that the notes would be there by tomorrow at noon."

He removed yet another flimsy from his waistcoat pocket and read: "Notes arriving by courier. Request Receipt.

"And we received this reply: Congratulations. Stop. AMA."

I will not be able to face any of the people in the CMS or my colleagues at Rush ever again. Again I must return to Ireland and hide.

"That shows, does it not, that Dr. Tierney's very notes must have been received . . ."

"I would think so."

"What has happened to them since? They seem to be lost."

"I have no idea. I believe, however, that is a problem for the AMA."

"It is unfortunate that you were unable to make copies of the notes before the courier carried them off to New York."

"Ah, but I did request Western Union to make two

copies on their machines and send them to me at home.
I put them in my safe . . ."

He reached into his pocket and produced a stack of
flimsy papers.

"And they are still quite legible. Here they are, little
sister, just as you wrote them. You will note Western
Union's date on them. The second copy is still in my
safe."

"Thank you, big brother. Yes, they are my notes,
Your Honor." Angela rose and gave them to the judge.
He glanced at them, shrugged, and passed them on to
the panel. Each member examined them carefully,
Len Fredericks most carefully of all.

"I don't think there can be any doubt on their au-
thenticity. I believe closer handwriting comparisons
with several other documents will demonstrate that
they are written in Dr. Tierney's businesslike handwriting."

"May I say one more thing, Your Honor, hopefully
to bring this hearing to an appropriate end," Timmy
said. "I toured Europe for several years in preparation for my new work. I have here a collection of six
articles in as many languages praising Dr. Tierney's
research. The authors of these articles would be astonished that in her own city charges could be made
against her.

"I was asked often if I knew her and I admitted
proudly that I did. A French physician and scholar of
the highest rank asked me what she was like. I dismissed the question with absolute truth: *Une femme
très irlandaise*. I was finally asked what she looked
like, a question a man is often asked about a woman
and to which he is well advised to remain prudent in
his reply . . . I happened to carry a picture of my family. They knew immediately which one was my little
sister. The same French scholar said, *Une femme très
formidable*. I could only add, *Mais oui, monsieur le*

médicin. I am delighted that you have confirmed that judgment today."

More cheers.

The miserable so-and-so was using this public, so public, event as a pretext for renewing our discussion about love. So ingenious, so clever, so offensively masculine.

I'd better be careful before I surrender myself to him.

Shay took charge once again.

"There is one more witness, Your Honor. I will call Dr. Leonard Fredericks to the stand. Dr. Fredericks has agreed to testify about certain matters concerning the origins of these patently false charges against the work and character of Dr. Tierney."

"Two members of the Association approached me this morning to report a confidential conversation they had at the end of yesterday's hearing with another member of the Association. He told them that there was no hope that the charges against Dr. Tierney would be dismissed because he had acquired the original notes from the files of the AMA and he had persuaded Sister Mary to silence the nuns who in fact testified today."

"Who is this man?" Hastings-Hudson arose in righteous wrath.

"My friends are prepared, Dr. Hastings-Hudson, to testify under oath, but only to you privately."

"What was the motive for such nefarious needs?"

"It was difficult to determine precisely, but apparently it was related to charges that Dr. Tierney, then a first-year student, had made about this individual after a procedure performed in this very room. Subsequently he has been unable to schedule any further procedures."

A name ran through the room. For all the pretense of secrecy, the cat was out of the bag.

Hopefully, in heaven, that Italian mother experienced some sort of vindication. Only the saints and the martyrs didn't need vindication.

"There remains only a determination of the verdict in this hearing," the Judge said. "By leave of the council, I ask the panel members to vote on that determination. I remind you that three votes are required to support the demand of the Chicago Medical Society. I remind you that three votes are required to approve expulsion. How many of you, therefore, vote to support Dr. Tierney's expulsion from the Chicago Medical Society? Please raise your hands."

He waited for perhaps twenty seconds. No hand was raised.

"Then the motion for expulsion fails, unanimously it would seem. Congratulations to you, Miss Tierney—pardon me, ma'am—*Doctor* Tierney. You have borne the assaults of this process with dignity and grace."

There was a huge cheer from the audience.

Angela thanked the Judge, the panel, and the various attorneys with gracious words and a warm smile. She pecked on Timmy's cheek with a proper kiss and embraced the rest of her family. She pled excuse from a celebration party but promised that she would come for pot roast on Sunday. The joy on her parents' faces was reward enough for the embarrassment of the day.

"You will serve on my staff here," Tim asked, "won't you, Angela?"

"I will need time to think about it, but I rather imagine that I might."

She went home, swallowed a lot of brandy, and slept till the next morning.

— 18 —

TIMOTHY INVADED Angela's mind and imagination and remained there for the next several days. The bond between them was stronger than ever. Tormented by what she would once have labeled as obscene thoughts about him, she could not sleep at night or concentrate on the lecture outlines she was trying to prepare for the second semester. He was her man. She had waited long enough for him. Now she wanted him. It was that simple. She had to wipe away the mistakes and cruelties of the past and open once more the wondrous mysteries of love. She would have to take the initiative because he was embarrassed by the mistakes of the past and probably intimidated by her cruelties.

The matter had to be resolved before the Sunday dinner at her mom's house or their mutual passions might erupt in anger. She had watched him at the lecture that morning to the faculty. She did not, could not, listen to what he said. Rather she worshipped what he was and imagined him naked and aroused for her. Was this a sin? She hoped not. She had no choice. In her office she paced back and forth. *What should I do?* It was not necessary that they consummate their love immediately. It was only necessary that the muck from the past be swept away so they both were free to make the decisions that had to be made.

Without any clear plan of action, she strode down the corridor to his office. There was a sign on the door which said PLEASE DO NOT DISTURB. She removed the sign, opened the door, and handed him the sign.

"I've come to disturb you, Timmy," she said.

He laughed.

"You don't have to be in the same office to disturb me, Angie. The same building is enough."

"Some time ago"—the words once again poured out of her mouth—"you wanted me as your wife."

"I still do, Angela, and always will."

She fell on her knees in front of him.

"Then please forgive all the terrible things I said."

He lifted her up.

"I'm the one who should be begging your forgiveness . . ." He spun her around in the air like she was a prize captured on the track field. "I let you get away from me once. I'll not make that mistake again."

"I observe that you were the one who ran away to Europe."

He set her down on the floor and extended her arms so he could drink her in.

"I'll not make that mistake again, I promise."

He was grinning broadly now, proud of his sudden conquest. Then he embraced her, held her tightly, and absorbed her in passionate kisses.

So that's what they're like, she mused.

Then he unbuttoned her blouse, eased it off her shoulders, and assailed her breasts with his lips. She did not resist, could not resist, did not want to resist.

"I've wanted to do this, Angela, since that day at the Central Depot."

She murmured something incoherent.

"Angela, we must marry."

Slowly he replaced the blouse and buttoned it again, his fingers lingering at every touch.

"I concur."

"We must marry soon."

"I concur."

She finished the last button which was baffling him.

"We must marry a week from Saturday. That will give you a whole week to choose a wedding gown and to make all the necessary preparations."

"More than enough time."

"You have beautiful breasts, Angela. I will look forward to a life of playing with them."

He brushed them with a gentle and reverent hand.

"I will resist that as fiercely as I have today."

She rested her head against his chest. A permanent captive and captor.

For a spontaneous seduction, she thought, that went pretty well.

"THE YOUNG woman wearing the crimson jacket in the center of the picture is Nellie. She is in seventh grade, but is the leading scorer in the North Side Catholic League. The three rather hefty girls immediately behind her are angry at that injustice. They have promised her that they will break her arm this afternoon. Such is the practice of liberation theology at this rather unusual Catholic school.

"The attackers seize her and pummel her. One of them grabs her left arm and tries to twist it.

"This woman here, we have learned, is the Principal of the school. Note that she makes no attempt to stop the fight. It will be interesting to hear comments from the Archdiocese chancery on this incident. The noise you hear is the sound of cheers. We have had to cut the cries of the attackers which are mostly obscene.

"Nellie, however, is slippery. She dances away from her foes, discards her crimson jacket, and assumes the stance of martial arts defense. One of them tries to capture Nellie with a stranglehold. She replies with a slice of her hand to the girl's throat, which in-

capacitates the attacker. A second heavyweight strives
to land a punch. Nellie fends her off with another slic-
ing hand. This attacker screams in pain and complains to the principal. The third one backs off. Nellie
walks away.

"Then the third one, a real heavyweight, picks up
a large stone and runs after Nellie. She intends to hit
Nellie's head with it. Nellie hears her coming, turns
around, and kicks her in the stomach. The girl collapses
and screams a curse, which we have cut out. Nellie
picks up the stone, walks over to the principal and
drops it at her feet. Then, accompanied by her brothers
and sister, she walks away."

"Your name is Nellie."

"Yes ma'am."

She is wearing her crimson jacket again.

"What were those obese young women trying to do
to you?"

"They said they would break my arm."

"Why?"

"So I couldn't play in the St. Wenceslas game tomorrow."

"Why would they do that?"

"They hate me."

"Why do they hate you?"

"Because I am in seventh grade and I play on the
eighth grade team. Coach and Captain asked me to."

"Why?"

"I rebound."

A boy next to her, much shorter, says, "Highest
scorer in the league."

Nellie ruffles his hair.

"How many points did you make last week?"

"I don't count."

Pert little girl: "I do! She made twenty-eight!"

Nellie ruffles her hair.

"My fan club."

"You have a black belt?"

"Yes ma'am."

"Do those other girls know it?"

"They do now."

Then this woman appears on the scene, running full speed at Nellie, and knocks her into the mud. Then she grabs the young basketball star by her long hair and pushes her head into the mud while screaming curses at her. Nellie's family rushes to her rescue and tries to pull this woman, not a lightweight, off their sister. The woman throws the little girl, Nellie's sister Socra Marie, onto the concrete section of the school yard. Nellie slips away from this new assailant and rushes to her sister, who struggles to her feet, fighting mad. Nellie picks her up. The woman charges again. Nellie spins around and kicks the woman in the stomach, sending her into the deepest muck. The woman, the mother of one of the original attackers, we learn, shouts the same obscene words. Security forces flood the yard. The assaulting mother is taken into custody. The parish priest emerges to join the principal in demanding her release. The security people ignore them both . . .

We encounter Nellie again, covered with mud and carrying her little sister, who has a muddy face with blood streaming down it.

"Will you play at St. Wenceslas tomorrow, Nellie?"

"Sure will," little sister shouts.

"Nellie, is there any future for you at this school?"

"I don't think so."

"Our school!" the little tyke exclaims.

"That woman who hurt both of you is the mother of one of the eighth graders who attacked you . . ."

"She doesn't take her meds anymore."

"So here at St. Joe's, a 'progressive' Catholic school, young women basketball stars are assaulted by obese girls who endeavor to incapacitate her and by adult women who throw little girls on a concrete basketball court."

The scene shifts to Dr. Fletcher, her eyes grim and her lips a straight line.

"The principal explained it to us."

"We believe in the fundamental equality of all Catholics. There should be no distinctions based on family background, intelligence, or athletic skill. Sometimes it takes a little revolutionary action to establish this equality."

"Violent attacks on other students? Bullies beating up on little kids and taking money from them?"

"We feel—and I include most of our laypeople—that Catholicism means a passion for equality."

"And the Cardinal?"

"He is a nonentity from whom this Catholic community has nothing to learn."

"This is Mary Alice Quinn, Channel 3 News, in the St. Joe's Catholic school yard."

Anchor: "Mary Alice, the chancery tells us that the Cardinal will have a comment for the six o'clock news."

We had been watching the 5:00 news on tape, most of us in horrified silence. Me wife, home from Madam's lessons, held Socra Marie in her lap and had her other arm around Mary Anne, who still wore her muddy crimson jacket as though it were a garment of honor.

Nuala had arrived just as the Channel 3 trucks pulled away and the police cars with the Finnertys left in the opposite direction. She rushed up the stairs to find Julie putting a large Band-Aid on Socra Marie's hairline. The whole family, including Julie, were covered with mud.

"It's good I wasn't here, Dermot Michael. I would have turned the dogs loose on them."

I switched off Mary Alice's tape, which had been spliced seamlessly with the tape I had removed from my TV monitor, and found Blackie gazing at us. He was wearing his silver Brigid pectoral cross and his New Grange episcopal ring.

"I was dismayed to see the report on Channel 3 from the St. Josephat school yard. The situation there violates all the traditions of Catholic education and is totally unacceptable. The parish buildings are the property of the Catholic Bishop of Chicago, a corporation sole. Oddly enough, I happen to be that person. Acting on the authority that comes with ownership I am locking down all the buildings on the parish property and closing the school pending the outcome of an investigation by the firm of Connor and O'Connor, which have reviewed suspect Catholic behavior in the past. I have removed both the Principal, Lorraine Fletcher, and the pastor, Father Frank Sauer, from involvement with the school for the present. I promise all the teachers employed by the school that they will be paid their salaries by the Office of Catholic Education. Father Richard Neal, Vicar for Education, will have de facto jurisdiction over the school. I dispense all members of the parish from the obligation of Mass attendance this weekend. They may of course attend the sacred liturgy at other churches if they wish. I have asked the relevant officers in the Chicago Police Department to protect the parish property. I promise the people of St. Joe's that I will reopen the school as soon as I am persuaded that the abuses there have been stopped and not resumed.

"We have received letters about the situation at St. Josephat." He gestures at a small pile of letters. "I have urged the pastor repeatedly to put an end to all bullying activities. It is evident that he has not done so. As someone who was a prime target for bullies when I was in school—one that had to be rescued frequently by big sisters—I do not like bullies. I will not tolerate them in schools for which I am responsible. I direct all questions to Father Neal, except one, Miss Quinn, that I will answer before you ask it. I do not have the authority to suspend athletic contests between Catholic schools. Therefore the games scheduled for this weekend may continue."

"Good on you," Finnbar Burke said. "I like the man!"

"He's great craic," his true love agreed.

"We can put all of them in jail," my sister announced, "on any number of charges. We can sue the Archdiocese for any number of reasons. I can prepare briefs over the weekend if you wish."

"Nuala?"

"Can we send them to Devil's Island for all eternity? All I want is that the school yard bullies have to pay back the money that they took from the little kids. And I want that awful Maureen Finnerty woman put under a heavy peace bond and on probation too."

"Nothing more?"

"We don't want revenge, do we Sorcie?"

"Jesus say no revenge except he do it."

"What about them two polecats?"

"I can call this Father Neal and tell him that unless they are banned from all contact with schoolchildren in the Archdiocese we will seek a court order."

"No problem with that," I agreed.

"And those three terrible girls have to be expelled," Nuala insisted.

"There's no room for them and me in the same school," Mary Anne, as she was now called again, said firmly.

"I think we can wait for the Archdiocese's report before we take action on individual cases, but I hope we find something for which we can drag them into court."

The phone rang.

"Dermot Coyne."

"Your big brother."

"You want to protect me from bullies in the school yard?"

He actually laughed.

"What did you think?"

"As priests in the diocese have been saying for years, never mess round with Blackie Ryan."

"I can't tell him that."

"I thought he was wonderful. Tell him that."

"Me too!"

"So does Socra Marie!"

"Great . . . Hi, Sorcie!"

"Hi, Uncle George!"

"Cyndi is already preparing motions."

"Tell Rick Neal a mountain is going to roll over him."

"He needs the experience."

Nuala Anne grabbed the phone before I could hang up.

"Your Riverence, tell that nice Father Neal that the bad guys will try to organize a riot tonight and there should be a lot of police there. We'll get some of Mike Casey's people to guard our house."

"We're all going to the game tomorrow, aren't we?" Finnbar Burke asked, waving one of his crutches like it was a broadsword.

We did, of course. Channel 3 reported that Nellie Coyne, who was beaten up by bullies yesterday in the St. Joe's school yard, had broken the North Side Catholic League record by scoring forty points. There were four shots of herself sinking three-pointers.

"Coach wanted me to start," Mary Anne told us, "and said he'd take me out only when I'd hit forty."

The cops snuffed out the riot the first night and

addressed a half dozen people for disorderly conduct. The three bully girls were arrested for throwing rocks at our windows. Saturday night was quiet. The worst was over.

Except on Sunday night, they set fire to our house.

— 20 —

NUALA WOKE me at about 1:30.

"Dermot, the house is on fire!"

I heard alarms from both back and front. An old wooden house like ours was a ready-made firetrap. Our alarms were connected to the local fire station, which was only a couple of blocks away. I had trained the family that there were three paths of escape: down the front stairs, down the back stairs, and through the kitchen, down the inside stairs to the basement, and out into the back lawn, where the dogs played. They were numbers One, Two, and Three.

I looked out the window of our bedroom. The front steps were ablaze.

"The kitchen is on fire too," Nuala shouted. "Number Three, everyone! Number Three down to the basement!"

Smoke was filling the house, but the center stairs were still clear.

Our plan called for Nuala to lead the group down the stairs into the basement—where we played—and for me to count the number of creatures as they started down the stairs. The dogs waited with me, barking in noisy protest. I counted the kids. There were seven people in the house, four kids and three adults. Mary Anne carrying Sorcie, Julie carrying Patjo—four people. Nuala down in the basement guiding them down the stairs. Five people. Mick, confused but ready to go.

"Downstairs, Mick. Number Three." Down the stairs he went. Six people.

"Down you go, doggies."

They charged down the stairs. Two dogs, six people. Who was missing? I counted the people and the bedrooms. Who was missing?

It dawned on me that it was Dermot Coyne. I followed the wolfhounds. In the basement confusion and panic reigned.

"I can't open the door, Dermot," my wife cried.

The back door. We had to open it before the smoke filled the basement.

Key? Key? Key?

Then I remembered. I pushed my way through the mass of humans and dogs, and grabbed the key from its hook next to the door.

"Everyone out," I ordered. "Nuala and Julie first— climb the steps to the backyard, Mary Anne and Sorcie and Mick, doggies, and now you, Dermot, you frigging eejit."

The firemen were waiting for us in the yard.

"How many humans in the house, Mr. Coyne?" the fire marshal demanded.

"Three adults, four kids. I believe they are all out."

"I counted seven. Now we'll save your house for you."

We watched, and a torrent of water doused the flames. The glowing red lights disappeared, the smoke soared higher and then disappeared. Our prize house and beloved home was a near wreck.

"Arson." Cindasue and Peter Murphy were in the yard with us. "Beyond any doubt. Gasoline spread on the staircase. Molotov cocktails through the kitchen windows." We were all shivering in the cold autumn air. Everyone was crying except Nuala and myself.

"Insured?" the Fire Marshal asked.

"Double the damage," I said.

"That should take care of it."

"Don't worry, Nuala," I said. "We'll rebuild it."

"I know we will, Dermot. It will be better than ever."

We walked down the alley around the corner and to the front of the house. Fire truck, police cars, crowds of people, cops, Reliable people. Commander Culhane, Mary Alice Quinn with her cameraman, Mike Casey, who rushed to embrace us.

Cardinal Blackie, lurking in the background with his useless Chicago Cubs rain poncho. Father George next to him, holding an umbrella over his head.

"A high cost for a basketball game," Mary Alice began her interview.

"We have no idea who started the fire," my wife, radiantly lovely as Ingrid Bergman playing Joan of Arc. "And we're making no charges. It is up to the police and the fire department to find the arsonists, our insurance company to rebuild the house, and the appropriate authorities to bring the arsonists to justice. We are jumping to no conclusions."

I was so proud of my wife, flaky as she might be on some occasions, she was rock steady in times of stress, now the strong West of Ireland country woman in a time of grave distress as solid as the rocks of Carraroe.

"Dermot, would you ever call me ma and pa and tell them we're safe. They won't believe me. I'll talk to them afterwards."

"George?"

"I called Mom and Dad, Nuala. Why don't you give them a ring. They have more confidence in you than in either of their sons."

"Naturally," she said, her wit returning and meself a lot more mature in crisis.

"You're going to rebuild it, then?" Mary Anne Quinn asked me.

"What about it, kids?

"A unanimous vote . . . Mary Alice, we will restore it. It's part of Chicago past as of Chicago present. We will restore it and make it even better, even more fireproof."

Cheers from my constituency.

With outside fire escapes, I thought.

"Ma, 'tis Dermot in Chicago. Everyone is fine, a little wet and cold but we escaped with no more problems than a whiff of smoke. Here's herself. You should be proud of her. She saved us all with her confidence in a very bad situation. I'll put her on."

Blackie was standing next to me.

"Tomorrow you might well go down to NWH to have the doctors check everyone's lungs . . . They all sound healthy to me. Thank God you have survived, we need people like you in this troubled city. But I will slip away now and talk to you tomorrow because I see my revered and eminent predecessor arriving."

The kids who had been swarming around Blackie ran to embrace Cardinal Cronin.

All except Mary Anne.

"Thank you Cardinal Blackie for saving us."

"You better get that jacket cleaned, Nelliecoyne. It's too cool to be covered with mud."

We spent the night at the Murphy's house and the next morning began moving our headquarters to the Belden-Stratford Hotel on Lake Shore Drive. We needed only four suites. On the top two floors. They put meself and herself into the honeymoon suite, causing both of us to blush.

"I haven't ever been in a honeymoon suite," she protested. "It must cost terrible dear altogether."

"Put it on the insurance tab," I said.

Our electronic equipment was undamaged. Some of our clothes survived the smoke and the water. We sent them off to a special cleaners. The library was in good shape, though we sent the books off to be dried out. Also the antiques in the parlor, which I hated and Nuala Anne loved because they were "so 1850."

We hired, at Cyndi's direction, a firm to estimate damage and loss and the cost of reconstruction. They in turn hired an architect to design a restoration and a contractor to build it.

We were busy unloading and unpacking when the president of the insurance company called us and offered to visit us with a check that "might relieve you of a lot of worries."

Nuala thanked him and said to me, "Get herself on the line . . ."

In this case Cyndi was undoubtedly herself.

"He's trying to cheat you. Don't sign anything or even appear to agree verbally. Double the loss, isn't it? You bought that because you want to restore it as a landmark home? Then they have to pay double the loss as estimated by a reputable evaluator of your choosing. We're not about to settle for anything less. Watch him! He's a genial Catholic layman of the Boston variety. He'd rob you blind."

So the man arrived, genial, silver-haired, Boston accent. We were both in jeans and sweatshirts.

"I'll do the talking, Dermot Michael, if you don't mind."

"I wasn't planning to say a thing."

We offered him a "morning cup of tea," which he declined.

"I'm Jimmy Flanigan," he said in a tone which, as Nuala later said, oozed bull shite. "When I read in the morning papers about your terrible tragedy, I remembered of course that you hold one of our policies. I got it out and spoke with some of my directors and we put together this offering which should eliminate most of the worries I'm sure you have."

Hit them when they're traumatized.

He handed me several pages of boilerplate to which was attached a check for what might be considered a very large sum of money, nowhere near twice the cost of restoration. I passed the file to herself.

She turned up her elegant nose at the check and read the offer. She sighed loudly and placed the offer on one thigh and the insurance policy on the other. Again she sighed loudly.

"Sir, Ms. Cyndi Hurley of Warner, Werner, Wanzer, Hurley, and Hurley will represent us in this matter. Any future, slick offers of this sort should be made to her. As you doubtless know the indemnity in this policy is very high because we feel an obligation to preserve and restore a historic landmark home. We paid a high, one might even say exorbitant premium for that security. It will not be pried loose from us by this kind of blarney. I put it to you this way, sir, one way or another, you are going to pay us a large sum of money determined by twice the losses as estimated by a reputable firm of our choosing, or that sum and more as determined by a court order after you have engaged in expensive litigation. It's entirely your decision. However, do not deceive yourself by thinking that I am a harebrained West of Ireland entertainer who will be taken in by this kind of—you will excuse my expression, sir—bull shite."

The man's face turned pale.

"There might be some questions about the origins of the fire," he said uneasily.

"There might indeed. We propose to proceed with the restoration of the house. Fortunately we can afford to do that. But you will pay for it too, sir. Of this I assure you."

She stood up in dismissal.

"This is your position too," he said to me, a hint of contempt in his voice.

"Yes."

"Well then, you'll be hearing from our lawyers."

"It would be more convenient," I said, "if you sent your further bull shite directly to Ms. Hurley."

His generosity mocked, his dignity offended, Jimmy Flanigan departed with as much dudgeon as he could manage.

He was followed by Commander John Culhane of Area 6 Detectives, a man in the physical condition of a lightweight boxer, which he was.

He did welcome a morning cup of tea. Fiona, our retired police dog who can smell a cop a mile away, ambled in and offered her paw to the commander.

"It was arson, of course," he said. "No question about it. We arrested those three young amadons and found gasoline on their hands and clothes. We also found four more paper milk containers filled with wicks ready to ignite. They denied all knowledge of the fire and accused you of planting the evidence in the Finnerty basement. We arrested them on the charge of attempted murder of seven people. They became hysterical. They insisted that four men with Irish accents had brought them the Molotov cocktails and showed them how to light them with fire starters. They were fortunate not to have killed themselves."

"Why are the evil always the lucky ones?" me wife complained.

"I'm not sure they're lying," John Culhane said slowly. "I don't think they would have known how to make such incendiary devices, much less what to do with them. Do you have any ideas we might pursue, anyone lately who might have wanted to kill you?"

"Not us," Nuala said, that far away, communing-with-the-powers look in her searing blue eyes.

"They might want to kill Julie Crean."

"Who is she?"

"The one with the long golden hair like a ripe wheat field in the rising sun."

— 21 —

IN THE week before her marriage, Angela was kissed, caressed, embraced, cosseted, and her sexual feelings enflamed. A week of foreplay, she complained to herself. And she had to see to the arrangements for the wedding when her need for love was intolerably active and her fiancé's fingers were so demanding and delightful. She kept lists of things to do, but often could not decipher what an item on her list meant.

Would her marriage be like that? Would she become the official family planner for the Gaughan clan?

Probably not. They were now giddy, drunk on the heady wine of the Holy Spirit, as Bishop Muldoon explained. They're enveloped in the exuberance of sacraments.

Their wedding would be on Saturday and Father Vinny's First Mass would be on Sunday. A great family weekend, Vinny exulted—little sister becomes big sister-in-law.

"Still little sister," she insisted.

Her mom and dad were ecstatically happy, dreams coming true all around them—one long expected and the other now an improbable surprise. So she did not mind organizing both events. If only her future husband was not so persistent in his affection. She was worried too, as any virgin bride might be about the possibly painful adventure of the first night. Her Timmy would be the most gentle of men, but how would it feel when he took possession of her?

The joy began when Tim had carried her into the family parlor, holding her in his strong arms.

"You know, I've been searching for a bride," he announced. "You know that I absolutely insist on long golden hair. I was wandering about the park and didn't I find such a woman and didn't I steal her from her guards and bring her here for your approval."

They both were being silly, giddy, laughing half the time and giggling the other half. *I must settle down,* Angela told herself. *Someone has to be sensible.* Then she realized that love is not sensible and that the romance between her and Tim would always be just a little madcap—and that would keep it alive through the years.

Father Vinny presided at the marriage and Bishop Muldoon said the mass. Shay and her beloved Rosina were the witnesses. Everyone giggled and laughed. She and Timmy had to repeat the wedding vows several times because they both could not contain their laughter. Even Bishop Muldoon, normally serious and sober during ceremonies, laughed often.

"Though we never doubted that this couple would marry, we laugh because their match is so comic. Please God that it will always be."

The dinner at the Palmer House, the dances, the wedding cake, the toasts, were all unintentionally funny.

Ma was there, of course, radiantly happy and laughing.

I didn't know that the Blessed in Heaven laughed.

"We see a lot more of the comedy in life. Anyway, God laughs all the time."

Timmy's toast was wonderful.

"I once said to you up at the lake that I had always loved you, Angela, and that I always would. Today I merely made that promise solemn."

And she replied, "I said the same thing to you, Timothy. Only you were in Prague, so I had to shout it."

More laughter.

"And I heard it."

We even laughed on our way to the bridal suite.

"Madam, may I assist you in removing your clothes?"

"If you don't, Timmy love, I don't know how I'll get rid of all this stuff . . . Just a moment."

She removed a blanket from one of the dresser doors. It was the old, faithful Irish tweed.

"You can always wrap me in this when you're finished with me."

"I'll never be finished with you, Angie. Never."

He did, however, wrap her in her own Irish tweed after their first love.

"You'll keep the bed warm on cold winter nights, Timothy. I can give up my nightly brandy."

And they laughed again till they slept.

NOTE

Their marriage was indeed filled with laughter. Together they helped to reform medicine in Chicago and made the city a much healthier place in which to live. They had three children—Mae, Patrick, and Vincent. Patrick died in the 1918 influenza epidemic. His parents suffered greatly because of his death, but recovered their laughter. They traveled often in Europe. Angela kept her promise to visit her friend Eileen in

Connemara. They received the Nobel Prize in 1935 and met Alexander Fleming, whose discovery of penicillin confirmed Angela's conviction that there were substances in nature which could defeat many more once-fatal diseases. She may have written another volume of memoirs, but it has yet to be discovered. They died within a month of one another just before the Japanese attack on Pearl Harbor.

— 22 —

"RUSTY LITZ, yes of course. I know him from the Board of Trade. He owns a tavern on North Avenue just east of Narragansett . . . I know the place . . . And he lives in Oak Brook . . . and the other fellow was Jerry Maginn. Yeah . . . I was so embarassed when I tried to introduce him to my friend from Cork . . . He's good, all right. *Almost* beat me."

"It's your man Litz," Nuala told us. "And his tavern is the same one that your man Martin McGurn owned. I bet there's always a group of Irish half-drunks lolling around there all the time and they were the ones who wanted to kill Finnbar Burke and set fire to our house so they could kill Julie Crean, who never did anything to anyone except smile at poor Finnbar."

"Astonishing," John Culhane said, as he often had when Nuala solved a problem.

I wasn't astonished. There was nothing uncanny about her solution. All she had to know was that the same people who wanted to kill Finnbar Burke would also want to kill Julie Crean. They had seen our battle with Gena Finnerty and her bunch on TV, spotted Julie's golden hair in the ruckus, and found a way to get rid of her without getting involved themselves. Junior high school kids are not the most reliable conspirators. They didn't dump their plastic Molotov cocktails, wash their hands, and throw their clothes in the laundry.

They were perfectly willing to wipe out a family to get Julie so they could punish the Burkes for something that had happened almost ninety years ago. That was weird, crazy, mad—but you didn't have to be a psychic to realize there were a lot of crazy people in the world.

They would also take the risk of ruining permanently the lives of the three young women they had sent to do the work. But what did they matter?

Nuala Anne certainly had psychic instincts. I would be the last to deny that, and meself with a silver-blue aura. However, she also had a gift of making quick connections and seeing the implications of these connections. Hence she was a first-rate detective. I told her so in bed that night.

"Sure," she said dismissing my insight, "and yourself knowing that all along."

Knowing from day one that there was evil haunting Finnbar Burke and Julie—that was not something that could be so easily dismissed. I didn't want to think about it.

So two days later a couple of very tough plainclothes dicks and I, dressed like an Irish oil drill rigger, dropped in to the Last Chance, which was, as we had learned, the descendant of Martin McGurn's Irish Saloon of years ago. We sat there, slowly and silently sipping our pints of Guinness, as is appropriate in such places. A sullen and suspicious woman bartender stared at us with a hostile glare.

We had a pretty good idea of the looks of the perpetrators for whom we were searching. John Culhane had pried loose from Immigration some pictures of suspicious Irishmen in town. He showed them to Gena Finnerty and company, all of whom were under charge of arson and attempted murder. They had been terrified by the cops' descriptions of what reformatories for women were like. They had no trouble identifying two of them.

Soon these two punks swaggered into the Last Chance with two others and arranged themselves around the table in the front corner of the bar.

"Four of the best, Amy, doubles."

"Coming up!"

One of them sneered at me. "You have a problem?"

"I don't think so," I said, "except you guys burned my house down."

The four punks were punks, undersized hoods who thought attitude could substitute for intelligence and strength. Two of them threw over the table and came after me with knives. I knocked both of them down and kicked them in their private parts. A half dozen plainclothes cops surged into the tavern and cuffed the four of them quickly. No windows broken, no more resistance.

"I'm sure that was necessary, Dermot," the sergeant in charge said to me.

"Get the knives out in the open at the beginning," I said airily. Perhaps that was a rationalization. I don't know.

"You're right . . . OK, you bunch of losers. We're arresting you on charges of arson and attempted murder . . . Anything you say . . ."

I had seen the ritual on television and did not need to hear it. My heart was pounding loudly from the tussle with the knife wielders. I'd better not tell me wife.

"Tell Rusty the cops will be coming after him next," I said to the bartender.

She was crying, her face now tender.

"It's his grandmother. She raised him after his mother had left them and his father remarried. She's dying of cancer over at West Suburban . . . All her life she was obsessed by the Cork Regatta. I warned him. Everyone did. His poor wife and kids . . . But he tried to kill you and your family too, didn't he? He never got over the story. His grandmother is a McGowan, you see."

"Yeah, I see. It was ninety years ago. His grandmother wasn't even born."

"The kid was her uncle. The whole family was consumed with hate. Martin McGurn kept after them about the need for revenge. I think poor Rusty may get over it now."

"Too late," I said.

I told Nuala the whole story.

"I shouldna let you you go."

"Probably not."

"Well, you might have saved some lives by disarming those with the knives."

And as we were getting ready for bed that night, she said, "I think it's a frigging shame that we are not taking advantage of this honeymoon suite."

"Men go crazy during the honeymoon."

"You didn't."

" 'Tis true."

Naturally we took advantage of the opportunity. Great craic.

The next morning Conor O'Connor came to visit us and talk to the kids . . . Nuala insisted on being present.

"Smart man," my wife said that night. "I imagine that the school will be open next week."

"New leaders and expelled bullies should be enough."

"And strong oversight from His Riverence and Father Neal."

"They just took a lot of notes," Mary Anne reported to me. "They wanted the names of all the bullies. Will they expel them, Da?"

"Some of them."

"Not all of them?" Mick asked.

"You think there should be exceptions?"

"Some were just dumb."

"Give your da," Nuala suggested, "a list of the just-dumb ones. They'll probably expel all of them and then review the cases."

"Were they really trying to kill me, Dermot?" Julie asked as she was leaving to return to the neighborhood with her fella.

"They were, the frigging eejits . . . Don't worry, they'll be in jail for a long time, and the poor woman who paid them is dying."

"It's so dumb . . ."

"Very dumb."

She paused at the door.

"Oh, there's a rumor I may get a ring at Christmas . . . Just a rumor. I already told Nuala."

Not that she needed to be told.

"Congratulations in order?"

"Only when I'm after getting the ring. You know what Irish men are like!"

Did I now?

Rusty Litz called me that evening.

"My grandma is dead, Dermot."

"I'm sorry to hear that, Rusty."

"I'm sorry about what we did to your house."

"And almost did to my family."

"She gave the orders. I learned only the next morning."

"I hope she's at peace now."

"So do I . . . She was always obsessed . . . But as her condition worsened, she became totally obsessed.

It's all over now. I'm turning myself in to the Chicago cops."

"Did you know about the attempt on Finnbar Burke?"

"No. I told her that I had met him at the Club. She said that he needed to die. I was horrified . . . and that poor little child with the golden hair who is your nanny."

"To say nothing of my own children."

"I went to church this morning to give thanks they are all still alive . . . That kid with the three-point shot is really good . . . You remember, Dermot, I went to St. Ignatius."

I said that I did, but I didn't remember.

"Well, I have to pay the price. My wife is sticking with me, though she shouldn't."

"I don't imagine," I said with unintended irony, "that the Burkes will want revenge."

"They're entitled to it, Dermot."

"Only God is."

"Poor dear man," Nuala observed as she hung up the phone. "And such a fool. We don't want revenge, do we, Dermot Michael?"

"Only against the insurance company."

"Och, Dermot, when your sister is finished with them, they'll pay quick and proper."

"'Tis true."

We had one more penitent that night—Hugh Finnerty.

"I'm so sorry, Nuala, so sorry. I didn't like what was going on at the school and I was concerned about my wife's explosions . . . That's not the way she really is or used to be anyway . . . ever since she had the hysterectomy she stopped taking her meds and has been increasingly crazy . . . She grew up in a family which believed in clout . . . All that mattered was who you know . . . Anything can be fixed . . . I told her that wasn't true . . . you couldn't be a good basketball player and be overweight . . . She was furious at me . . . If your daughter had weighed as much she wouldn't play either . . . She attacked me physically for saying that . . . We're going to ask that she be institutionalized . . . She was so happy when she heard the fire sirens . . . I'm not sure she will ever recover . . . She has to take her meds . . . Anyway, we will move to another city . . . also they will give the children time in a training school which will be much better than boarding school."

"We won't stand in the way of any of those decisions, will we, Dermot?"

"No," I agreed. "It would be wise if you get a job in some other place . . ."

"I'm thinking of California."

"Good idea."

"Poor devil," I said when he had left.

"Three obsessed women," Nuala replied. "Maureen, Dr. Fletcher, and Grandma McGovern . . . What sad, wasted lives."

"I hope they can turn themselves around."

"All we can really do," my wife said, "is forgive them and have Mr. Casey keep an eye on both of them—and say the occasional prayer for them."

"It's a good time to teach the kids about forgiveness."

On Monday the Cardinal released the Conor and O'Connor report. It blamed the situation on the Superintendent of Schools, the Pastor, and the Principal and detailed how discipline and order slowly collapsed at St. Joe's, and then suddenly crashed. The Pastor was placed on sick leave, which he accepted, we were told, with considerable complaint. Ms. Fletcher was removed as principal but received her pay for the rest of the year. A new principal from the Notre Dame program was hired and a new Pastor was appointed, both as it turned out, people of great charm and prudence. St. Josephat won the girls' basketball championship in Catholic North. Cardinal Ryan presided at the confirmation rites in the parish . . . Julie did collect her huge diamond at Christmas. The wolfhounds were spoiled rotten by all the attention at the Belden Stratford. Herself and meself both enjoyed the honeymoon suite. We all flew to Ireland for Christmas, and I managed, by a miracle of great power, to avoid my usual Ireland cold.

Long before we left for Ireland we gathered in the parlor of the honeymoon suite for another kind of ceremony, which Mary Anne had convened. It was a big deal and a very solemn one.

"I want to ask everyone's permission to change my name back from Mary Anne to Nelliecoyne which is my real name. I can be Mary Anne officially on my driver's license if I have to, but I'm really a Nellie and I'm proud to have the real name of my great-grandmother. If any of you object then I'll change my name back."

The vote was unanimous.

Her mother began to sing the appropriate song, "My Nellie's Blue Eyes" by W. J. Scanlan:

> *My dear Nellie's eyes are blue*
> *Hair of red and golden hue*
> *Like her heart, her eyes are true*
> *My Nellie my own*
> *My Nellie's blue eyes*
> *My Nellie's blue eyes*
> *Brighter than the Stars that shine at night*
> *My Nellie's blue eyes*
> *Never was culled from nature's bower*
> *Half so rare or sweet a flower*
> *My Nellie, my own my own*
> *My Nellie's blue eyes*

My Nellie's blue eyes
Brighter than the Stars that shine at night
My Nellie's blue eyes

It was promptly decided by unanimous vote that would be the theme of our Christmas program.

"'Tis not me eyes," Nuala insisted. "They're your great-grandmother's eyes. A lot more complicated than mine."

And so they were.

— Afterword? —

TIM AND Angela took their three children to Europe in 1905. On their way, they stopped at both Castle Garden and Ellis Island. Angela had not wished to burden their imaginations too early in life with the details of her life story.

"You had to stay in this terrible place all day, Mom?" Mae was the oldest and most sensitive of the three.

"Some had to stay here much longer and they didn't let them in. I was lucky."

They studied the photographs which hung from the stark walls.

"These poor people . . . how terrible! Are you in any of the pictures?"

"I don't think so. I was hardly worth noticing. You can see why so many Americans were worried. How could people like these ever become good Americans?"

Then they went to the Statue of Liberty. From memory Angela recited the ending of Emma Lazarus's sonnet:

"Keep, ancient lands, your storied pomp!" cries she
With silent lips. "Give me your tired, your poor,
Your huddled masses yearning to breathe free,
The wretched refuse of your teeming shore.
Send these, the homeless, tempest-tost to me,
I lift my lamp beside the golden door!"

"Are we these huddled masses, these wretched refuse, these tired poor, these tempest-tost?" Mae asked.

"No, dear, you're a Yank. I'm the wretched refuse."
Mae hugged her protectively.

"Here your mom is, Mae. This is the fourteen-year-
old we picked up at the Central Depot the next day."

"Mom," Patrick exclaimed, "look at the light in your
eyes!"

"All of us fell in love with her when we saw that
glow," Tim said proudly. "We never got over it."

"How could you . . ." Mae said softly.